Also by Aimée Carter

Simon Thorn and the Wolf's Den

SIMON THORN
AND THE
VIPER'S PIT

AIMÉE CARTER

BLOOMSBURY

NEW YORK   LONDON   OXFORD   NEW DELHI   SYDNEY

First published in the United States of America in February 2017
by Bloomsbury Children's Books
www.bloomsbury.com

Bloomsbury is a registered trademark of Bloomsbury Publishing Plc

For information about permission to reproduce selections from this book, write to
Permissions, Bloomsbury Children's Books, 1385 Broadway, New York, New York 10018
Bloomsbury books may be purchased for business or promotional use. For information
on bulk purchases please contact Macmillan Corporate and Premium Sales Department at
specialmarkets@macmillan.com

Library of Congress Cataloging-in-Publication Data
Names: Carter, Aimée, author.
Title: Simon Thorn and the viper's pit / by Aimée Carter.
Description: New York : Bloomsbury, 2017. | Series: Simon Thorn ; [2]
Summary: Simon Thorn only recently discovered that he's an Animalgam—one of a secret race
who can shift into animals. Now, for the first time in his life Simon has real friends to train and
study with at the secret Animalgam Academy. The only missing part is his mother, held captive
by his evil grandfather, Orion, who's bent on taking over the animal world.
Identifiers: LCCN 2016023118 (print) | LCCN 2016036824 (e-book)
ISBN 978-1-61963-715-3 (hardcover) | ISBN 978-1-61963-716-0 (e-book)
Subjects: | CYAC: Human-animal communication—Fiction. | Shapeshifting—Fiction. |
Animals—Fiction. | Adventure and adventurers—Fiction. | Kidnapping—Fiction. | BISAC:
JUVENILE FICTION / Action & Adventure / General. | JUVENILE FICTION / Fantasy &
Magic. | JUVENILE FICTION / Animals / General.
Classification: LCC PZ7.C24255 Sh 2017 (print) | LCC PZ7.C24255 (e-book) |
DDC [Fic]—dc23
LC record available at https://lccn.loc.gov/2016023118

Book design by Donna Mark and John Candell
Typeset by Newgen Knowledge Works (P) Ltd., Chennai, India
Printed and bound in the U.S.A. by Berryville Graphics Inc., Berryville, Virginia
2 4 6 8 10 9 7 5 3 1

To Courtney

SIMON THORN
AND THE
VIPER'S PIT

EARLY BIRD

"Simon, *duck!*"

Simon Thorn took one look at the gigantic moose swinging its antlers at his head, and he hit the sand beneath him hard. Scrambling toward the edge of the pit, he stared wide-eyed as the moose threw its head back and laughed.

"What are your options, Simon?" said his uncle Malcolm from the bleachers surrounding the sand pit. Simon's heart pounded as he huddled against the stone barrier, but his hulking dark-haired uncle didn't look concerned. He never did during these early-morning training sessions no matter what kind of animal Simon encountered, and Simon was beginning to resent him for it.

"Yeah, Simon," taunted the moose, prancing across the sand toward him. "How are you going to get out of this one?"

Simon climbed shakily to his feet, never taking his eyes off the moose. It towered over him, and Simon was sure that if his uncle were in the pit, it would tower over him, too. Simon might have been small for his age, but Malcolm was tall and broad. There weren't many humans or animals who would willingly tangle with him. "Run," said Simon plainly.

"You can't run now. Try again," said Malcolm. He was right, of course. Even if Simon hadn't been trapped inside the pit, he was still stuck inside the L.A.I.R.—the Leading Animalgam Institute for the Remarkable far beneath Central Park Zoo, where Animalgam students trained. It was a place that, up until recently, Simon would've never guessed existed, let alone that he might one day attend.

For most of his life, Simon had grown up in New York City thinking he was perfectly ordinary. However, over a year ago, he'd suddenly developed the ability to talk to animals, which had been weird enough. He hadn't told anyone, not even his mom or Darryl, the uncle who had raised him. For a whole year, he let the kids at school think he was crazy, and at first he thought they were right.

But Simon wasn't crazy. Unbeknownst to him, he was really an Animalgam—a human who could not only talk to animals, but developed the ability to turn into one, too. He hadn't believed it at first, of course, like most rational seventh graders. But when he had seen Darryl shift into a huge gray wolf right in front of him, everything in his world had changed.

Now, two months later, instead of studying math or geography like most normal twelve-year-olds, Simon was facing down a moose. If he couldn't run, then what *could* he do?

"Fight?" he guessed. The edges of his vision were growing fuzzy as he tried not to blink. The instant he showed any sign of weakness, he knew the moose would attack again.

"Against those antlers? I don't think so," said Malcolm. Out of the corner of Simon's eye, he thought he saw his uncle whittling a small piece of wood. Great. He was barely paying attention.

"I'm not shifting," said Simon firmly as he inched around the edge of the pit toward the exit that led into the rest of the school. The doorway was narrow, and there was no way the moose could follow him into the hallway with those antlers.

"You need to get over this sooner or later, Simon," said Malcolm. "You can't ignore your Animalgam form forever."

Watch me, thought Simon, though he didn't dare say it out loud. Instead he muttered, "At least I'm not a moose."

The moose made a strange noise that sounded like a cross between a groan and a whine. "You don't like my antlers? Fine. Let's see how you like this."

Rapidly, almost too fast for Simon to follow, the moose morphed right in front of him. Its antlers disappeared, its body and long legs shrank, and its brown fur turned black with a long white stripe running down the middle. By the time Simon blinked, the moose had vanished, and a skunk stared up at him.

Simon turned and bolted toward the door. Yanking on the handle, he groaned when it didn't budge. He was locked in. "Malcolm!" he protested. His uncle glanced up.

"Can't have anyone walking in," he reasoned, even though it was early enough that Simon was sure none of the other students were awake.

The skunk ambled toward him, raising its bushy tail. "Guess what I can do."

"I know what you can do. You don't need to prove it," said Simon, his voice tight as he looked around for an escape route. His only option was climbing over the wall and into the bleachers, but the skunk had him backed against the door now.

"I had a lot of beans for dinner last night," said the skunk, turning to point its rear end at Simon. "I think I feel a massive fart coming on."

Having no other choice, Simon darted forward and leaped over the skunk right as it released a cloud of stink. Covering his nose, Simon scrambled up the bleachers, climbing as high as he could get. The smell was overpowering, and as he reached the top, he was gagging.

"Nolan!" *That* had gotten Malcolm's attention, and he stood, covering his nose as well. "What do you think you're doing?"

"I'm *trying* to make him fly, like you said," said the skunk, his tail puffing indignantly. "The smell isn't that bad."

"Try shifting back into a human and seeing how you like it," said Simon from the top of the pit.

The skunk huffed. "You're just being a baby," said Nolan, and as if to prove his point, he began to change again. This time, instead of shifting into another animal, the black and white fur on his head turned into brown hair, his four legs elongated into human limbs, and his muzzle and beady eyes morphed until a boy identical to Simon stood where the skunk had only seconds before, wearing the same black student uniform the L.A.I.R. required.

Simon had only met Nolan two months ago, on the night he'd unsuccessfully tried to sneak into the school to search for his missing mother. Before that, Simon had lived his entire life on the Upper West Side just a couple of miles away, while Nolan had lived with their mother beneath Central Park Zoo. Simon had only gotten visits from her on Christmas and his birthday, something that still bothered him whenever he thought too much about it. And never, not once, had she ever mentioned the fact that Simon had a twin brother.

The sounds of gagging interrupted Simon's thoughts, and he refocused on his brother at the bottom of the pit.

Nolan could only pretend the smell didn't bother him for so long, and at last he bolted up the bleachers, toward a spiral staircase. "That's *disgusting!*" he shouted as he disappeared into the upper level of the school, where Malcolm's office stood.

"Simon—" Malcolm began.

"Nolan did it, not me!" he called, darting after his brother and leaving their uncle to grumble on his own.

As soon as Simon exited the pit, he took a deep breath, only to discover the foul stench was clinging to his clothes. Terrific. He was enough of a social pariah as it was. If he went to breakfast smelling like skunk, that would give even his best friends a reason to avoid him.

Simon adjusted his black armband, turning the silhouette of an eagle in toward his arm so it was hidden. He had shifted into a golden eagle for the first time two months ago, and while he could think of few things cooler than being able to fly, he was the only member of the bird kingdom who attended the L.A.I.R. His grandfather, Orion, the leader of the bird kingdom, had been at war with the mammals for longer than Simon had been alive, and since the mammals ran the school, they had banned birds from attending. Simon was only allowed because he was Nolan's twin.

"You should help Malcolm clean the pit," said Simon as he found his brother lingering in the upper hallways. Only faculty was allowed up here, but since Malcolm not only ran the L.A.I.R., but was now also the Alpha of the entire mammal kingdom, no one ever gave Simon and Nolan a hard time about being there.

Nolan made a face. *"You* help him. If you had just shifted, I wouldn't have had to spray you."

"I told you, I don't like flying in the pit," he said. And while technically that was true, there was another reason—a much bigger reason—Simon didn't like shifting in front of other people.

Nearly all Animalgams could only shift into a single animal, and they belonged to one of the five Animalgam kingdoms: mammals, birds, insects, reptiles, or underwater creatures. But Nolan was different. He was the heir to the Beast King, a tyrannical ruler who had gained the power to shift into any animal he wanted, making him almost impossible to defeat. Though the five kingdoms had banded together half a millennium ago to overthrow him, his line had continued in secret, and Simon and Nolan's father had been the Beast King's heir before being murdered. Two months ago, they had discovered Nolan was the twin who had inherited his abilities, and that was why Malcolm had locked the doors of the pit even though it was so early that the sky was still dark. If anyone else found out that the Beast King's line still existed, it would start another war between all five Animalgam kingdoms— and this time they would all be trying to kill Nolan.

Simon couldn't let that happen, but he also couldn't tell

anyone his secret and the real reason he was so reluctant to shift in front of everyone while he still wasn't very good at it. Not even Nolan. *Especially* not Nolan. Despite their tentative cease-fire after what had been, to put it lightly, a rocky start to their relationship, Simon was sure that the moment Nolan found out he wasn't as special as he thought he was, he would hate Simon all over again.

"All you have to do is flap your wings a few times, and Malcolm will be happy," said Nolan, annoyed. "I don't get why you won't do that."

"He'll get there eventually," said a voice behind them—Malcolm. He must have followed them. "Just like you'll stop relying so heavily on your mammal forms and start working with the other kingdoms, too."

"I shift into animals from other kingdoms all the time," said Nolan, shoving his hands in his pockets as the three of them stood outside the doorway to Malcolm's office. "I shifted into a hawk yesterday, and an alligator the day before that."

"Mammals make up the smallest kingdom," said their uncle, "yet you almost always revert to a mammal form during morning practice. If you have any hope of protecting yourself someday, you're going to need to be proficient and comfortable in forms from all five kingdoms. And," he added, "you're going to have to start cleaning up after yourself. I can't open the pit until that skunk stench is gone."

"Make Simon do it," said Nolan.

"You're the one who made that mess," said Simon. "I'm not cleaning up your skunk juice, no way."

"But you're the one who made me—"

"Enough." Malcolm pinched the bridge of his nose. "Nolan, you're cleaning up your own mess. Simon, go change. I can smell you from here. But if I don't see your wings in the next twenty-four hours, you'll be the one taking care of any future skunk messes in the pit."

And if Simon knew his brother at all, he was positive Nolan would skunk him every chance he got just to make him clean up.

"That's not fair!" cried Nolan. Malcolm set his hand on his shoulder and started to lead him down the hallway.

"It's perfectly fair. Now come on, the kitchens must have a few extra gallons of tomato juice lying around."

As the sound of their argument faded, Simon headed through the hallway and down into the Alpha section. The underground L.A.I.R. was called the Den, and it was shaped like a pentagon, one side for each kingdom. Since the birds weren't invited to attend, the Alpha and his family stayed in their section instead. Once Simon changed into a clean uniform, he would have the whole place to himself, minus a handful of pack members posted as guards.

He wasn't interested in a nap before breakfast, though. He could hardly believe his luck at getting the rest of the early morning off, and he knew exactly what he was going to do with that extra forty-five minutes: practice shifting the way he couldn't in the pit, not in front of Nolan and Malcolm. Because while his uncle only wanted to see him stretch his wings, Simon could do much, much more.

And that was Simon's big secret, the one he kept from everyone, even Nolan. Somehow, someway, his twin wasn't the only one who had inherited the Beast King's abilities. Simon could shift into any animal he wanted, too. He hadn't had nearly as much practice as his brother, however, and every time he shifted in front of others, he was painfully aware he risked thinking of the wrong animal and exposing his secret. That was why he refused to shift in the pit.

But while he didn't have the experience his brother did, he knew all the lectures Malcolm gave Nolan were right. If he wanted any chance of protecting himself and his brother from the people who wanted to destroy the Beast King's line, he had to learn how to fight in the style of all five kingdoms. If he couldn't do that in the pit, then there was only one other place he could safely practice.

After saying hello to the wolves standing guard near the tall trees that filled the Alpha residence, he headed up the winding glass staircase and into his bedroom. Their section, which had been built to house the bird students, was several stories high, and while it would have been easy enough for Simon to fly around, he wouldn't be able to practice shifting into other animals. Not with the pack members watching.

"You're back early," said a sleepy voice from Simon's bed. Curled into a ball on his pillow lay a tiny brown mouse. Felix was, in many ways, his best friend, but Simon knew where he ranked when it came to the little mouse's priorities: right below naps and television.

"Yeah, Nolan tried to skunk me. Malcolm's making him clean up the pit right now," said Simon, heading over to his dresser.

"That explains the smell," muttered the mouse. "You need a shower."

"And you need to sleep another hour if you're going to be this cranky."

Felix grumbled to himself, not disagreeing, and Simon grabbed a fresh change of clothes and ducked into the bathroom. As soon as he closed the door, however, he headed straight through into the adjoining bedroom: Nolan's.

Beneath Nolan's desk in the far corner of the room was one of several tunnels that led to the Central Park Zoo above. While the Den was one of the safest places in New York City for Animalgams, it had its fair share of secrets, and Simon had discovered this one shortly after arriving. Moving the chair out of the way, he bent down and nudged open the secret panel. On the other side was an opening barely big enough for Simon to crawl through, but he didn't need much space. As soon as he closed the small door and was engulfed in darkness, he closed his eyes and focused. Within a heartbeat, he began to shift.

The cold tunnel expanded as he grew smaller. It didn't hurt, but it did tickle, especially as fur sprouted all over his body. His face grew pointed, and his spine elongated into a tail, leaving him unbalanced for a moment. But before it could bother him, his transformation into a mouse was complete. Simon wasn't sure exactly how many animals he could shift into, but between watching his brother in the pit and the experiments he tried when he sneaked out on his own, he had yet to find any exception.

He scurried through the rest of the tunnel, careful not to make a sound. As soon as he reached the grate that let out into the middle of the Central Park Zoo, he shut his eyes and imagined a golden eagle, and his body once again transformed. His front legs twisted and lengthened into wings, feathers replaced his fur, and his nose and whiskers turned into a hard beak. He hopped out of the tunnel, his long talons scratching the paved stones. The sun was only beginning to creep up between the skyscrapers surrounding Central Park, and with his vision sharpened, he could see everything even in the low light of dawn. Twisting his head around, Simon searched for the wolf pack that patrolled the zoo while it was closed. No signs of life. At least not the kind that would get him grounded.

Confident he was alone, Simon spread his wings and took off, soaring into the sky. At first he meant to only fly around the zoo for a little while, but he climbed higher and higher, his feathers adjusting to take advantage of the wind. He soared above the park, dipping down to swoop among the trees, not realizing where he was headed until he could see the building. His old apartment—the one he had lived in almost his whole life with his uncle Darryl.

It had been two months since Darryl had died on the roof of Sky Tower, and they had been the hardest months of Simon's life. While Simon missed his uncle fiercely, most days he went through the motions and pretended everything was okay, and no one knew just how deeply he was grieving. Sometimes Simon even managed to fool himself into thinking he had adjusted, that the biggest loss of his life was in the past instead of only an errant thought away. But as he circled above his old building, that gnawing ache returned full force, hitting him so hard that he almost forgot how to fly.

He couldn't stand seeing their apartment, not when he knew it would be one more reminder that Darryl wasn't there anymore. Instead, with his insides in knots, he landed on a branch in Central Park near the path he'd taken to go to school. Glancing around, he half expected to see the boys who had bullied him, but it was far too early. Instead he ruffled his feathers and tried to pull himself together. If he spent the morning upset, Malcolm might demand an explanation—or worse, ask if he wanted to talk.

A robin settled onto the branch beside him, puffing up nervously. "Gonna eat that worm?" she said, and Simon spotted a particularly fat one poking out of the dewy grass.

"It's all yours," he said, but the robin made no move to take it.

"You're Simon, right?" she said. "Simon Thorn?"

Suspicion crept through him, and he eyed the robin. "How do you know that?"

As he spoke, several more robins settled onto the trees nearby, along with a handful of blue jays and crows. Not the kind of birds who usually shared breakfast. He dug his talons nervously into the branch.

"Orion said if we find you, we'll have all the worms we want," said the robin, hopping closer to him. "And seeds, and bread. Do you like bread? I like bread."

"I, uh—" He may have been an eagle, but he had no idea if he could fly faster than the others. Over a dozen had gathered by now, all watching him with their beady eyes, waiting for him to make a move.

Perfect.

"I'm late for breakfast," he said to the robin, trying to sound as casual as possible. "But you can have that worm. It looks extra juicy."

For a split second, the robin's attention turned toward the grass, and Simon pushed off the branch and flew toward the zoo once more. Behind him, he could hear the flap of wings as the smaller birds followed. The wind whipped his feathers as he sped up, flying faster than he ever had before. He couldn't risk slowing down, not if Orion was after him.

His grandfather wasn't just the leader of the bird kingdom—he was dangerous, too, and though Simon had been foolish enough to believe Orion had been on his side at first, he now knew the truth. Orion had murdered Darryl, and in the chaos that had followed, he'd also kidnapped Simon's mother, leaving Simon with little hope of seeing her again. It was no surprise the birds were following him. Simon had shifted into a golden eagle in front of Orion, and now his grandfather thought he was the heir to the bird kingdom's throne. But Simon would have rather pulled out all his feathers one by one than ever help Orion again.

It took Simon several minutes of weaving through the trees at dangerously high speeds, but at last he lost sight of the other birds. As soon as he was positive they weren't following him anymore, he dived toward the Central Park Zoo and landed in the courtyard, hopping into the tunnel and pulling the grate shut with his beak. Shifting back into a mouse, he darted through the cold passageway as fast as he could, and by the time he reached the secret door into Nolan's bedroom, he was panting. He stopped, listening hard for the sounds of anyone following him. Silence. Taking a deep breath, he concentrated on shifting back into a human. The tunnel shrank around him, and he had to duck his head, but he relaxed as he grew into himself once more. Being able to turn into any animal he wanted was the coolest thing that had ever happened to Simon, but at the same time, there was nothing like being himself.

Simon shook out his tingling hands and pushed the panel open. He hadn't been gone long. He still had time to read a chapter before meeting his friends for breakfast and—

"Enjoy your flight?" said a deep voice, and Simon froze. In the middle of the bedroom stood Malcolm.

CAT GOT YOUR TONGUE

Simon hunched over in the mouth of the tunnel, staring up at his uncle. No doubt Malcolm knew where the tunnel led—the Alpha knew every inch of the Den, and Simon would never get away with playing dumb. The only thing he could do was own up to it.

"I'm sorry," he said, feeling strangely exposed. Malcolm had moved the desk, leaving Simon no place to hide. To make things worse, he spotted Nolan in the doorway, his face red with fury.

"You know the rules," said Malcolm, crossing his arms over his broad chest. "No one goes into the zoo without being accompanied by the pack. Especially not you two."

"I—" Simon shivered. His shirt was soaked through with sweat, and he was still catching his breath. "It's been *weeks* since you've let me go outside."

"I don't care how long it's been. You'll stay in the Den for months if that's what it takes to keep you safe," said Malcolm. Despite the anger in his voice, he offered Simon his hand and helped him to his feet.

"But I'm not—I'm not *Nolan*. It's not dangerous for me," said Simon.

His brother snorted. "No one knows what *I* am. The whole world knows *you're* Orion's heir," he shot back. "By now Orion's probably got the whole flock searching for you."

Nolan had no idea how right he was, and Simon wasn't about to tell him, not in front of Malcolm. "You can't keep me cooped up here. It isn't fair, not when there's no room to really fly," he said, shoving his hands in his pockets. He still smelled like skunk.

"I don't care if it's fair," said Malcolm. "Do you understand what will happen if Orion catches you? Or my mother?"

Simon grimaced. Celeste Thorn, the former Alpha of the mammal kingdom and Simon's grandmother, had already proved she would do anything to defeat Orion and the bird kingdom, even if it meant killing Simon.

"But they didn't catch me," said Simon. "I'm fine."

"They have nothing to do but wait for you and Nolan to appear," said Malcolm. "All they want is to get their hands on you, and when they do—"

"I won't let them touch Nolan," said Simon fiercely, and the grief he'd pushed aside during his flight back to the park crept through him again, hollowing out his insides. The night Darryl had died, Simon had promised himself he wouldn't let the same thing happen to his brother, and he'd meant it.

"I'm not the one who sneaked out, so I don't know why you're both dragging me into this," snapped Nolan. And while Simon could practically feel the heat of anger radiating from his twin, he also thought he detected a hint of hurt in his voice.

"Don't pretend you haven't used that tunnel a hundred times before, too," said Malcolm. "If you'd gone with Simon earlier, I don't doubt you would have both left the Den."

"No, he wouldn't have, because I wouldn't have let him," blurted Simon. Instantly he realized his mistake. Resentment and betrayal cast a shadow on his brother's face, and Nolan clenched his hands into fists.

"No, you wouldn't have, would you?" said Nolan, his voice shaking. "I'm not one of your precious *friends*, so why would you ever bother spending any time with me?"

"That's not what I meant and you know it," said Simon, scowling. If Orion or Celeste managed to kidnap Nolan like Orion had kidnapped their mother—

"Enough." Malcolm's voice cut through the air, and Simon clamped his mouth shut. "Nolan, go shower and change."

"But—"

"Now."

Muttering to himself, Nolan grabbed a clean black uniform from his dresser and ducked into the bathroom he and Simon shared, slamming the door so hard the lamp on his nightstand rattled. Simon winced.

"Look at me, Simon."

Though there was a growl in Malcolm's voice, he didn't sound as angry as before. Simon reluctantly met his stare. He had blue eyes, unlike Darryl's black ones, but there was still something painfully familiar about them.

"This isn't just about Nolan," said his uncle. "This is about you, too. You're as much a part of this family as he is, and I won't let anything happen to you."

Simon had to bite the inside of his cheek to stop himself from saying what he really thought. Malcolm could pretend all he wanted, but they had only met two months ago, and he hadn't raised Simon the way he'd raised Nolan. Simon *wanted* to be part of their family—he'd felt like an outsider looking in his whole life, and all he'd ever wanted was a place to belong. But he wasn't one of them, and as hard as it was to admit, he knew there was a possibility he never would be. Not completely.

"I'm not the one you should worry about," said Simon at last, his mouth turning to sandpaper. "Nolan's the one they want."

Malcolm studied the opening behind Simon. "I'm going to have the tunnel blocked. No one will be getting in or out that way again. But Simon—it isn't about keeping you cooped up."

"Feels like it," he mumbled. Malcolm sighed.

"I get it. You may not believe me, but I do. As soon as it's safe—"

"But what if it never is?" said Simon. "What if Orion's never caught? What if Celeste takes control of the kingdoms again?"

"That won't happen," said Malcolm, though he didn't look too sure. "The packs have been hunting down every lead we have on Orion and your mother—"

"But you still haven't found her."

"No, we haven't," said Malcolm reluctantly. "We're doing our best, though. Mammals all over the country are searching for them. They can't hide forever."

"Maybe not forever, but long enough."

Malcolm rubbed his eyes and muttered something under his breath. "Trust me, Simon. That's all I ask. I'm doing everything in my power to make sure nothing happens to you and Nolan, but I need you to help me, all right? I need you to not do anything stupid—like go flying outside the Den without telling me."

"So if I tell you before I go, it's all right?" he said. Malcolm gave him a look, and Simon slumped his shoulders.

"We both want the same thing, Simon. We both want to keep Nolan safe. But as long as you're running around ignoring the rules, you're only tempting Nolan to do the same thing. Despite what you may think, Orion and Celeste would be more than happy to get their hands on either of you, so do me a favor and don't risk it. Fly around the atrium if you'd like—that's what it's there for. But let me keep my promise to Darryl and protect you."

Simon deflated. That was it—that was the reason Malcolm was trying so hard to pretend like Simon was family. Because as Darryl lay dying on the roof of Sky Tower, Malcolm had promised him he would look after Simon. Considering they had known each other all of three days at that point, it was a lofty promise to make, let alone one to keep. And now he and Simon were both stuck.

No matter how much Simon wanted to help him keep his promise, he couldn't. Not completely. His mother was still out there, and if Simon ever wanted to see her again, he would have to break a few rules to find her—and likely face his grandfather down, too.

Malcolm seemed to take his silence as agreement, and he gave him an awkward pat on the shoulder before letting him head back to his bedroom. As soon as Nolan was done in the bathroom, Simon showered and finished getting ready while enduring Felix's chastisements.

"What were you *thinking*?" said the little mouse as Simon brushed his teeth. "You could have been killed, or captured, or *eaten*—"

"I'm pretty sure there aren't any animals native to New

York that eat golden eagles," mumbled Simon with a mouth full of toothpaste.

"Orion still could have caught you," said Felix. "What would happen to you then? What would happen to *me* then?"

Simon sighed and turned on the water, spitting into the sink. "You'd find someone else to feed you. Someone who has a TV."

Felix dipped his tiny paw beneath the running faucet and cleaned his whiskers. "I do miss my shows," he admitted before shaking himself out of it. "No. I won't allow you to talk like that. You may not be the Beast King's heir, but you're still important to me. You're important to Nolan, to Malcolm—"

"Don't pretend you weren't listening in on what Nolan said. He can't stand me right now. And Malcolm is only being nice because Darryl asked him to." Simon replaced his toothbrush beside his brother's and combed his shaggy hair.

"Malcolm doesn't have to love you in order to protect you." Felix scampered onto Simon's shoulder as he walked out of the bathroom and into the bedroom in search of socks. "He could keep his promise and still be a nasty piece of work about it, but he isn't."

Although Simon didn't know his uncle well, he couldn't imagine Malcolm being nasty about much. "If you're trying to convince me we'll eventually be one big happy family, I don't believe it." He didn't want to be one big happy family, not without Darryl. And not without his mother. "Besides, I can't just wait around, not while my mom's still missing."

While Simon was stuck in the Den, Orion was dragging his mother across the country in a desperate search for the pieces of the Predator, the five-pointed weapon the Beast King had used to steal other Animalgams' abilities. They weren't exactly easy to find, though. When the kingdoms had overthrown the Beast King, they had broken the weapon into five pieces. Each kingdom had agreed to protect one, preventing anyone from putting the whole thing together again. However, after spending Simon's whole life traveling across the country to research the Predator, his mother was the only person who knew exactly where they were all hidden. That was why Orion had kidnapped her—to track them down and put the Predator back together. And no matter how much Simon wanted to rescue her, he had no idea where to start.

He opened his sock drawer, his hand hovering over a clean pair. But before he could pull it out, he instead dug toward the back for the pocket watch his mother had given him, turning it over in his hands. The silver face wasn't particularly remarkable, but on the back was a symbol—five animals drawn together to form a single crest. The sign of the Beast King.

Simon didn't know what it meant. He only knew his mother had made him promise to keep it on him always, and he felt a twinge of guilt for hiding it in his sock drawer instead. But he had nearly lost it once already, on the rooftop of Sky Tower during his fight with Orion. Darryl had managed to steal it back, returning it to Simon in the final moments of his life, but even after Simon had cleaned it thoroughly, he could still imagine his uncle's blood staining the silver surface.

He'd promised his mom, though, and reluctantly he tucked the watch into his pocket. He had other reminders of her—other gifts that weren't so painful to think about. On the wall above his desk, he had displayed his collection of the one hundred and twenty-four postcards his mother had sent him while she'd traveled throughout his childhood. One for every month she'd been gone. Each boasted a different animal native to North America, and he had long since memorized the careful handwriting on the back where she'd given him facts about each species and occasionally mentioned how much she missed him. He had also found her old notebook in September, which she had filled with everything she knew about the Beast King. Simon had pored over every inch of it, searching for any clues to where the pieces might be hidden. While he'd discovered a list of locations and a few tantalizing clues, he had yet to put any of them together. If it was even possible.

Despite the turmoil of the morning, Simon's stomach let out a loud rumble, and he quickly pulled on his socks and shoes and headed into the atrium. Rather than take the spiral staircase to the ground level, Simon shifted into an eagle and flew down, hoping he would feel the same freedom he'd experienced beneath the sky. He didn't.

The dining hall was already crowded with students who all wore black armbands with silver animals on them, declaring their Animalgam forms. Almost all of them were Simon's age or older, since Animalgams could only attend the five-year program once they'd shifted, but unlike middle school, where the older kids never paid attention to the younger ones, every head seemed to turn his way as he entered. Keeping his eyes firmly on the buffet that offered every breakfast food he could imagine, including a morning sushi platter for the underwater kingdom, Simon quickly filled his plate and weaved through the dining hall. Each kingdom sat with their own kind, and not even the seventeen-year-old Animalgams mixed despite knowing one another for years.

Thankfully not all the students were like that. Somehow, Simon had managed to make friends despite who and what he was, and he set his tray down across from a blond boy wearing glasses and an armband displaying a silver dolphin.

"Morning, Jam," he said, stifling a yawn. Jam pulled his nose out of the book he'd been reading and grinned.

"Morning. You have feathers in your hair," he said.

"What?" Simon ran his fingers through his hair, and

several eagle feathers came out. He must have shed them while shifting. "Oh. Thanks."

"What are you doing here so early?" said another voice. Winter, a small, pale girl with long dark hair, sat down beside Simon with a plate full of fruit. "You don't normally get to breakfast until five minutes before it ends. And why do you smell like skunk?"

"I, uh—"

"He went for a fly around the park this morning." Another girl joined their table, but unlike Winter, everything about her was vibrant, from her freshly dyed purple hair to the mischievous look in her eyes. She'd even colored in her black widow armband with pink Magic Marker. "The Alpha yelled at him for ages."

"Malcolm didn't yell," said Simon, scowling as he tried to remember if he'd shifted into a mouse where Ariana could have seen him. "And you promised you wouldn't spy on me anymore."

"Did not," said Ariana, taking a bite of bacon and smirking. No, he decided, she hadn't seen him shift into anything but a bird. He probably would have noticed her in the tunnel if she'd been there, and if she knew his secret, she would have mentioned it to him by now. Or at least not so openly admitted to following him. If he knew anything about Ariana, it was how good a spy she really was.

A loud chorus of laughter echoed through the dining hall. Nolan sat at a table on the opposite side of the room with a handful of the biggest and most brutish mammals at the L.A.I.R. Simon caught his brother's eye, and Nolan glared at him before turning away.

Simon refocused on his plate, stabbing a piece of sausage. Apparently Nolan was still upset.

"The Alpha put my name down for the pit this morning," said Jam, his voice shaking slightly. "If he puts me up against anyone but an insect—"

"Not everyone in my kingdom is an insect, you know," said Ariana. "Spiders are arachnids. We're all arthropods, though."

"If he puts me up against anyone bigger than a cricket, I'm dead meat," amended Jam. "I can't shift on the sand. I'd be useless."

"Completely," agreed Winter, brushing her dark hair from her eyes, and Simon gave her a look. "What? Have *you* ever seen a dolphin in the desert?"

Simon ignored her. "You won't be useless," he said to Jam. "You're great at self-defense."

"Yeah, against humans," said Jam, pushing his glasses up his nose. "If Malcolm pits me against a mammal or a reptile—"

Behind him, Simon sensed a flurry of activity, and something soft and white dropped onto the table. He turned in time to see Garrett, one of the mammals Nolan had been laughing with, finish tipping a bucket full of goose down directly over Winter's head.

"Hey!" cried Simon, but there was nothing he could do. The fluffy white feathers clung to her hair and spilled into her lap, and Winter sputtered, her eyes widening with confusion.

"Thought I'd help you out, Mutt, since you want to grow feathers so badly," said Garrett. Behind him, the other mammals laughed, and Simon clenched his fists when he saw Nolan's mocking smirk. Simon had endured plenty of bullying from Garrett and the other mammals when he had first arrived at the L.A.I.R., but up until today, Nolan had kept them under control. Apparently he was mad enough to let them off their leashes now.

But Simon's attention quickly returned to Winter, who had gone from pale to scarlet. Garrett and Nolan might have thought it was a hilarious joke, but Simon could see the pain and humiliation swirling in her green eyes. Winter was a Hybred. Instead of her parents being from the same kingdom, her father had been a bird Animalgam, and her mother had been able to shift into a reptile. Being a Hybred didn't seem like much of a big deal to Simon, but Winter, who had been raised by Orion and had spent her entire life wanting nothing more than to shift into a bird, had been desperate to keep her parentage a secret from everyone, even Simon. She'd only revealed her real Animalgam form in order to protect him, and now the entire school knew that she was a cottonmouth snake.

It was one of many things Simon felt guilty about, but at

least this time he could do something to help. While Winter sat still, her hair shielding her face and her shoulders tensing as if she were about to cry, Simon stood and gripped the back of his chair so tightly that his fingernails left indents in the wood.

"You know who else is a Hybred?" he said. "Me and Nolan. Would you dump feathers over our heads, too?"

Garrett stepped closer, towering over Simon. "I wouldn't have to, birdbrain. You've already got them. And if the teachers had any sense, you wouldn't be here right now, not after you let Orion kill Darryl Thorn. *Traitor.*"

As soon as Garrett said his uncle's name, something inside Simon snapped. The world went dark around the edges, and it felt as if there was a molten-hot hand squeezing around his heart. Without warning—without even realizing what he was doing until it was too late—Simon launched himself at the bigger boy with a feral cry.

Garrett fell, his elbows knocking against the wooden floor with a hard *crack*. Simon scrambled over him, trying to pin his legs and arms, but before he could get any kind of grip, Garrett began to shift. His body sprouted tan fur, his hands and feet turned into paws, and his face twisted into the muzzle of a mountain lion, complete with a set of razor-sharp teeth.

In an instant, the massive cat flipped over, and he shoved his paw so hard against Simon's chest that Simon felt as if his ribs were about to snap. "You think you can take me on and win? Your wings are useless if you can't fly."

Simon wheezed, struggling to breathe as his vision went red. He didn't have to fly. If he wanted, he could shift into a bear and show Garrett what a real fight was like. He could turn into a venomous viper and make the rest of the day excruciating for him. Or he could will his body to become as small as a flea, and when Garrett least expected it, he could strike.

The temptation to do all of that and more was enormous, and Simon had already formed the image of a tiger in his head when a massive gray wolf tackled the mountain lion, sending Garrett flying. Simon sat up, half expecting the wolf to pin Garrett, but instead they both shifted back into their human forms.

"What did I tell you about laying a paw on my nephews?" growled Malcolm, casting a shadow over Garrett, who had turned ghostly pale.

"Simon attacked him," said Nolan from the edge of the crowd that had already gathered. "Garrett was just defending himself."

Simon glanced at the table where his friends sat, opening his mouth to insist Garrett had attacked Winter. But while Ariana and Jam were on their feet, both ready to jump in and defend him, only a pile of white feathers remained where Winter had sat seconds before.

"I don't care who started it. We do not use our

Animalgam forms against each other, period," said Malcolm. "No more pit privileges for the rest of the month, Garrett. And if you ever attack another student again, you'll be expelled."

Simon didn't hear Garrett's response, if he managed one at all. Instead, as Simon climbed to his feet, he caught sight of his hands, and his blood ran cold.

His fingernails had shifted into claws.

3

HYBRED

For the rest of breakfast, Simon only half listened to his friends' conversation, staring at his hands instead. His fingertips had returned to normal, but that had been too close. If Malcolm hadn't interrupted the fight when he had, Simon didn't want to think about what he would have done.

On the way to the pit for morning practice, Simon trailed behind his friends, all too aware of Garrett complaining about the loss of his pit privileges in a booming voice that rose above the crowd. Simon, unfortunately, hadn't received the same punishment—or any punishment at all—which undoubtedly meant Garrett would make Simon's life as miserable as possible for the foreseeable future. There wasn't much he could do to make it worse, though. Not unless he was smart enough to keep targeting Simon's friends.

The pit reeked of vinegar, but better that than skunk. Simon joined Jam and Ariana at the top of the bleachers, where they sat as far from the action as possible. Ariana looked annoyed, while beside her, Jam appeared vaguely ill. Simon thought it was from the smell until he remembered what Jam had said at breakfast.

"At least you won't have to fight against Garrett," said Simon as he sat down.

"That's something, I guess," said Jam, though he didn't look terribly reassured. "I thought for sure I'd be matched against him in the pit."

"Not today. Do you see Winter anywhere?"

Both of them shook their heads. Simon searched the sea of students around them, but there was no sign of her. Before he could try to sneak away to find her, however, Malcolm strode onto the sand with a pair of pack members in wolf form trailing after him.

"Sophie Fitzgerald and Geoffrey Lee," he called, and two older students stood. "You're up."

He and the pack members cleared the sand, leaving room for the pair to face off. As soon as Malcolm blew the whistle, they shifted into their Animalgam forms—a wasp and a rattlesnake—and the fight began. Other students shouted support for their favorites, but Simon couldn't muster up much interest, not with Winter missing. Despite Jam's anxiety, most students enjoyed pit practice. It was the only time they were allowed to shift into their Animalgam forms outside of sanctioned training and when they were inside their sections. Simon knew most of the others ignored those rules, though; he'd seen for himself how Ariana spent half her time as a black widow spider, and most of the mammals shifted whenever a member of the pack wasn't looking. Simon didn't blame them. If he could, he would have run around as a different animal each day just to see what it was like. As it was, he was stuck as either an eagle or a human in front of others, and both seemed to catch him an equal amount of grief.

The wasp won the match after the rattlesnake tried to capture the insect in his mouth, only to wind up with a stinger in his tongue, forcing him to yield. The students cheered, and Simon's attention wandered even more with each successive match. Beside him, he could feel Jam growing tense, but there was nothing he could do other than quietly reassure his friend that he would be fine. When they'd sneaked into Sky Tower two months earlier, Simon had seen Jam take on a grown member of the pack and win. A student would be a piece of cake.

As Simon seriously considered whether anyone would follow him if he excused himself to use the bathroom, Malcolm called the names of the next pairing.

"Benjamin Fluke and . . ."

Simon held his breath.

"Nolan Thorn."

His eyes widened, and he looked over at Jam. "At

least it's not Garrett," he managed, but that wasn't much consolation. While Nolan was really the Beast King's heir, almost everyone in the L.A.I.R. believed he could only shift into a massive gray wolf like their uncle. And with the mood Nolan was in that morning, Simon wouldn't have put it past his brother to draw blood.

With his hands trembling, Jam made his way down to the sand, where Nolan stood waiting, determination radiating off him. Simon anxiously leaned forward for a better view, all thoughts of Winter temporarily pushed aside. This couldn't possibly end well.

"He'll be fine," said Ariana, but even she didn't sound convinced.

Malcolm blew the whistle, and the match began. Instantly Nolan shifted into a gray wolf. Jam stumbled back, nearly tripping over his own feet. Even from a distance, Simon could see the panic on his face.

"Grab him by the scruff!" yelled Ariana, but Simon remained silent as Nolan advanced. If the mammals were willing to publicly humiliate Winter in the dining hall, he couldn't imagine what Nolan had in mind for Jam now.

In a flurry of fur and teeth, Nolan snarled and jumped, his paws landing against Jam's chest as they fell to the ground. Jam's glasses flew off into the sand, and Nolan bared his teeth an inch from Jam's throat. While he didn't bite him, Jam winced with pain, and Simon noticed wolf's claws digging deep into Jam's black uniform.

"Nolan's hurting him!" he shouted, but the cheers from the crowd drowned him out. Why wasn't Jam yielding?

The wolf pushed off Jam's chest, tearing his shirt with his claws, and he grabbed Jam's boot with his mouth. Before Simon could shout again, Nolan began to drag Jam through the sand around the edge of the pit, as if showing off his prize. As he paraded around, he purposely stepped on Jam's glasses.

Simon's blood boiled with fury, and he began to shift before he could stop himself. For one terrifying moment, as his vision changed and his limbs twisted, he wasn't sure which animal he was about to become. But as soon as he opened his mouth and an eagle's cry escaped, he spread his wings and flew down into the pit, consumed with anger. It was one thing for Nolan to go after Simon, but Jam hadn't done anything to deserve this humiliation.

"Let him go," he demanded, landing on Nolan's back and grabbing his ear with his beak. He must have squeezed harder than he'd thought, because the wolf yelped and immediately released Jam's boot.

"What are you *doing?*" cried Nolan, trying to shake him off.

Now that he'd let Jam go, Simon released his brother and flapped his wings, rising several feet. "You were hurting him. The match is over."

"He hasn't yielded!" Nolan leaped into the air and snapped at him, his muzzle missing by inches. Simon rose even higher. "You can't do this!"

"*Enough*, both of you." Malcolm lumbered across the sand, and from Simon's vantage point, he could see the cords in his uncle's neck standing out. "Simon, you know better than to interfere in someone else's match."

"But Nolan—"

"I saw it, too, Simon. Shift back, both of you, and meet me upstairs."

Simon landed easily beside Jam, and though he was still furious, he forced himself to turn back into his human form. "Are you all right?" he said, kneeling beside Jam in the sand.

Jam nodded, though the scratches showing through his torn shirt told another story. "Do you see my glasses anywhere?"

Simon fished around in the sand until he found them—mangled and broken, exactly like he'd feared. "Nolan stepped on them," he said apologetically, offering them to Jam.

"The general won't be happy about this," said Jam. The left lens had cracked in the center, while Nolan had managed to snap the opposite arm clean in half. There was no salvaging them.

"So tell him the truth—that it wasn't fair," said Simon. "Your dad will understand."

"Simon. Upstairs. Now," called Malcolm from halfway up the staircase. Groaning inwardly, Simon stood and offered Jam his arm. Jam wobbled a little, but managed to find his footing in the uneven sand.

"I'll see you in class," said Simon as Ariana joined them from the bleachers. "Go to the infirmary first."

"I'll make sure he doesn't fall over on the way," said Ariana, and though she was nearly a head shorter than Jam, she wrapped her arm around his middle and led him toward the door.

Simon joined his brother upstairs in Malcolm's office, keeping as much distance between them as possible. As soon as Malcolm closed the door with a soft *click*, the hair on the back of Simon's neck stood up.

"I don't know what's going on between the two of you, but whatever it is, it needs to stop," said his uncle.

"Why are you yelling at me?" said Nolan, even though Malcolm hadn't raised his voice. "Simon's the one who—"

"I saw what happened. I don't need you to tell me," said Malcolm, perching on the edge of his desk. "I'll say it a hundred times if I have to—you're brothers. You will be a part of each other's lives from here on out, and you can either learn to get along, or you can suffer for it."

"I don't see how you expect me to get along with him when he does things like *this* all the time," said Nolan, crossing his arms.

"And I don't see how you expect *me* to get along with *you* when you're bullying my friends," said Simon hotly. Malcolm sighed.

"We have thirty minutes of pit time left before you need to be in class," he said. "I'm going back down to observe. You two will stay in here and talk it out, and you will not leave until you're behaving like brothers. Is that understood?"

Though neither Simon nor Nolan nodded, Malcolm strode out of his office and closed the door behind them. For several minutes, Nolan refused to look at him, let alone say anything. Simon knew without a doubt that his brother would accept nothing less than a total apology, and even then he'd probably argue with him just to drive the point home. As far as Simon saw it, there was no point—what little headway he'd managed to make with Nolan the past two months had been destroyed in a single morning.

"That was the first time in six weeks Malcolm's let me fight in the pit, and you had to go and humiliate me in front of everyone," spat Nolan at last.

"I wouldn't have done it if you hadn't been hurting Jam," said Simon. "You didn't have to drag him around like that. He hasn't done anything to you."

Nolan scoffed. "He's weak."

"Not when he's underwater." Simon shook his head. "He's my friend. If you'd been set up against anyone else, you would've never—"

"You think I care that he's your *friend*?" said Nolan.

"Yes. Just like I think you only told Garrett to pull that prank on Winter because she's my friend, too."

His brother's nostrils flared exactly like Simon's did when he was upset and trying to think of what to say.

Seconds passed, and finally Nolan burst. "The entire school knows you like your friends more than you like me and Malcolm. You're always with them, and you never even bother talking to me unless Malcolm makes you. Sometimes I think—I think if you had to choose between us, you'd choose your friends."

Simon stared at him, speechless. That wasn't a choice he ever wanted to make, but if he did . . . if he was being honest with himself, Nolan was right. He *would* choose Winter and Jam and Ariana.

"It's not the same for me," said Simon, a knot forming in his throat. "You've known Malcolm your whole life. He's already your family. Me, I'm not—"

"You're not what? Our family?" Nolan narrowed his eyes and finally looked at him. "You could be, you know, if you tried. But you don't. You don't sit with me—"

"Because your friends hate me," said Simon. "Did you or did you not hear what Garrett called me?"

"You *are* a traitor," snarled Nolan. "You're a traitor against me. Against Malcolm. Against Mom. *You're* the reason she's gone."

Simon would have preferred a sucker punch to the gut than having to listen to the venom Nolan was spewing, and he could feel that familiar hot anger surge through him. Willing himself not to shift, he took a deep breath, trying to calm himself down. It didn't work. "I didn't betray you. *You're* the one who already has a family. My family died on the roof of Sky Tower, and you and Malcolm are never going to replace him. And yeah, maybe I spend more time with my friends, but that's because they like me and *want* me around. You just want someone to tell you how awesome you are all the time. But you're not," said Simon, and he stood, glaring at his brother. "Awesome people aren't bullies. Awesome people are accepting and nice and don't call people traitors or Mutts or act like the world should revolve around them, because it doesn't. My world has never revolved around you, and never will, got it?"

"Yeah, I got it," said Nolan nastily. "Good to know what you really think of me. I guess you think Mom made the wrong choice, don't you? Keeping me instead of you."

Simon didn't bother replying. Instead he stormed out of the office and slammed the door behind him, not caring if Malcolm would be upset with him. His uncle was already upset, and if things kept going this badly between Simon and Nolan, he always would be.

While everyone was finishing up in the pit, Simon wandered the Den, checking empty classrooms and the musty library for Winter. He even ducked into the dining hall again to see if she'd tried to sneak breakfast once everyone had left, but it too was empty. Frustrated, he headed toward the reptile section. He doubted she would hide in there, considering how much she hated being a cottonmouth, but with most of the students in the pit, there was a chance she would try. Each of the five Animalgam sections was designed to create a familiar environment for that specific kingdom, and the reptiles lived in a desert, complete with sand and suffocating heat. Simon had only been inside a couple of times before, and he instinctively looked down, not wanting to step on anyone's tail.

Inside the reptile dormitory was an oasis—for the reptiles that didn't thrive in the desert, Simon figured. An older crocodile gave him an odd look as he passed, and he stepped around a patch of swamp. But Winter wasn't in her room, and she wasn't in the common area, either.

By the time he exited the reptile section, pit practice was about to end, and he had no choice but to brush the sand from his clothes and head toward his first class of the day: History of the Animalgam World. It was much more interesting than the wars and revolutions he'd studied in a normal middle school, and it was also Winter's favorite subject.

But when he reached the classroom, her desk was empty. He sat between Jam and Ariana, trying to ignore the back of Nolan's head three rows ahead of him. "Did you go to the infirmary?" he said to Jam, who was wearing a fresh shirt and a spare pair of glasses.

"All bandaged up," said Jam. "The nurse said I shouldn't go in the water for a few days. The general won't be pleased."

But Jam would love an excuse to have the extra reading time rather than doing endless underwater drills. Simon flashed him a smile, and Jam returned it.

As class began, their teacher, Mr. Barnes, a tall man with a scraggly goatee and hollow cheeks, cleared his throat. Simon sat up a bit straighter, pen poised to take notes for Winter. If nothing else, that would give him an excuse to look for her later.

"Throughout history, what it means to be an Animalgam has changed," said Mr. Barnes, pacing slowly in front of the class with his hands clasped behind his back. "We have adapted to modern technology and shrinking natural habitats. We have learned how to live seamlessly as human or animal, and despite the many wars we have had to overcome, our kind continues to thrive. Though the rules governing our people have changed over the centuries, there are three core foundations shared by all kingdoms that have not. Who can tell me the three laws of the Animalgam world?"

Jam's hand shot up, but Mr. Barnes's gaze landed on Ariana instead. She twirled her pen around and leaned back in her seat, propping her combat boots up on the edge of the chair in front of her.

"First rule: respect nature and the natural order of the world. Second rule: never hunt other Animalgams. And the third and most important rule: never, ever reveal the Animalgam world to a human."

"Very good, Miss Webster," said Mr. Barnes. "Can you tell the class why secrecy is so important to our kind?"

"Experiments," said Nolan before Ariana could get a word out. "Even back in the Dark Ages, if an Animalgam was discovered by humans, they were usually tortured to death or burned at the stake as witches."

"Life would be infinitely easier if I could cast a spell on you and make you disappear," muttered Ariana, still twirling her pen. If Nolan heard her, he didn't let on.

"And that is why secrecy, above all else, is valued by our kind," said Mr. Barnes. "Those who have made the mistake of shifting in front of others or confessing their secrets to non-Animalgam friends and loved ones always pay a dear price. Many of your families no doubt instilled this in you as young children, long before you were able to shift, and it is a law we uphold to this day."

"But what about the first time we shift?" said Simon. Nearly every head in the classroom turned to look at him, but he held Mr. Barnes's stare and balled his hands into fists, imagining how it would feel if claws instead of nails were digging into his palms. "Most people can't control that, right?"

"Though there are rare instances of Animalgam children being raised among humans—such as, ah, yourself, for instance, Mr. Thorn—you will find nearly all Animalgams choose to rear their young among their own kind," said Mr. Barnes. "Each kingdom has habitats and communities spread across the country, and they cater to the specific needs of their population."

"What if they don't know which kingdom their kids will belong to?" said Simon. Several students shifted uncomfortably and glanced at one another.

"You mean—Hybreds, yes," said Mr. Barnes, clearing his throat. "Being raised in an environment unnatural to their eventual Animalgam form, which of course will not be discovered until after they shift for the first time, can lead to . . . confusing results. That is why relationships between members of two different kingdoms are so highly discouraged," he added. "It has even reached a point where some communities ban Hybreds altogether, as their presence can often lead to exclusion and other negative behaviors."

"But that isn't the Hybreds' fault," said Simon. "They shouldn't be punished for it."

"I agree," said Mr. Barnes, peering down his nose at Simon with something akin to pity in his eyes. "But I fear there are few solutions present that would satisfy all. Until then, it is a deep shame, but Hybreds often remain on the fringes of society long after they have shifted, particularly if they were raised in the wrong parent's kingdom."

Silence permeated the room, and once it became clear Mr. Barnes was waiting for Simon to react, he nodded stiffly. While Mr. Barnes quickly changed the subject, Simon turned his attention to his notebook, keenly aware of the stares burning holes into his head.

He ignored them. At least now he understood why Winter was so ashamed to admit she was a snake raised in the bird kingdom, and he spent the rest of his morning classes trying to come up with a way—any way—to help her. He would stand up for her as many times as it took for Nolan and the mammals to get the picture, and he would be there for her as much as she would let him. More than anything at that moment, he wanted to talk to her—he wanted to make sure she knew she wasn't alone. But after spending his whole life being bullied by kids bigger and stronger than him, Simon knew how useless it was to be told it gets better. Of course it would get better eventually, once school was over, but it wasn't better now, and that was all he wanted. It was probably all Winter wanted, too.

"Where do you think she went?" said Simon as he, Jam, and Ariana made their way to their zoology class. "I've checked everywhere for her."

"Sometimes she sneaks outside," said Ariana, who was carrying Jam's backpack for him despite his protests. "There's a tunnel in the reptile section, too."

Jam blinked, his eyes wide behind his glasses. They were thicker than the other pair and made him look more owlish than usual. "How do you know that?" he said.

"Someone has to keep an eye on her," said Ariana. "It's not like she goes to Sky Tower or anything. She just hangs around in the zoo."

"I'll check during lunch," said Simon. It was a risky move, leaving the Den again after Malcolm had caught him that morning, but he couldn't stand the thought of Winter being alone right now. Earning a detention or two would be worth making sure she was okay.

As soon as zoology class let out and lunch began, he said a quick good-bye to Jam and Ariana and headed back to the Alpha section. Once he dropped off his backpack, he ducked into Nolan's room, stopping when he saw the heavy bookcase that now covered the entrance to the tunnel.

"It's completely blocked," said Felix, scrambling up Simon's leg and into his cupped hand. "I already checked. Besides, don't you think you've been in enough trouble today?"

He didn't know the half of it, but Simon quickly told the little mouse everything that had happened at breakfast. "I think Winter's out there," he said at last. "I have to go through the other tunnel, but the pack's going to come back any minute. Can you be my lookout?"

Felix's whiskers twitched. "If the Alpha finds out, he'll roast me with garlic for an afternoon snack."

"Malcolm won't find out, and if he does, I'll protect you. Please, Felix—I won't ask anything from you again for the rest of the year."

"We both know that's a lie." He sighed heavily. "Fine. But if you get caught, I'm out of there, got it?"

"Thanks, Felix," said Simon, and he slipped the mouse into the pocket of his black uniform, ignoring his mutterings.

At the far edge of the atrium, beyond the green grass

and tall trees, stood a door that led into the Alpha's office. Simon had only been inside a few times before, and never for pleasant reasons. Originally it had belonged to Celeste Thorn, before Malcolm had banished her and taken the title of Alpha. Now it technically belonged to Malcolm, but Simon had only ever seen his uncle use the one above the pit.

Simon scooped Felix out of his pocket and set him down. "Squeak if anyone comes," he said, and he opened the door. The hinges creaked, and Simon winced, but there was no going back now.

It was an ordinary office, with a large mahogany desk and a cold, empty fireplace. Three portraits hung from the walls, and though Simon couldn't make out the details in the darkness, he knew exactly what they looked like. One was of Celeste herself, and the other two were of the sons she had lost: Darryl and Simon's father, Luke, whom she'd adopted and raised as her own. Part of Simon was tempted to turn on the lights and stare at his father's face. It had been months since he'd seen the portrait, and he worried he'd forgotten what his father had looked like. But he didn't have much time before lunch would be over, and right now, he had to focus on Winter.

He tugged on the edge of Celeste's portrait. The frame clicked open, revealing the entrance to another tunnel, and Simon climbed in. He hadn't taken this one before, but Winter had, and she'd insisted the tunnel let out somewhere inside the zoo above. Simon only hoped she was right.

Despite his close call with Malcolm—and Ariana—that morning, he closed his eyes and urged his body to shrink into a mouse once more. He couldn't see the tunnel in the darkness, but he could sense it growing bigger until he was Felix's size. Blinking, he twitched the end of his tail, making sure he had his balance before scurrying up to the surface as fast as he could.

A few minutes later, he reached the exit, which was choked with foliage and clearly hadn't been used recently. That was no surprise—only those with access to the Alpha section would be able to get to the portrait, and the pack members wouldn't bother, not when they could go into the zoo anytime they wanted. Simon shifted back into a human and, pushing the leaves aside, he crawled out onto the cold ground and squinted in the sudden onslaught of sunlight.

Winter had been right. The tunnel let out at the very back of the Central Park Zoo, near a pond filled with turtles. Relieved, Simon stood and brushed the dirt off his knees. A few feet away, a little girl no older than four stared at him with wide eyes. Simon pressed his finger to his lips and hurried past her.

The zoo wasn't very crowded, not in the middle of a November weekday, but Simon searched every winding path and building and still couldn't spot Winter. Deflated, he stopped near a vendor selling stuffed animals. Maybe she wasn't there after all, but where else could she possibly be? Had she finally run away? He glanced at the city skyline, where he could see Sky Tower a few blocks from the park. If he flew, he might have time to make it there and back before the end of lunch.

Simon was about to search for a dark corner to shift when he spotted a familiar statue out of the corner of his eye. The stone wolf didn't appear to be anything special, and most visitors passed it without a second look, but Simon knew better. It marked his uncle's grave, a headstone that blended in with the rest of the statues in the courtyard. A second wolf figure beside it marked his father's, but it was Darryl's grave that Simon approached. He couldn't leave without visiting, not when he was this close.

"Hi," he whispered, rubbing the wolf's muzzle and brushing his fingertips against the scar that ran down the wolf's left cheek. "I'm sorry I haven't been around lately. Malcolm's keeping his promise to you, and it's getting harder to sneak out—"

He stopped. At the base of the statue, half-obscured by a loose stone, he spotted something colorful that looked almost like trash. Kneeling, he moved the stone, and a piece of stiff paper poked out of the hidden compartment.

It was a postcard.

With his heart in his throat, Simon picked up the colorful picture of the Arizona desert and flipped it over. There, written in his mother's familiar handwriting, were four simple words.

Wish you were here.

BIRDS OF PARADISE

Simon's hands shook as he read the words on the postcard over and over again, searching for a clue that this wasn't some big joke. His mother was with Orion. There was no way she could have come back to New York to hide this for him.

A sparrow landed on his shoulder and trilled. "Simon Thorn has found it!" she declared, puffing up with pride.

"This?" he said, holding up the postcard. "You left this for me?"

"A bird from the sandy place did," she said, and she pecked at his ear. "Food?"

Hope surged through him, and he dug in his pockets and handed the sparrow half a cracker he'd meant to give

Felix. She flew off, and Simon stumbled toward the center of the zoo, his mind reeling.

His mother was in Arizona. That was where Orion had taken her to search for the pieces of the Predator. He looked at the card again. There was a rattlesnake in the picture—they must have been hunting for the reptiles' part of the weapon, he reasoned, running his fingers over her looping handwriting. He doubted any of the other kingdoms would have tried to hide their piece in the desert.

Simon swallowed hard. He had to find a way to get to Arizona. Maybe he had enough allowance money saved up over the years to buy a plane ticket, or maybe he could borrow—Simon didn't want to think of it as *stealing*—from Malcolm. Either way, his mother needed his help, and he wasn't going to let her down again. He had no idea how long it had taken for her postcard to reach him, and there was a chance they'd already found the piece and moved on to the next. But this was the only lead Simon had, and he had to follow it. As soon as possible.

He didn't realize he'd run across Winter until he nearly tripped over the flock of pigeons at her feet. She sat rigidly on a bench across from the seal exhibit with a bucket of stale popcorn on her lap, and she stared at the pigeons in front of her as they pecked at the kernels scattered across the cobblestones. Without even glancing his way, she said in a biting voice, "It's about time. You've passed me twice."

"I was—distracted." Simon tucked the postcard in his pocket and sat beside her without asking. She didn't move away. "I thought you hated pigeons."

"They're the only birds that'll come anywhere near me now," she muttered. "Why are you here?"

He hesitated. "I'm sorry about what Garrett and Nolan did."

"Don't be. I'm surprised it took them this long." She tossed another handful of popcorn on the ground, and a half dozen more pigeons joined them. Her light green eyes were rimmed with red. "I don't want to be here anymore."

Simon nudged a pebble with the toe of his sneaker. "Sometimes I don't want to be here, either."

She scoffed. "Darryl and your mom didn't want to leave you. They didn't decide to forget about you just because you shift into a snake instead of a bird. At least they still love you. At least you still have family."

"Loved," he said, all his excitement from receiving the postcard evaporating. "Darryl loved me. And now he's dead." He didn't have to point out that if it hadn't been for Winter, his uncle would probably still be alive. That cold, hard fact had wedged its way between them the day Darryl had died, and though they'd both done their best to move past it, neither of them had forgotten. Simon wasn't sure he ever could, just like he was sure Winter would never forget that Simon was the reason Orion knew she was really a snake.

A pigeon waddled over to his feet, already nearly twice the size of a normal bird. "Food?"

Simon grabbed a few kernels from the bucket and tossed them over to the pigeon. "I'm trying to help you," he said to Winter.

"How? By putting my life back together for me?"

"By—I don't know. Being your friend."

"Look where that's gotten you so far," she spat. "Just leave me alone, Simon. I don't know why you're trying so hard."

"Because someone should. Bad things happen every day, and sometimes—sometimes it feels like the end of the world. But they always get better eventually."

Winter gave him a withering look. "Do you really believe that?"

He ran his fingers across the glossy postcard in his pocket. "Yes," he said firmly, even though ten minutes ago, he hadn't been so sure. "The only way any of this will get better is if we keep going. Maybe—maybe it'll be a while before I find my mom. Maybe we won't be able to stop Orion from getting all the pieces of the Predator. But no matter what happens, you have me, and I have you. Right?"

For a long moment, she said nothing, but finally she rubbed her cheek and reluctantly nodded. Though she didn't look at him, she mumbled, "Thanks for standing up for me. You didn't get in trouble, did you?"

"Malcolm has other reasons to be mad at me," said Simon. "Garrett's a jerk. We'll get back at him somehow."

"That'll just make him come after us even harder."

"We'll be ready for him."

The pigeons cooed for more food, and Winter tossed them another handful of popcorn. At last Simon pulled the postcard from his pocket, and without letting go, he showed it to Winter. "I found this at my uncle's grave. It's from my mom," he said. "She used to send postcards when it was just me and Darryl."

"I've seen them on your wall." Her brow furrowed as she examined the handwriting. "'Wish you were here'? What does that mean?"

"She sent it from Arizona," he said, flipping it over to show her. "Paradise Valley, wherever that is."

"And what are we supposed to do about it?" she said. Simon stared at her, and her eyes widened. "Simon, no. We can't."

"Why not?"

"Why do you think? You obviously remember what happened last time you tried to take on Orion. Do you really want the same thing to happen again?"

"She needs my help," said Simon, guilt gnawing at his insides. The last time he had tried to take on Orion, Darryl had died. "I can't ignore her. She's my mom."

"How do you know it's really her?" said Winter.

"Because I know her handwriting. She wrote to me my whole life. I could recognize it anywhere."

"And you don't think anyone could duplicate it?"

He scowled, staring at those four words. It could be a trap. Maybe it was. Orion was desperate to get his hands on him, and he must have known Simon wouldn't hesitate to rescue his mother. Still, that was a risk he had to take. Even if Orion was waiting for him, he wasn't prepared to face the Beast King's heir. As long as Simon didn't reveal his secret, he would have the upper hand. "Please, Winter. I need your help. I think they're going after the reptile kingdom's piece."

For a fraction of a second, her annoyed expression slipped, revealing a hint of terror underneath. "No. Absolutely not. I don't care how many pieces of the weapon they're hiding—"

"You swore you'd help me," said Simon. Winter dug her hand into the popcorn again, but he pulled the bucket away, spilling kernels all over her lap. "After Darryl died, you said you'd do anything to help me find my mom."

"Anything except this," she said, throwing the kernels she'd managed to snatch on the ground.

"Why?" said Simon. "I thought you'd jump at the chance to leave the city. You hate it here."

"I'd hate it more there," she muttered.

So this, too, like everything else, was about her Animalgam form. "You're upset about not being a bird. I get it—"

"You don't have the slightest idea."

"Maybe not, but I'm trying." There was an edge to his voice that caught in his throat, sharper than his usual tone.

"You know you're going to have to accept it sooner or later, right? You're a cottonmouth. Yeah, you'd rather have wings, but that doesn't mean you're useless or have nothing to offer. You're venomous, which means people will leave you alone when you want them to—"

"You mean like right now?" she said. Simon ignored her.

"You're smart and creative, you never let anyone else tell you who you are, and you love to read like the rest of the reptiles at the L.A.I.R.—"

"I am *not* one of them, and I never will be," she snarled. "I'm not going to Paradise Valley, Simon, and you can't make me."

"I'm not trying to—" He raked his fingers through his hair and let out a frustrated huff. He'd fought enough with Winter over the past couple of months to know a losing battle when it stared him in the face. "Fine. If you're not going to help, then I'll find someone who will."

"You do that," she said bitterly, brushing the popcorn off her lap. "It won't be me."

Standing, he shoved the postcard in his pocket. "If you're not back for afternoon training, Malcolm's going to come looking for you."

"I don't care."

"Fine, then be expelled. Doesn't matter to me."

He started to walk off, but before he could get more than a few steps, he stopped. It did matter to him. It mattered to him a lot, and while she acted like it didn't bother her, he knew he was Winter's only real friend. Even Jam and Ariana put up with her because of Simon, and if he abandoned her, she would have no one. He turned around, and though she looked as if she was about to cry, the moment their eyes met, her expression turned stony.

"If you don't want to come, then—okay. I get it," said Simon. "But you can't change who you are. You're a cotton-mouth, and that's okay. It doesn't make you a bad person, and it doesn't make me like you any less. Anyone who does care—they don't matter, and they never will."

"Easy for you to say," she mumbled.

"No, it isn't." He didn't think it would help to point out the fact that he was the only bird Animalgam in the entire school and that everyone hated him for it, not when being a bird was all Winter wanted. He didn't have to, though. She already knew how bad it was for him, and it passed unsaid between them. "But as long as you're my friend—as long as Jam and Ariana are still my friends, people like Garrett . . . they don't matter, because they'll never be able to see who I really am. Or who you really are. And you're pretty cool, you know. Sometimes you're not very nice—"

She scoffed.

"—but if I had to choose between being your friend or being an eagle, I would choose being your friend every time."

He took a step backward. The groups and families milling around didn't seem to be paying any attention to them, but he knew it was only a matter of time before a member of the pack came by and recognized them. He couldn't be caught in the zoo again today, not if he wanted to have any hope of sneaking out a third time.

"You'll still be my friend whether you come with me or not," he continued, even though she was now staring resolutely at the pigeons instead of him. "But if you change your mind, I'm going to try to leave tonight, after dinner. My mom needs me, and I can't lose her again. And I don't want to lose you, either."

With that, he turned and walked away, leaving Winter on the bench with a flock of pigeons and a half-empty bucket of stale popcorn.

Simon returned to the Den ten minutes before afternoon classes began. Felix assured him no one had come by or noticed his absence, and once Simon fetched his backpack, he headed down into the bottom level, where the Tracking and Survival classroom took up more space than the dining hall and pit combined. It was by far his favorite class. Vanessa, a member of the wolf pack with curly dark hair and an expression that always made Simon think he'd done something wrong, taught them to survive in the wild not only as a human, but in their Animalgam forms, too. It was the closest Simon ever got to feeling like a real Animalgam and not an impostor among the rest of his classmates, who always seemed to be three steps ahead of him. Most of them had grown up in communities, so they seemed to know as much as Simon when it came to surviving the wild on their own.

The Tracking and Survival classroom had a combination of multiple terrains, with a forest in one corner, a swamp running along another wall, and a patch of desert toward the opposite end of the room. Though he doubted Winter would bother attending, not after she'd skipped their morning classes, Simon searched for that familiar head of dark hair as he entered the room. There was no sign of her, and instead, a loud burst of laughter caught his attention. Nolan was once again in the middle of a knot of mammal students. Making a point to avoid them, Simon trudged toward the back of the room, where Ariana was perched on a log.

"Any luck?" she said as he sat on a mossy rock beside her, dropping his backpack at his feet.

"Found her feeding pigeons," said Simon. Winter liked pigeons about as much as Simon liked Orion, and the fact that she'd voluntarily gone anywhere near them spoke volumes about how much she must have missed her old life in Sky Tower.

"I don't know why she stays here if it makes her so miserable," said Ariana, studying the ends of her purple hair. "She must have family somewhere."

Simon shrugged and tossed a pebble into a gurgling

creek that cut through the center of the room. "The only family she wants is Orion, and he's never going to let her back now."

"I wouldn't want to go back if I were Winter, not after Orion abandoned her," said Ariana, while Jam plopped down between them.

"I saved some lunch for you, Simon." Jam offered him a wrapped sandwich. "It's dolphin-safe tuna. I hope that's okay."

"As long as I'm not eating one of your relatives. Thanks," said Simon as he peeled back the waxed paper. Before he took a bite, however, he pulled the postcard from his pocket and handed it to Ariana. "I found this at the base of my uncle's statue. My mother sent it to me."

"Your mother? How do you know it's from her?" said Jam. Ariana flipped it over to reveal the words on the other side. *Wish you were here.*

"The handwriting matches the other postcards she sent Simon," she said before he could answer. "It's definitely from her."

Simon took a bite of tuna and swallowed. "She had a bird bring it to me, but I don't know how long ago she sent it." Wiping his mouth, he added, "I'm going after her."

Neither of them looked surprised. Instead, Ariana examined the picture, while Jam peered curiously over her shoulder. "When are we leaving?" he said.

"We?" said Simon.

"Yes, *we*." Ariana handed the postcard to Jam. "You didn't think we'd let you leave by yourself, did you? You can't even fly around the park without being attacked."

"But—"

"Whatever you're going to say, helping you find your mom is more important," said Ariana. "Besides, if she's in Arizona, that means they're looking for the reptiles' piece of the Predator. Do you even know the first thing about the reptile kingdom?"

Simon hesitated. "They're, uh—creative? And they have a council instead of an Alpha or a queen or anything."

"And do you know who the head of that council is?" said Ariana. He shook his head. "Robert Rivera. No one likes him, not even his own kind. Usually the reptiles stay neutral in Animalgam wars, but Councilman Rivera threw his support behind the mammal kingdom years ago. My mother always says she's surprised he's lasted this long, but the reptiles that don't agree with him have a nasty habit of disappearing."

A shiver ran through Simon. "We won't have to go anywhere near Rivera."

"Except Paradise Valley is where the council is based," said Jam, handing the postcard back to Simon. "And if Orion's after the reptiles' piece of the Predator, the council's probably protecting it."

Simon deflated. Terrific. "So we'll just have to find a way around Councilman Rivera."

"Or you could just ask Winter," said Ariana. Simon blinked, and she blinked back. "You do know her name's Winter Rivera, right?"

As far as he knew, Rivera had been a fake last name she'd given Malcolm the day they'd tried to sneak into the L.A.I.R. She had claimed Councilman Rivera was her grandfather, Simon remembered. Simon had assumed that she was lying, but now he couldn't ignore the possibility that she wasn't.

"But Winter doesn't want to come," said Simon. "I already asked. She refused."

"Then I guess you'll have to find a way to convince her," said Ariana. "She's our best shot at finding out what's really going on. When *are* we leaving, anyway?"

"After dinner," said Simon, tracing his mother's handwriting on the back of the postcard once more. His chances of convincing Winter to come along were slim, but he had to try. "I don't know how we'll get there, though."

"We can take a train from Penn Station," said Ariana with the air of someone who had run away plenty of times in her life. "I have some extra money saved. It should be enough to travel to Arizona and back."

If they came back at all. "You know it'll be dangerous even if Winter does come with us, right?" said Simon. "Orion still has my mother. I don't think we'll be able to rescue her without seeing him again."

Ariana cracked her knuckles. "Good. This time, we'll make sure he gets what he deserves."

"The general won't be happy when he hears I've left," said Jam, pushing his glasses nervously up his nose. "But there's no way I'm letting you go without me."

"Even though we'll be in the desert?" said Ariana. Jam gulped.

"It can't be that bad, right?"

"Keep telling yourself that," she said.

Jam turned a vague shade of green. Simon felt a pinch of guilt, but he knew it was pointless trying to talk his friends out of joining him. And selfishly, he wanted them to come. He wasn't sure he could do this without them.

Instead of trying to start a fire without matches, like they were supposed to, Simon, Jam, and Ariana spent the entire lesson whispering over their dry kindling. Whether or not Simon could convince Winter to come, they would meet by Darryl's statue after dinner, they decided—that way, if one of them was caught leaving the Den, the remaining two would be able to escape. And Penn Station wasn't far. If they could make it there without the pack following them, they'd be home free.

Near the end of the lesson, Vanessa began to hover, insisting they should have at least produced a little smoke by now. Ariana grabbed the sticks and, in under a minute, she'd started a fire. As Jam warmed his hands by the flames, Simon felt the back of his neck prickle, and he looked over his shoulder. Nolan sat two campfires down, watching him.

Simon turned away. He knew he should tell his brother about the postcard, but Nolan would want to come to Paradise Valley, too. And no matter how much danger Simon was putting himself in, he couldn't do the same to his brother.

Once afternoon classes ended, Simon said good-bye to Jam and Ariana and headed back to the Alpha section, where he had every intention of packing and pretending he was doing his homework. As soon as he walked inside, however, a member of the pack with scars peeking out from the collar of his shirt stopped him.

"Malcolm wants to see you in his office," he said gruffly.

"Right now?" said Simon. The man nodded.

"He wanted me to escort you—"

"I know the way," said Simon shortly. He didn't mean to be rude, but the last thing he wanted was to visit Malcolm's office yet again.

Reluctantly Simon headed out of the Alpha section and up to the second level above the pit, trying not to panic. There was no way Malcom could have found out about his plans. He, Ariana, and Jam had made sure Vanessa hadn't overheard their conversation, and he was pretty sure Winter wouldn't have told.

Maybe someone had spotted him talking to Winter in the zoo earlier. Simon trudged down the hallway, his boots sinking into the green grass that acted as carpet. Or had his mother sent word to Malcolm, too? Did he know where she was?

Simon picked up the pace, but when he reached Malcolm's office door, it was closed. Frowning, he raised his fist to knock, but a muffled voice on the other side stopped him. Malcolm was talking to someone.

Taking a deep breath, Simon checked over his shoulder to make sure he was alone, and then, against his better judgment, he pressed his ear to the door.

". . . spotted in the park. There's no telling how many there are," said Malcolm in a deep growl. "I need reinforcements."

There was a nervous edge to his uncle's voice that wasn't usually there, and a prickle of anxiety ran through Simon. Anything that made Malcolm uneasy couldn't have been good.

Several seconds passed in silence before Malcolm spoke again. "I don't care who you send. I'm not asking for your entire reserve. But the pack won't be able to hold off an onslaught, and if she's found allies in another kingdom—"

"What are you doing?" said a voice inches from Simon's ear. He jumped back, stumbling away from the door and nearly tripping over his own boots.

Behind him, his arms crossed, was Nolan.

5

FLY THE COOP

"I—" Simon opened and shut his mouth as he and Nolan stared at each other in the middle of the grassy hallway. His brother wore a triumphant smirk, and Simon got the distinct impression that he had been hiding out in one of the empty offices, waiting for him. That would explain why Simon hadn't heard him coming. "I think someone's trying to attack the school."

Nolan gave him a withering look. "Maybe if you paid attention to someone other than your friends, you would know that Celeste is trying to take the kingdom back from Malcolm. She's been closing in on the zoo for weeks."

Simon blinked. "Why didn't anyone tell me?"

"Guess you're not as important as you think you are," said Nolan with a sneer.

Suddenly the door opened, and Malcolm loomed over them both. Simon spotted dark circles under his uncle's eyes that he was sure hadn't been there before. The worry lines in his forehead looked more pronounced, too, and he rubbed his neck wearily. "Inside, both of you."

"Simon was eavesdropping," said Nolan as he passed. Malcolm sighed.

"I suppose you two aren't so different after all."

Simon slipped inside the office. "I'm sorry, I heard you talking and—"

"And you couldn't help yourself." Malcolm closed the door. "I know. I was your age once, too, so believe me when I say eavesdropping is a habit you're better off breaking sooner rather than later, before you find yourself in real trouble."

Nolan slouched in the chair nearest the exit. "I have homework," he said.

"This is more important."

"Did something happen?" said Simon anxiously. "Did you hear anything about Mom?"

As Malcolm leaned against his desk, he studied Simon with a look that was all too familiar. Simon didn't want his uncle's pity. He didn't want anyone's pity.

"Not yet," said Malcolm slowly. "I have the entire mammal kingdom looking for her, though. Eventually we *will* find her."

"You'd better," said Nolan. "Else I'm going to track her down myself."

Malcolm shook his head, the lines on his face deepening. "That's exactly what I want to talk to you about. I need you both to swear to me you'll stay in the Den. No more trips outside. Not to fly, not to find a friend"—here, Simon shifted uncomfortably—"and definitely not to swim with the polar bears. Got it?"

"*I'm* not the one who sneaks out all the time," said Nolan with a sniff.

"Really?" said Malcolm, eyebrow raised. "Is that how you want to play this?"

"I don't," insisted Nolan, but he didn't sound as sure of himself this time.

Simon cleared his throat, and his uncle refocused on him. "Is—is this because of Celeste?" he said. "Nolan said—"

"Yes, this is because of my mother. And Orion. And every other threat facing us in the five kingdoms." Malcolm leaned forward, clasping his hands together. "I cannot tell you how important it is for the both of you to stay where I can protect you."

"I can protect myself," said Nolan. Simon rolled his eyes, but secretly, he agreed with his brother. Malcolm was formidable, and any Animalgam with half a brain obeyed his orders. But Simon and his brother weren't normal Animalgams. If they were being attacked by a bird, they could turn into a bear; if they were being attacked by a wolf, they could fly away. Their abilities were what made the original

Beast King so dangerous and powerful all those centuries ago. The only difference was that Simon and Nolan had no intention of forcing the five Animalgam kingdoms to bow to them. Or at least Simon didn't. He wasn't so sure about his twin.

"You *think* you can protect yourself, but you can't, not yet," said Malcolm. "Your education, just like your father's, is going to be immeasurably more difficult than every other student's simply because you won't be focusing on one Animalgam form over the other. You, Nolan, will have to learn how to navigate all five kingdoms seamlessly before you'll be ready to face the rest of the world. It took your father years to be comfortable with shifting between them. And you, Simon . . ." Their eyes met. "There is no bird in the sky that can defend itself alone against Orion's flock. I can't protect you up there, so I need you to stay down here, too."

Simon nodded wordlessly, his conscience already eating away at him. He couldn't stand lying to his uncle, but what other choice did he have? He couldn't stay and lose what might be his only chance at saving his mother. But he couldn't tell Malcolm he was leaving, either. Not when his uncle would stop him.

He tuned out the rest of the lecture, and as soon as Malcolm dismissed them, Simon made a beeline for the Alpha section. Instead of doing his homework, however, he locked his bedroom door and began to pack. His book bag could only hold so much, but somehow he managed to include enough clothes to last him a week and the notebook he'd discovered with all of the information about the Beast King. As he gazed around his room, his eyes fell on the collage of postcards his mother had sent him. Even if he was probably coming back, he couldn't bear to leave them behind, so climbing onto his desk, he began to unpin them one by one and sort them into a neat stack.

"Are you going to tell me where you're going this time, or are you going to sneak off again and forget about me?" said Felix, scampering up onto the chair. Simon groaned.

"I didn't forget about you, Felix. I just figured I'd spare you a trip to the desert, since you don't like snakes."

Felix shuddered. "You found Orion?"

"I found my mother," he said. "Or she found me, I guess. She sent me this." He held up the Paradise Valley postcard for Felix to see. "It says 'wish you were here.' She wants me to come find her."

"And you're going without telling anyone?" said Felix, his whiskers twitching disapprovingly. "Malcolm would help you."

The memory of Darryl lying in a pool of his own blood flashed through Simon's mind, and he clenched his jaw. "Malcolm would never let me leave the Den. Besides, if Mom wanted his help, she would have written him, too. She probably doesn't trust him."

"That doesn't mean you shouldn't, either," said Felix. "Having a wolf on your side wouldn't hurt."

Simon set a handful of pins down on his desk. "I'm not telling him, all right? So just drop it."

"You know you can't go out there without someone watching your back—"

"I said *drop it*."

Silence rang throughout the room, and Simon stopped, hunching over. He'd never yelled at Felix before. Not like that. But as he opened his mouth to apologize, the little mouse interrupted him. "What is this really about?"

Wordlessly Simon finished gathering his postcards and climbed off the desk, not looking at Felix as he tucked them securely into the side pocket of his backpack. "The last time I asked someone for help, Darryl died," he mumbled. "I'm not letting the same thing happen to Malcolm."

Felix sighed. "You know that wasn't your fault."

"I'm not giving Orion the chance to kill the only uncle I have left," he said. "Are you going to tell Malcolm?"

Felix sniffed, clearly offended. "I am not a *rat*."

"Then help me," said Simon. "I need to get out through the tunnel again after dinner. The zoo will be closed, and the pack will be patrolling."

"I'll help you if you let me go with you," said Felix. Simon shook his head.

"I'm not taking you to Arizona. You're an appetizer to

half the reptile kingdom. Besides, someone needs to keep an eye on Winter," he said.

"She isn't coming with you?"

"Not unless I can convince her before the end of dinner."

Felix snorted and flopped onto the pillow. "Great. I'm never going anywhere again."

"You never know," said Simon.

However, as optimistic as he tried to be, by the time he walked into the dining hall, he knew his chances of convincing Winter were slim. His hopes dimmed even more when he spotted her in the corner, as far from their usual table as she could get. He headed over, but before he could say a word, she spoke.

"I'm not coming with you."

"I—" Simon paused. "We can't do this without you, Winter. We need you."

"Not my problem." She turned the page of the book in front of her, and Simon bit the inside of his cheek.

"Okay," he said. "I just thought you should know that Robert Rivera is the head of the reptile council, and there's a really good chance he's the one who knows where the reptiles' piece of the Predator is. I don't know if he's really your grandfather or not, but if he is—"

"Simon." At last she looked at him, her expression a mask of coldness. "*I don't care.*"

He exhaled, deflated. "Okay. If you change your mind, we're meeting by Darryl's statue after dinner."

Winter shifted her resolute stare to the page once more. Resigned, Simon returned to their usual table, where Jam rambled nervously throughout dinner, barely touching his sushi. While Ariana broke the monotony of his one-sided conversation every now and then, Simon remained silent, occasionally glancing over at Winter. She left the dining hall twenty minutes before dinner ended, and while he was tempted, he didn't follow her. They would just have to figure out how to save his mother and find the reptiles' piece of the Predator without her.

Though Felix was still grouchy about not getting to come along, he once again stood guard, ready to distract the pack while Simon sneaked out through the tunnel behind Celeste's portrait. Nolan must not have come back from dinner yet, and to Simon's relief, Malcolm was nowhere in sight. He supposed there was some silver lining to Celeste causing trouble after all.

The sky was already dark when Simon crawled out of the tunnel and onto the bridge near the pond. He crept across the zoo toward the wolf statue, careful to listen for any signs of the pack. No doubt they would be on high alert thanks to Celeste's threat, and sure enough, before Simon could reach his uncle's grave, he heard the telltale click of claws against stone.

Ducking into a nearby bush, Simon remained as still as possible in the cold November breeze. He could see the wolf through the leaves, coming closer and closer as he sniffed the air. Simon's palms began to sweat, and for a moment, he considered shifting into a rat or a cockroach to escape. But if he was caught shifting, that would only make everything infinitely worse, so instead he held his breath, silently willing the wolf to leave.

Suddenly the wolf's ears perked up. Tilting his head, he howled a warning to his fellow pack members and, much to Simon's relief, ran off toward the edge of the zoo.

As soon as Simon was sure he was alone, he hurried across the courtyard, jumping from shadow to shadow until he reached the wolf statue. In the darkness he spotted a gleaming black spider clinging to the stone ear. "Did anyone see you?" he said.

"No, but if you keep talking, someone's going to hear *you*," said Ariana in a tiny voice.

Soft footsteps sounded against the stone nearby. Before Simon could hide, Jam appeared with a backpack slung over his shoulder.

"Something's going on. I saw seven members of the pack gathering near the polar bears," said Jam. "They looked like they were waiting for something."

The spider dropped from the statue, and Ariana shifted back into her human form. "We need to leave while they're distracted."

Simon opened his mouth to agree. The sooner they left, the better, but before he could say anything, someone behind them cleared his throat. "Going somewhere?"

Ariana cursed, and Jam shrank behind the statue. With dread coiling inside him, Simon turned.

Nolan stood on the cobblestones, his arms crossed and his lips twisted into a smirk. He must have followed them, Simon realized. "Go back inside, Nolan. It's dangerous out here," he said coolly.

"I can protect myself. What can you do? Fly away?" said Nolan. "That's great until a peregrine falcon catches up to you and—"

Suddenly a huge hand appeared out of the shadows and grabbed Nolan's shoulder, making him jump half a foot in the air. It would have been funny if Simon hadn't also been terrified, and his heart pounded as Malcolm stepped out from a dark path.

His uncle was more furious than Simon had ever seen him before, and for a moment, the three of them stared at one another. Simon's mind raced as he tried to think of how to get out of this one. Sprouting feathers wasn't the worst idea in the world right now, but he couldn't leave Jam and Ariana behind.

"Simon's the one who sneaked out," said Nolan quickly. "I was only following him to make sure he didn't do anything stupid."

The anger didn't fade from Malcolm's eyes. "Tell me, both of you," he said in a deep growl that made the hair on the back of Simon's neck stand up. "Do you think this is all some sort of joke? Do you think your life is a game?

And you, Benjamin, Ariana—do you not understand the danger Simon is in? Do you think you're enough to protect him?"

Simon tightened his grip on the strap of his backpack. "You don't understand. We have to go—"

"The only place you have to go is back into the Den, where a member of the pack will be assigned to watch you at all times for the rest of your school career," said his uncle, advancing on him. "You can either come quietly, or you can clean the toilets in the mammal section for the next five years. It's entirely up to you."

Simon let out a hiss of frustration. "Malcolm, if you'll just *listen*—"

A shrill cry filled the air, and goose bumps prickled over Simon's skin. That wasn't a wolf.

He looked up. An entire army of birds of prey was gathering above the zoo. There had to be hundreds, a dark cloud that blotted out the moonlight.

"The flock!" called Malcolm in a booming voice. With his hand still on Nolan's shoulder, he started to drag him toward the safety of the nearest brick building, but when he reached for Simon as well, Simon dodged his grip, stumbling backward over the cobblestones.

"I can't. I—" He couldn't go back, not when they were so close to freedom. If he didn't leave now, he never would.

In a split second, he took in the terror on Nolan's face as the flock circled above them. His brother would be safe with

Malcolm. Their uncle would protect him. And Simon—Simon would protect him by going to Arizona. He would find their mother and the reptiles' piece of the Predator, and he would figure out a way to stop Orion from putting the weapon together and using it to kill his brother. In order to do that, he had to go.

"I'm sorry, Malcolm," he said. And before his uncle could protest, Simon darted across the open square toward the zoo exit.

6

WILD-GOOSE CHASE

"Simon, wait!" shouted Malcolm, but Simon didn't stop. With Jam and Ariana at his heels, he dashed past the zoo border and toward the Arsenal, the old brick building that marked the entrance to the underground Den. Beyond it was Fifth Avenue and the glittering city, with street lamps illuminating the bustling sidewalk. If Simon could just run fast enough—

"Where do you think you're going, Simon Thorn?" A red-tailed hawk landed on the concrete in front of him, blocking their path. Before Simon could dart around, the hawk shifted into a thin man with beady eyes. Perrin, Orion's lieutenant.

"Not with you," said Simon, aiming a swift kick at Perrin's knee before taking a sharp turn into the park. Perrin howled with pain, and Ariana and Jam quickly caught up with Simon, her hair whipping wildly behind her and his glasses askew.

"We need to lose them," said Ariana evenly, as if they were walking down the sidewalk instead of running at breakneck speed. "We can try the subway—"

"No, that's the rats' territory," gasped Simon. Celeste was already allied with the rat army; no doubt if the three of them stepped foot down there, she would capture them in an instant. "What about the bus?"

A screech cut through the night sky, and Simon glanced up long enough to see the silhouette of a red-tailed hawk above them, along with a handful of falcons and other raptors. The rest must have been going after Malcolm and Nolan, he realized, horror spilling through him.

"We can't stop," he managed, sucking in great gulps of air. "If we do, they'll catch us. Is there another way to shake them before we get to Penn Station?"

Ariana dodged a couple walking hand in hand down the path. "I have an idea," she said. "We need to find a taxi. They won't come after us if we're with humans."

"Are you sure about that?" said Simon. The rats had had no problem attacking him in front of half of New York City. But Ariana nodded, and together they darted toward Fifth Avenue.

It took them three blocks before Ariana managed to hail a cab without stopping. As they ducked inside, Simon once again shot a nervous look into the sky. Perrin and his soldiers circled the taxi, but none of them made a move to attack.

As soon as Simon slammed the door shut behind him, Ariana said, "Times Square, fast as you can."

She shoved a crisp fifty-dollar bill under the driver's nose, and he snatched it and slammed the gas pedal so hard that the tires squealed. Simon flew back against his seat, and he exchanged a look with Jam, who was squeezed in beside him. At least Ariana knew what she was doing.

Minutes later, they reached their destination, and the three of them spilled out of the taxi and into the huge crowd. Times Square was chaotic and claustrophobic, with people pushing up against them from all sides and bright lights coming from every direction. Jam grabbed the handle of Simon's backpack so they wouldn't get separated, and Simon followed Ariana through the masses as best he could, losing her half a dozen times before he spotted her purple hair again. Whatever she was trying to do, it wasn't working—the flock appeared overhead nearly as soon as they arrived, and from their vantage point in the sky, Simon and his friends had no chance of shaking them out in the open.

"Ariana," he said, his voice rising. She glanced up and cursed.

"Hold on," she muttered, stopping under an awning big enough to hide them from view. Leading them into an abandoned corner behind a sandwich board sign, she said, "I'm going to shift."

"In front of all these people?" said Jam, looking at the crowds passing by.

"I'm a spider, not a bear. Everyone's walking too quickly to notice, and even if they do, it's hectic enough that they'll think they imagined it," she said. "You two wear these and head to Penn Station."

She produced a pair of hats she must have stolen from a vendor, and both Simon and Jam pulled them on. As a cluster of sightseers passed, all staring upward at the bright billboards decorating Times Square, Ariana knelt behind the sign like she was going to tie her shoelace. Instead she shifted into a black widow and immediately crawled up Simon's clothes, settling near his collar.

"Where are we going when we reach Penn Station?" said Simon as he walked out from underneath the awning and back out into the open. He didn't dare look up at the birds and give them away.

"Chicago," said Jam. "We'll pick up tickets to Arizona there, just in case. I researched the route on the captain's computer during afternoon drills, while everyone else was in the water. It'll take us a few days, but the train will bring us as far as Flagstaff, Arizona. We'll figure out how to get to Paradise Valley from there."

"Why don't we just fly?" said Simon as they hurried along, pushing their way past tourists with cameras and puffy jackets. Someone jostled him, and he quickly checked his shoulder to make sure the black spider still clung to his sweatshirt.

"Do *you* have enough money for three airline tickets to Arizona?" said Ariana, her tiny voice barely audible. "Taking the train is much cheaper."

"It's better like this anyway," said Jam, his voice suddenly higher than usual. "The birds might take down our plane or something."

"Don't lie. You just hate flying," she said. Jam's cheeks turned pink.

"And you hate water, so I guess we're even."

Ariana leaped from Simon's shoulder to Jam's, and the pair of them bickered for the next nine blocks. Simon tuned them out. All he cared about was the fact that he hadn't heard a single squawk since the awning. Once they were clear of Times Square, he dared to look up again. There was no sign of the flock.

Penn Station came into view, and Simon broke into a jog. "Follow me," he called. A crowd surrounded the entrance, and he squeezed a path through them, closer and closer to the escalator that would take them inside the train station.

"Simon!" yelled Jam, his voice distant. Simon stumbled to a stop, looking around wildly. Where had he gone?

"Jam!" he shouted, pushing his way out of the crowd. "*Jam!*"

"Simon, run!" he cried, and Simon froze. The people in front of him parted, revealing Jam standing on the sidewalk, rigid as a statue.

Perrin stood beside him, his hand tight around Jam's shoulder—the same one Ariana had clung to since Times Square. Simon's pulse raced, and he searched Jam's expression for any hint of whether Ariana was okay.

"I'm not doing this all night," said Perrin, his thin lips curling into a sneer. "Either you come with me, or I squeeze your friend's shoulder a little harder. Your choice, Simon Thorn."

Simon exhaled sharply. She was still alive. Out of all the choices he had made today, this was by far the easiest. "Let them go, and I'll come with you." Nothing was worth his friend's life, and underneath Perrin's hand, Ariana would be entirely defenseless. Even if she bit him, Perrin would kill her before the venom took effect.

"Very well," said Perrin, and he beckoned for Simon to cross the distance between them. Simon did so slowly, one step at a time, his eyes glued to Perrin's hand. Simon didn't trust him to keep his word, but right now, he didn't have a choice.

"Hey, beak nose," said a familiar voice in the crowd. Winter appeared from behind a pack of businessmen, and she marched right up to Perrin, grabbing his free hand. "You're going to let them go right now."

Fear flickered across Perrin's face. The last time Winter

had been this close to him, she'd sunk her fangs into his leg and dosed him with so much venom that Ariana had had to administer an antidote to save his life. Right now, part of Simon—a terrible part of him that wanted nothing more than to get on that train—wished Ariana hadn't.

Perrin stood straighter, his hand on Jam's shoulder tightening. "Winter. What a delight. I'm sure Orion will be thrilled to hear how you're thriving among your own kind."

Her expression darkened. "Simon, stay where you are."

"But—" he began. Before he could finish, she opened her mouth and let out an earsplitting shriek.

Simon had never heard anyone so loud in his life. Even several feet away, he thought his eardrums might explode, and Jam winced. Winter tugged on Perrin's arm, her glove slipping under his sleeve to make it look like he was the one holding on to her.

"Kidnapper!" she screamed. "Someone help! He's trying to kidnap us!"

It took Simon a moment to catch on, but he and Jam exchanged a look, and in unison, they both joined her.

"Help!" shouted Simon. "Someone help us!"

The crowd began to take notice. Several pedestrians and travelers coming out of Penn Station stopped what they were doing and surrounded Perrin, who had paled. "Hey, why don't you let them go?" said a beefy man with a thick moustache.

"They—they're lying," said Perrin, stumbling over his words. "I'm their uncle, you see. They're trying to run away—"

"Someone call the police!" shouted another voice, and an angry woman grabbed Perrin's hand, yanking it off Jam's shoulder. Simon's heart nearly burst from fear. Jam sprang free and hurried over, and Simon quickly checked his coat.

A shiny black spider clung to the wool, and even in the uproar from the crowd, Simon could hear her sputtering curses.

"She's all right," said Simon, and he headed toward the entrance to Penn Station once more. Glancing back, he caught Winter's eye, and she nodded, letting go of Perrin now that a dozen adults had surrounded them. She slipped into the crowd, and Simon lost sight of her.

"Do we wait?" said Jam, and Simon shook his head.

"If she's coming, she'll find us," he said. She'd managed to follow them this far, after all.

Penn Station was packed with evening commuters. Jam led him over to the monitors displaying the train schedule, and Simon stared at it, his vision swimming. "Which one are we supposed to take?"

"That one," said Jam, pointing. Simon still couldn't figure it out, so he let Jam lead him over to a kiosk. "Have you ever taken a train before?"

"Does the subway count?" he said, and Jam shook his head.

"Long-distance trains are different. They've got bed-rooms and stuff." He hesitated when the screen asked how many tickets he needed. "Three or . . . ?"

"Four." Winter appeared at Simon's elbow, smirking. "That was almost too easy. Perrin's trying to explain him-self to a police officer right now."

It took every ounce of willpower Simon had not to hug her. "You came after all."

"You said you needed me. And I promised I'd help."

There was something else in her voice—something that Simon couldn't identify—but whatever it was, he didn't care. "Thanks, Winter."

"Don't thank me yet." She pulled out a piece of plastic from her designer purse. "Here. I am *not* squeezing into a tiny room for two."

"A credit card?" said Jam. "How do you have a credit card?"

"How do you not?" said Winter, giving him a strange look. She swiped the card, and the printer spit out four train tickets to Chicago. "We should buy an Arizona guidebook, too."

"We're not going to sightsee," said Simon.

"No, but it might give us an idea of where the reptile council is," said Winter. "Unless your mother told you about that, too."

Simon opened and shut his mouth. *Wish you were here.* That was all he had to go on. "Okay. We'll find a guidebook."

"Good." Winter tossed her dark hair back. "I know exactly where to get one."

As they followed Winter, Simon couldn't help but wonder what had changed her mind. But as long as she was willing to help, he wasn't so sure it mattered. They weren't on the train yet, and until then, he didn't want to say anything to spook her.

She led them through the busy terminal to a tiny bookstore crammed between a café and a travel shop, and in all of thirty seconds, she'd located a colorful guidebook to Arizona. As soon as she bought the book, she dragged them to the café next door to buy sandwiches—all on her, she insisted.

"Wonder why she's being so generous," mumbled Jam as they made their selections.

"Just go with it," whispered Simon, who figured free sandwiches were better than no sandwiches at all. He had brought all the money he had saved from his weekly allowance from Darryl, but it wouldn't be enough to get them to Paradise Valley, and he was in no position to refuse Winter's generosity. Or Ariana's. Or Jam and his willingness to come along. He knew how much his friends could be sacrificing by going with him, but the guilt wasn't enough to make him break away and do this alone. He would find a way to pay them back somehow, but right now, he needed them.

While Winter was making her purchases, Simon spotted a man lurking nearby, looking around suspiciously as if he was searching for someone. That wasn't too unusual, but as soon as he turned around, Simon spotted a few hawk feathers clinging to his trench coat.

Simon quickly ducked his head to hide his face. "That man out there, the one with the blond hair and goatee—*don't look!*—I think he's one of Orion's." He glanced at the counter. "Winter!"

"Hold on, I'm doing something," she said, and she flashed the cashier a charming smile as she handed her card over to him.

Simon's palms began to sweat. Any moment, the man could spot them, and there was nowhere to run in the café. He silently willed Winter to hurry, but she took her time gathering the bag with the sandwiches and tucking her credit card back in her purse. When at last she reached them, Simon felt like he was about to burst.

"What?" said Winter as she approached him. "We have plenty of—"

She stopped, her face draining of color as she focused on something over Simon's shoulder. She must have spotted the man.

"Perrin wasn't alone," said Simon through gritted teeth. "We need to go."

For once, Winter didn't argue. Simon pulled his hat tighter over his head and, exchanging silent looks with Jam, they moved to either side of her as they exited the café and dashed toward the staircase that led down to the platforms. Simon was recognizable, sure, but he hadn't lived in Sky

Tower his entire life. If the man in the coat was going to spot one of them, it would be—

"Winter!"

Simon cringed and, without looking back, he grabbed her hand and broke into a run. This time he made sure Jam was keeping up before rushing down the stairs.

"Who is that?" said Jam as they darted around a group of tourists wearing I ♥ NY shirts.

"Rowan," she said in an oddly high-pitched voice. "He's Perrin's son. He used to babysit me when Orion was out of—"

"Winter!" called Rowan, sounding desperate. He was getting closer. "Winter, stop, it's me—please. We all want you to come home."

A flicker of uncertainty passed over Winter's face. As they stepped onto the platform, Simon tightened his grip on her hand. Two trains sat on either side of them.

"Right or left, Winter?" he said firmly, trying to distract her. She twisted her head around, and he repeated, *"Right or left?"*

"I—"

"Winter, please—Orion's sorry—he wants you back—he loves you—"

She stopped now, her heels digging into the concrete, and a dozen different emotions played out in her eyes. Simon knew that look. He'd never seen it before, not on anyone else's face, but he knew exactly what was going through her mind. Rowan wasn't only offering to return her to her old life, one where she had been raised as Orion's granddaughter. He was offering her a family again. He was offering her a place to belong. If Celeste herself had chased after Simon, saying she could return him to early September, when Darryl was alive and he had no idea what an Animalgam was, Simon would have stopped, too.

"He's lying," said Simon.

"He's not lying," said Winter, her voice catching. "He's practically my older brother. He wouldn't lie to me."

"Orion left you behind," said Simon. "He killed Darryl, he kidnapped my mom, and he took off without you. The only reason Rowan is here right now is because Orion wants me. Not you—me. Do you get that?"

"Simon . . ." said Jam, but he didn't have to say anything. Winter's eyes were glassy, and she stared at Simon with such horror on her face that he felt a sick stab in his gut. But with each second they wasted, Rowan grew closer, and they didn't have any time to spare on Winter's feelings. Simon would apologize later. Right now, they had to board their train before Rowan reached them.

"If he really means it, he'll find you again," said Ariana as she joined them from behind a pillar and tucked her purple hair underneath her hood. "If he's just after Simon, he won't bother. So if you want to prove he really wants you back, then your only choice is to get on the train and see what he does. Preferably before he catches us."

Winter's lower lip trembled, and for one terrible moment, Simon thought she was going to burst into tears in the middle of the platform. Instead she dug into her purse with shaking hands and pulled out the tickets. "It's—it's that one," she managed, nodding to the train on the left.

Without another word, Simon led her farther down the platform. The crowds began to squeeze together, forcing them through narrow spaces and over pieces of luggage. "Sorry, sorry," said Simon, pushing his way through the crush of travelers and creating a hole big enough for the others to follow. Only when Simon was absolutely sure they'd lost Rowan did he lead them onto the train.

It was just in time, too; when Simon peered through the window, he spotted Rowan's long blond hair only a few yards down the platform. His brow was furrowed, and he looked around before pressing through the crowd and passing their car.

Simon exhaled, but his relief was short-lived. Winter stood beside him, her jaw clenched and her eyes stormy as she also watched Rowan go. She looked as if she was about to spring off the train and race after him, and Simon's hand twitched, ready to grab her if she tried.

"I'll be in the room," she said at last, and she walked stiffly past him and headed down the train. Jam hurried after her, his mouth open like he wanted to say something, but they were gone before Simon could hear what it was.

Ariana lingered beside him, watching them go. "If Rowan doesn't come back for her . . ."

"He would have taken her with him the first time if that's what they really wanted," said Simon. And though he would've given nearly anything to be wrong, he knew he wasn't.

Maybe he'd made a mistake, asking Winter to come, but it was too late now. The train began to move and, shoving his hands into his pockets, Simon followed his friends through the car. If Rowan didn't come back for her, it would destroy Winter. But if he did, that would mean the birds had found them again, and Simon wasn't sure how long they could keep running before their luck ran out.

7

CREATURE COMFORTS

Their assigned room in the sleeper car was smaller than Simon had pictured. The beds folded out from the wall, and there was a tiny private bathroom, but otherwise they were crammed together on two benches—or, rather, Simon, Ariana, and Jam were crammed together while Winter sat on the bench opposite, staring resolutely out the window as the train left the city. She hadn't spoken to anyone since Simon had arrived.

He too stared out the window once they emerged from the tunnel, watching the city disappear. They were doing this. They were really leaving New York. None of it seemed real, and Simon wiped his sweaty palms on his jeans. He had every intention of coming back as soon as he had rescued his mother, but it still felt like he was saying good-bye to something important.

"You look like you're about to throw up," said Ariana. "Even if they figure out which train we took, there are a million stops between here and Chicago, let alone the number of trains we could take when we get there. As long as we're careful, they won't figure out where we're going."

Simon wasn't so sure he believed her, but they were heading directly to Orion anyway. They would inevitably have to face the flock again. "It's not that. I've never been out of the city, except for the trip to the Stronghold."

"Never?" said Jam, adjusting his glasses. "But—what did you do for vacations and holidays?"

"We stayed in New York," said Simon with a shrug, suddenly self-conscious. "Darryl worked a lot, and I guess he must have thought we were safer there than on a beach or something."

"Your uncle was right," said Ariana as she flipped through the guidebook Winter had bought. "Not many Animalgams live in the city, but there are tons of them near the coasts. They would have picked you off in a second if they'd figured out who you were."

Jam turned red. "No one in my kingdom would ever hurt Simon."

"I'm sorry, *how* many teeth does a shark have?"

"Darryl didn't trust any of the kingdoms," said Simon

quickly. Their compartment was small enough without adding more tension. "He hated spiders, too."

"That's because he was smart," said Jam.

Ariana grumbled. As she flipped through the pages, Simon craned his neck to get a glimpse. She was searching for hotels. "What are you looking for, exactly?" he said.

"I'm looking for the council. Reptiles are weird," she added, and Winter huffed. Ariana continued as if she hadn't heard her. "They have a horrible reputation, right? No one sees a snake and wants to cuddle it. But they're really the most laid-back, peaceful kingdom in the Animalgam world. They don't usually form communities—most of the time they travel from place to place, or if they do settle down, it isn't in an area populated with other Animalgams."

"Wonder why," muttered Winter. Ariana cleared her throat.

"Most of the leaders of the five kingdoms rule from somewhere only their kind would go, so you might think the council would be in a cave in the desert or something. But reptiles are creatures of comfort. They like the finer things in life. Art, good food, culture—"

"Designer handbags," said Simon, eyeing Winter's purse. She pulled it onto her lap and hugged it.

"Exactly. And you try to find the equivalent of a Fifth Avenue socialite willing to stay in a hovel. The council's location is supposed to be secret, but I know for a fact that even though reptiles are nomads, the council is always in the same place. Otherwise they'd be too hard to find."

"But they're supposed to rotate members every year," said Jam from the other side of Ariana. "That's how their government works. You serve on the council for a year—sort of like jury duty, I guess. It's supposed to keep everything equal and honest. Except ever since the treaty with Celeste, the members of the council have mostly stayed the same. I remember the general talking about it. He doesn't like Councilman Rivera."

"Right." Simon glanced at Winter, but her expression remained impassive. "So we're looking for someplace fancy. Someplace a reptile Animalgam would want to stay."

"Someplace *comfortable* in the middle of a desert," said Ariana. "They'll have to be in their human form at least part of the time. There are thirteen members of the council, and if you want to petition them, you have to visit, so—"

"They're not staying in a house somewhere." Simon took the book from Ariana and scanned the pages. "You're thinking a hotel?"

She nodded. "Five stars. Expensive. A resort, probably. Think someplace Winter would stay. Paradise Valley is close enough to Scottsdale that we can count those, too."

There were too many luxury hotels to count in the Scottsdale area, but only a handful near Paradise Valley itself that looked promising. "Winter, if you had to choose, would you rather stay in the . . . Desert Flower Resort, or the Stilio?" said Simon.

Instead of ignoring him like he expected, she snapped her head around to look at him. "The what?"

"The . . ." Simon eyed the word. "The Stilio. Am I saying it wrong, or—"

Winter snatched the book from him. "The Stilio. I used to get letters from them."

"Really? What kind of letters?" said Simon hopefully.

"I don't know. I never opened them." She squinted at the page. "I remember the logo on the envelope, though. That's definitely the same one."

She handed the book back to Simon. Beside the column detailing the amenities at the Stilio Resort and Spa was a circle—or at least he thought it was a circle. Taking a closer look, he noted that it was actually a snake eating its own tail. He shuddered inwardly.

"So that's where we're going," he said. "To the Stilio."

While Ariana and Jam pored over every detail the guidebook had to offer about the hotel, Winter refocused on the window and rested her cheek against the back of the seat. Simon didn't realize he had been staring until Winter's eyes suddenly locked on his.

"What?" she said.

Simon blinked. "I—" He leaned closer to her, as if that would somehow stop Ariana and Jam from overhearing. "I was just wondering why you threw the letters away."

"Because some of us were actually happy before this whole mess started," she muttered. "Just because you were pining away for a life you didn't have doesn't mean I was, too."

"You weren't curious at all?" said Simon. He couldn't imagine not reading one of his mother's postcards.

"Why would I be? I already had a family—I didn't need another one. Especially from the reptile kingdom."

"You do know every time you put them down, you're putting yourself down, too?" said Ariana.

Winter's face grew red. "I'm not one of them."

"Maybe you weren't raised a reptile, but that's what you are, like it or not. It's not a bad thing, you know."

"Do I?" snapped Winter. "Because as far as I can tell, calling someone a *snake* isn't a compliment."

Ariana snorted. "*I* think being one of the most venomous snakes in the country is pretty awesome. But even if someone else doesn't, so what? When it comes to you, the only opinion that matters is your own. We can't decide what kind of Animalgam we are, but we can control what kind of person we are. I don't know why you settled on *whiny spoiled brat*, but it's getting really old."

Winter's jaw dropped, and her eyes filled with tears as if no one had ever spoken to her like that before. Simon scowled at Ariana. He didn't disagree with her, but that didn't mean she had to say it out loud. Ariana merely shrugged, while Jam stared down at the guidebook, clearly trying to look like he wasn't listening.

"I was supposed to be able to fly," said Winter, and her

voice caught. "Don't you get that? You have no idea how lucky you are, Simon—I was supposed to be you. I was supposed to be a bird. Orion said so my whole life—I was too smart to be a reptile. Too level-headed, too logical. I did all the right things. I studied the right subjects. I read the right books. I did everything they told me to do. We were a family, and I was supposed to be one of them. But instead of feathers—instead of feathers, I got *scales*."

She spat out that last word as if it were poison, and angrily she wiped her eyes. Simon plucked a few tissues from a dispenser attached to the wall and wordlessly offered them to her. At first she glared at him, but after several long seconds, she finally took them and dabbed her cheeks.

"I was happy before. That's why I didn't open the letters. I told you, I already had a family—I had everything I wanted, and those stupid letters didn't matter. And now . . ." She shook her head and blew her nose so loudly that Simon briefly wondered if she was part goose. "And now I have nothing but an adoptive grandfather that doesn't want me anymore and letters I never read."

"You have me," said Simon. "You have us, and we're not going to leave you. I promise."

Winter was silent. It didn't matter—she didn't need to speak for Simon to know exactly what she was thinking. They weren't the family she wanted.

"And maybe Rowan was telling the truth," added Simon.

"Just because Orion's a horrible person doesn't mean they all are."

She took a deep, shuddering breath, and for a moment Simon thought she might start sobbing. Instead she exhaled slowly and stood in the narrow space between the seats, hugging her purse.

"Don't get my hopes up, Simon," she said. "It hurts too much."

Taking a few more tissues from the dispenser, she then walked out of the compartment, leaving the three of them behind. Simon tried to follow her, but Ariana grabbed his sleeve.

"Don't," she said. "If she wants to be alone right now, there's nothing you can do to help. She'll come back when she's ready."

That wasn't what Simon was worried about, but against his better judgment, he sat back down. He knew what it was like to feel like an outsider, and he knew how much it hurt to watch his mother walk away from him time and time again.

Simon had always had Darryl, though. He had never doubted how much his uncle loved him, and that had given him the strength to keep his chin up when everything else in his life was going wrong. He had been Simon's rock.

Orion had been Winter's rock, too, and now he wasn't just gone; he had abandoned her, leaving her questioning everything. It was worse than death somehow. It was rejection—rejection of something Winter couldn't help, something she desperately hated about herself, and Simon felt awful for her.

The steward pulled their beds down for them while Ariana lied about their parents staying nearby, and by the time the three of them had brushed their teeth and changed in the tiny bathroom, Winter still hadn't returned. Simon opened the door and stuck his head out, glancing up and down the narrow corridor. "I should go after her," he said.

"She's probably waiting until we're all asleep so she doesn't have to talk to us," said Ariana. "Come on. The sooner you go to bed, the sooner it'll be morning, and maybe by then she'll be in the mood to talk."

Ariana was right about the first part. Nearly an hour passed as Simon lay awake, staring out the window and trying to will himself to sleep, but eventually light from the hallway briefly filled the compartment as Winter slipped back inside. He wanted to say something, but Jam was snoring softly, and Winter didn't make a sound as she crawled into the bed directly below Simon's bunk. He listened as her breathing evened out, and only when he was sure she was asleep did he let himself drift off, too.

But by the time Simon woke up right after dawn, Winter was gone. He would find her before breakfast, he decided, and he roughly dug through his backpack for a change of clothes.

"Ouch!" came a tiny cry from inside his bag, and Simon jumped back, knocking into Winter's empty bunk. As a tiny mouse wriggled out from between his balled-up socks, his surprise turned to anger.

"What—*Felix!* I told you not to come," said Simon, scooping him into his hands. "Don't you ever listen?"

"About as well as you do, I'd imagine." Felix stretched, his nose twitching.

"But—I left you in the Alpha's office," said Simon. "How did you even find us?"

"I hitched a ride with Winter. Do you mind? I'm dying of thirst."

"Do *you* mind? Some of us are sleeping," muttered Ariana. She pulled her pillow over her head, and Simon got the hint, retreating into the bathroom and closing the door. He turned the tap on low, and Felix tilted his head back, drinking directly from the faucet. Simon would have thought it was funny if he wasn't so upset.

"You shouldn't be here," he said.

Felix didn't reply right away. Instead he drank his fill before straightening out his rumpled whiskers. "Someone has to watch your back."

"Oh, like you were a huge help against Perrin and Rowan," said Simon. "You're going to get yourself killed."

"Look on the bright side—then you won't have to worry about feeding me anymore," said Felix, and he climbed up the sink to perch beside the soap. "We both know I was never going to let you go alone, so stop acting surprised. I'm here. Short of leaving me in Chicago, there's nothing you can do about it, so you might as well let me help you."

"And how do you expect to do that?"

"Haven't figured that part out yet."

"Great." Simon grabbed his toothbrush. "When you do, let me know. In the meantime, stay in the compartment. If anyone catches you . . ."

"Don't have to tell me twice," muttered Felix, and he returned to the nest he'd made in the backpack and sulked.

Once Simon had changed, he began his search for Winter. There were only so many places she could go on the train, and it didn't take him long before he spotted her in the dining car, alone in the corner as she scribbled something into a notebook. Despite the early morning, several other passengers sat scattered at other tables, reading newspapers or chatting over cups of coffee, and Simon skirted around them, making his way straight for Winter. As soon as he reached her table, he stopped, but she was so busy writing that she didn't look up.

For a moment, Simon wondered if giving her more time alone wouldn't be the worst thing in the world. They wouldn't reach Chicago until that evening, and she didn't look like she wanted company. But he remembered the look on her face the night before, after her argument

with Ariana, and his resolve hardened. She needed someone right now, and Simon was the only person on that
train who cared enough to put up with whatever attitude
she would fling his way.

As he opened his mouth to apologize, however, he spotted a few pages of discarded notebook paper sitting at the
end of the table. And while Simon didn't *mean* to snoop,
as someone who had spent his whole life escaping into
books, he couldn't help but read the first line of her neat
handwriting.

Dear Orion.

8

SHAKE A TAIL FEATHER

Simon grabbed the piece of paper bearing Orion's name, and Winter started.

"Simon? What are you—give that *back!*" She snatched the unfinished note away with such force that it ripped. "That's *mine*."

"What are you doing?" said Simon. He'd been planning on apologizing to her, but now he was too confused and angry. "Are you telling him where we're going?"

"Of course not," said Winter, but there was an edge to her voice that Simon didn't trust. "How many times do I have to prove I'm on your side?"

"Then why are you writing him?"

"Because—" Winter faltered, and she looked away,

crumpling her discarded letter into a ball. "I just wanted to, okay? Sometimes it helps. I wasn't going to send it."

Right now she had a better chance of convincing him that she was secretly a flamingo, and he'd hallucinated the whole cottonmouth thing. "I don't believe you."

Her expression hardened. "Then I guess you shouldn't have guilted me into coming with you."

"I shouldn't have had to," said Simon. He dropped what was left of the notebook paper onto the table. "Do whatever you want to do, Winter. Just don't mess this up for the rest of us."

With all the times Winter had betrayed him, he shouldn't have been surprised that once again he was questioning whether she was on his side, but disappointment and frustration formed a knot in his chest. He *knew* Winter wasn't the kind of person she wanted everyone else to think she was. She was stubborn, yes, but she made good choices most of the time, and when she didn't, her heart was always in the right place. But he'd already lost his uncle because of her betrayal. How many chances could he give her before she took everything else from him, too?

By the time he reached the compartment, where Ariana and Jam were arguing over who got to use the bathroom first, he had resigned himself to no longer having Winter on their team. Maybe they wouldn't need her after all. He could always pretend to be a member of the reptile kingdom if he had to. The last thing he wanted was to reveal his secret to anyone, but if it gave him and his friends the opportunity they needed to infiltrate the Stilio on their own and find his mother, he would do it.

"Is breakfast good?" said Jam, who had lost the fight. He sat on the edge of his bed, fiddling with a padlock as he waited none too patiently for his turn.

"I don't know. Didn't eat anything," said Simon, climbing onto his bunk. Felix was curled up in the middle of his pillow, snoring softly. "What are you doing?"

"Ariana's teaching me how to pick locks," said Jam. Sighing, he pulled a thin metal object from the padlock. "I can't get it right."

"That's because you're going too fast," called Ariana from the bathroom. She stuck her head out the door, a green toothbrush in her mouth. "Technically lock picks aren't allowed at the Den, but after what happened in September, I had my mom send me some. You should learn how to use them, too, Simon."

"Maybe later," said Simon, trying not to picture Darryl's beat-up and bloodied wolf form trapped in a cage. "I found Winter in the dining car. She—"

He stopped suddenly. He couldn't say it. He couldn't tell them that Winter had been writing to Orion, because what if he *was* wrong? What if Winter really never intended to send her letter?

"She's what?" said Jam curiously.

"She's just—writing stuff," said Simon with a shrug. "She looked mad, so I didn't want to interrupt."

Ariana disappeared long enough to spit out her toothpaste. "She better get over this before we reach Paradise Valley."

"I'm not sure you just get over losing your entire family," said Simon.

"You know that's not what I mean," she said. "This isn't all about her right now. This is about your mom and the Predator. She might be the center of her web, but she isn't the center of mine. Or yours."

"I know," mumbled Simon. He would find out eventually if Winter had been telling the truth about being on their side. Until then, all he could do was hope that no matter how upset she was, she wouldn't jeopardize their plans.

Simon spent the rest of the trip in the compartment, staring out the window or trying to read the book he'd brought with him. Eventually he gave up and studied the postcard, tracing his mother's words over and over again. Though Simon didn't ask for privacy, Ariana and Jam left him alone, only coming back to bring him lunch.

He didn't see any hint of Winter until the conductor announced they were thirty minutes out from Chicago. Only then did she return to wordlessly pack her things, but she didn't so much as glance at Simon. He wasn't sure whether she felt guilty for betraying them to Orion or if she was still upset he thought she would, but either way, by the time the four of them stepped off the train and onto the busy Chicago platform, Simon didn't expect her to ever talk to him again. And he wasn't so sure he minded.

"We have an hour and a half before the train to Arizona shows up," said Ariana, examining the schedule on a monitor overhead while Winter lingered behind them. "I don't know about you guys, but I'm dying for a cheeseburger."

"There's a food court on the upper level," said Simon, spotting a sign. Lunch had been hours ago.

"Uh, guys? I think that cheeseburger is going to have to wait," said Jam. "Look."

Perrin stood on the platform, scanning the crowd as passengers exited the train. The four of them were close enough toward the end that Perrin hadn't spotted them yet, but a sick feeling overcame Simon, and as he pulled his hat back on, he searched the platform. He counted four other men lingering nearby, none of them carrying luggage and all of them facing the train, waiting.

Simon rounded on Winter. "Did you tell them where we were?"

"What? Who?" she said, clutching her purse.

"The flock," said Simon. "They have us surrounded."

Winter's face lit up, her green eyes bright, and she stood on her tiptoes. "Is Rowan with them?"

Ariana tugged her down with one hand while pulling

her hood up with the other. "Are you crazy? They'll recognize you instantly."

"That's probably why she's doing it," blurted Simon.

Winter sputtered as if he'd slapped her. "If you really think I'd—"

"How else did they find us?" said Simon. "Someone must have told them. You could have easily asked a bird to deliver the message for you."

"There were only two trains on the platform in New York, genius," said Winter. "Maybe they split up."

"Enough," said Ariana, and Simon's retort died on his lips. "*We* need to split up. They're probably expecting all four of us together. If we can blend in with other groups, we'll have a better chance of sneaking past the flock."

Simon swallowed his anger and nodded, looking at her purple hair. Even underneath her hood, it was a dead giveaway. "It might be better if you shifted," he said.

"Right. On it." She ducked behind a pillar nearby, bending down as a large group of people passed. A few seconds later, a shiny black spider crawled up Simon's pant leg to his shoulder. He almost suggested she join Felix in his backpack, but he wasn't sure how the mouse would react to unexpected venomous company.

"We'll meet up at the front of the station," he said. "If you want to leave, Winter, here's your chance."

Winter's face twisted, her expression sharp with hurt and resentment, but he didn't have any sympathy left. Not when they were seconds away from being discovered. He caught Jam's eye and managed a quick, reassuring nod before ducking into the crowd.

Simon fell into step beside the first family he found. Keeping his head down, he stuck close to them, trying to look like he belonged as they passed a member of the flock. Simon didn't dare sneak a glance at him—if he accidentally caught his eye, the game would be up.

"Almost there," said Ariana in a tiny voice from his shoulder. "He's looking the other way—I think it's working. Just keep walking."

Simon held his breath as the family headed into the station terminal. As soon as it was safe, Simon broke off from them and hurried to the nearest exit. "Are you sure they didn't see me?" he said.

"Positive," said Ariana, sounding enormously pleased with herself. "Jam shouldn't have a problem. They barely know what he looks like."

"It's not Jam I'm worried about," said Simon, leaning casually against the railing of a staircase as he searched the bustling crowd. "Do you think she'll come back?"

"Who, Winter?" said Ariana. "Do you really think she tipped Perrin off?"

"I don't know," said Simon. Maybe Winter was right—maybe the flock had split up. "This morning, in the dining car, I—"

"Simon!" Jam's voice echoed through the station, and he burst through a group of men wearing suits. "Simon, run!"

It took Simon a beat to realize what was happening. With his face flushed and his mouth hanging open, Jam sprinted across the tiled floor, a man in a trench coat hot on his heels.

Perrin.

Simon darted down the stairs and burst through the station doors, spilling out into the cold Chicago air. It was already night out, and yellow pools of light illuminated the unfamiliar street as cars drove past, tires splashing through piles of slush. He looked around wildly. "Which way?"

"Does it really matter right now?" said Ariana in her tiny voice as she clung to his shoulder. "Just run!"

Simon bolted down the sidewalk, dodging pedestrians in overcoats and hurtling around corners. Behind him, he could hear Jam's loud footsteps against the sidewalk, and Ariana groaned.

"What is he *doing*? He's leading Perrin straight to you!"

"He doesn't want to lose us," said Simon, only narrowly avoiding a mailbox. The streets of Chicago seemed more frightening somehow—darker, narrower, and missing everything that was familiar about New York. Icy fear settled over him, driving its way deep into his bones. "How do we shake the flock?"

"Normally I'd suggest you fly away, but since they have wings, too . . ." Ariana paused. "I've got an idea. I'm going to jump. You duck into that alleyway up there. Meet us back at the train station in ten minutes."

"But—" By now Simon was so lost that he couldn't have gotten back to the train station if his life depended on it. However, Ariana had already leaped off his shoulder, and he didn't have any choice but to trust her. He took a sharp turn into the alleyway, only to barrel straight into a dented trash can and knock it over.

"Hey!" cried a voice, and a raccoon wriggled out of the overturned bin, bits of rotting food stuck in its fur. "What was that for?"

"Sorry," said Simon, looking around. The alleyway was a dead end. If Ariana didn't find a way to get Perrin off their trail, the flock would have no problem cornering him.

"No *way*," said another voice, and a second raccoon emerged from the pile of garbage now strewn across the concrete. "You can understand us? Bonnie, check this guy out!"

A third raccoon poked her head out of a nearby Dumpster that reeked of rotting Chinese food. "Calm down, Billy. You act like you've never seen another Animalgam before."

"Not out in the wild," said the second raccoon, and he bobbed his head eagerly, his striped tail twitching. "What are you?"

"I—" said Simon, but a flash of purple bolted past the alleyway entrance, and he crouched behind the overturned trash can. Ariana.

Half a second later, Jam followed, and Simon held his breath. Though Jam glanced into the alleyway, meeting

Simon's eye, he followed Ariana instead. She was leading Jam away from him. They were risking their own safety to give him a chance to escape.

Two men in trench coats sprinted after them, and Simon crept toward the entrance again. If he left now, there was a chance more members of the flock were following them, but if he waited, it wouldn't be long before they realized he wasn't with Ariana and Jam and doubled back. Either way, he had to take a risk.

"Hey, don't run—we've got plenty of food if you're hungry," said Bonnie. "You'll have to dig for it, but it's good stuff."

"Thanks, but I just ate," lied Simon. He slowly stood, watching people pass on the street. Why wasn't Perrin running after Jam with the others?

A screech echoed above him, and horror spread from the tips of Simon's fingers to his toes. He looked up, but he already knew what he'd see. A hawk perched on a fire escape, watching him.

"You have nowhere to go, Simon Thorn," said Perrin. The raccoons cursed and scrambled into a nearby Dumpster.

"Yeah? Watch me," said Simon. Clutching the straps of his backpack, he darted out of the alley and back onto the sidewalk, running the other way now. He still had no idea where the train station was, but he tried to retrace his steps, cutting corners and darting between cars stopped at traffic lights in hopes of losing Perrin.

Simon had no idea how to shake a tail, though, and Ariana wasn't there to give him any clever ideas this time. Perrin followed him easily, soaring through the city sky. The most he had to dodge were cables, but Simon couldn't count the number of pedestrians and cars he nearly plowed into, only to dart around them at the last second. A symphony of car horns followed him, and he swore to himself.

At last he had no choice but to admit he was thoroughly lost. He stopped, leaning over with his hands on his knees as he caught his breath. Perrin circled above him, unnoticed by the people milling around, and Simon took some small comfort in the fact that, while Ariana might be able to get away with disappearing in a crowded room, Perrin would never be able to shift back into a human in front of all these people and not be spotted. But if Simon stopped long enough and gave him the chance to shift in one of the dark alleyways nearby, Perrin would undoubtedly grab him the first chance he got. Simon had to keep moving.

He straightened and surveyed the area. A bank stood opposite him, while the other corners were taken over by a drugstore and two restaurants. He recognized a café sign with a cat on it, which had to be a good thing—he must have passed this way earlier.

"Excuse me," he said to a woman waiting at the crosswalk. "Where's the train station?"

She pointed him in the right direction. Simon was only a couple of blocks away. Reenergized, he hurried across the street. When he found his friends, they would figure out what to do from there.

Except when Simon glanced into the sky again, he froze. Perrin was gone.

He spun around, searching the crowd of unfamiliar faces. Had Perrin sneaked off to shift back? Or was he perched on a balcony somewhere, watching him?

Simon couldn't afford to wait around and find out. He hit the pavement again, running as fast as he could toward the station. Before he could get more than half a block, however, a hand grabbed him by the collar, pulling him into a dark alleyway.

"This would have been so much easier if you hadn't run, Simon Thorn," said a deep voice. Perrin.

Simon twisted, trying to break Perrin's grip, but the stronger man shoved him deeper into the alley. "I'm not alone," blurted Simon. "The Alpha's with me—"

"Is he? My flock must have chased his double into the Den while you were busy running away," said Perrin, a hint of amusement in his voice. "Try again."

Simon gritted his teeth. He could try shifting, but turning into anything but a golden eagle in front of Perrin would give away his secret and only make Orion even more eager to find him. And if Simon did shift into an eagle, Perrin already had a handful of his feathers. He wouldn't have a chance of getting away.

"How many times does the kid have to tell you?" squeaked a voice from Simon's backpack. Felix. "Let him go."

Simon turned his head just in time to see Felix sink his teeth into the soft space between Perrin's thumb and finger. With a cry, Perrin released his grip, snatching his hand away.

"Filthy rodent," he growled, making a grab for Felix, but Simon jerked his backpack away.

"I don't care what you do to me, but if you touch my friends, I'll peck your eyes out," he said, stumbling backward. Perrin rubbed his hand and chuckled.

"I don't want to do anything to you, Simon Thorn. All I want is to deliver you safely to your grandfather. Why you have to make it so difficult, I've no idea. I can have you on a flight tonight. By midnight, Orion will have his whole family to protect, and you'll be with your mother. Everyone wins."

Simon hesitated. It was tempting. Going with Perrin meant his friends could go back to the safety of New York. And as much as Simon didn't trust the birds, he knew Perrin wasn't lying—he would see his mother again.

But Orion didn't want to protect them. He wanted to use them. He'd imprisoned Simon's mother because she knew where to find the real pieces of the Predator, and he only wanted Simon because he thought he was the heir to the bird kingdom. If Simon wanted to help his mother and stop Orion from putting the Predator back together, then he couldn't afford to walk straight into Orion's trap. And he needed his friends' help. He couldn't leave them behind.

"I'm good on my own, thanks," he said, taking another step back. Nearby, something rustled, but the alley was so dark he could barely see Perrin's silhouette. If he shifted, he might stand a chance of going undetected. Perrin would be looking for an eagle in the sky, not an ant on the ground.

Or you could end this now.

Simon didn't know where that voice in the back of his mind came from, but it made his skin prickle. If he shifted into the right animal, it wouldn't matter if Perrin could see him or not. All it would take was one bite, one deep scratch in the right place, or one dose of venom, and—

Simon forced the thought out of his mind. If he used his powers against Perrin, that made him no better than the original Beast King, who had slaughtered his own kind. Simon wasn't a killer. And he wouldn't let Perrin turn him into something he wasn't.

Suddenly his back hit a wall. A sliver of light appeared under a door ten feet in front of him, but Perrin stood in his way, and the alley was too narrow for Simon to go around.

He was trapped, and this time there was no one here to save him.

SHIFTY BUSINESS

"It can't be easy being the only bird attending the L.A.I.R.," said Perrin, his voice silky now that he had Simon cornered. "We've heard stories of how you've been treated. I saw for myself how even your brother isn't your friend."

"You have no idea what you're talking about," said Simon as Perrin stepped closer.

"Don't I? I was raised in the insect kingdom. I know how hard it is to be a Hybred—to live among those of another kingdom. You're a bird. Your uncle is a mammal, and your brother is the most powerful person in our world. Surely you're ready to be surrounded by your own kind. By your family, and by people who care for you."

"And how long is that going to last?" Someone snapped

behind Perrin. Simon's eyes widened. He would have recognized that waspish voice anywhere.

"Winter?" Perrin shuddered. "What are you—"

"If you don't want to be followed, you shouldn't fly high enough for everyone to see you," she said. "Answer me. How long are you going to keep him? Until you find all the pieces to the Predator? Until he's no longer useful to you? Don't tell me Orion actually wants to be surrounded by family, because we both know that's a lie."

Simon felt Perrin's bony hand on his shoulder, holding him in place as he turned to face Winter, but Perrin didn't move toward her. He must not have been able to see her, either. "Simon is Orion's grandson. He loves him—"

"He called me his granddaughter my whole life," she spat. "And the first time I wasn't as perfect as he wanted me to be, he ditched me."

"Winter, sweetheart, leaving you behind broke Orion's heart. Surely you must understand—"

"I understand everything just fine," she said. Simon heard the dry whisper of scales against concrete, and he lowered his gaze. She'd shifted. "Orion's trying to put the real Predator together, and when he does, he's going to kill the Beast King's heir. Who, in case you've forgotten, is Simon's *brother*."

Perrin sniffed. "Orion has no intention of killing anyone, least of all his own grandson."

"Yeah?" blurted Simon. "Then why did he drop me off a skyscraper?"

"Because you are his heir," said Perrin, a note of anxiety in his voice as that dry whisper grew closer. "Of course you were going to shift and save yourself—"

"*Liar!*" A loud hiss filled the air, and thanks to the sliver of light from underneath the door, Simon spotted a dark blur flying toward them. Perrin must have spotted it, too, because with impossibly fast reflexes, he snatched the snake out of the air and hurled her against the wall. She hit the brick with a sick *crack*, and there was a loud ringing in Simon's ears as panic overtook him.

"Winter!" shouted Simon, and he fought against Perrin's grip. "Help! Somebody *help!*"

"Enough," he said, pinning Simon against the wall with his elbow. "One way or the other, you are coming with me."

A pained squeak sounded from his backpack, and Simon stopped moving, if only to save Felix from being squished. Perrin bared his teeth.

"What will it be, Simon Thorn? The easy way, or the hard—*argh!*"

Something dropped onto Perrin's head, and though Simon couldn't see it, he could feel its fluffy tail brush against his nose—and smell the soy sauce in its fur. The raccoons.

The door burst open, and light flooded the alleyway. "In here," said a girl who couldn't have been older than fifteen, and she gestured for Simon to join her. He ducked underneath Perrin's flailing arms, narrowly avoiding having Perrin's elbow connect with his nose, and he crouched down long enough to gently pick up the cottonmouth slumped against the brick wall. Winter was unconscious, and Simon wished he knew enough about snakes to tell whether or not she was breathing.

"Are you coming or what?" said the impatient girl. Simon glanced at Perrin. While one raccoon bit his ear, another climbed up his leg, and Simon didn't wait around to see what it would do. He hurried through the doorway and into what looked like a storage room for a restaurant, stopping dead in his tracks when he saw who was waiting for him.

"Jam? Ariana?" he said. Ariana looked annoyed, and Jam clutched Winter's purse. "How did you find us?"

"This one knows Chicago like the back of his hand," said Ariana, nudging Jam in the ribs.

"I told you, I've never been here before," said Jam, his face turning red. "We just followed the raccoons."

"Are they going to be okay?" said Simon, peering over his shoulder at the now-closed door.

"They'll be fine," said the girl, tucking her short bleached hair behind her ear. It was uneven, like someone had cut it without caring much about making it look good. "But *we* need to get out of here before the manager catches us."

"We need to find a doctor," said Simon, looking down at the cottonmouth coiled in his hands. "Or—a veterinarian."

"You are *not* taking me to the vet," came Winter's muffled voice, and Simon breathed a sigh of relief.

"Stay like this—I'll carry you," he said, and though her tongue flicked out in a halfhearted hiss, she didn't argue.

The girl with the bleached hair led them through the storage room, grabbing items off the shelves as they went and stuffing them into a ragged tote bag slung over her shoulder. By the time they exited into a bustling restaurant kitchen, her bag was overflowing with tin cans and whole vegetables, but she walked in as if she had every right to be there.

The smells emanating from the ovens made Simon's mouth water, but he was too worried to be hungry. The girl seemed to have no such hang-ups, and she grabbed a roll off a waiting plate as they passed into the dining room.

"Hey!" cried a woman dressed in a pantsuit. "I told you not to come back!"

"Time to run," said the girl, and the four of them bolted through the dining room, weaving between tables and customers enjoying their dinner. As the woman—the manager, Simon presumed—continued to shout at them, they burst onto the sidewalk and sprinted down the street.

Simon did his best to keep Winter steady, but by the time they finally slowed down, she was moaning. "I think I'm going to be sick."

"She could have a concussion," said Ariana as they

followed the girl into another alleyway. "When we stop, she can shift back. That might help."

"Where are we going, anyway?" said Simon, who didn't want to think too hard about what sort of injuries Winter might have. She'd gotten them trying to protect him from Perrin yet again, and he felt guilty enough already.

"Bonnie said we can crash at her place for the night," said Ariana. "There's a train in the morning we can catch. With any luck, the flock will be looking for us on the streets, not the station. It's a risk, but we have to take it."

"Where—" Simon cut himself off. "Bonnie? The raccoon?"

"Only when digging through trash and running from the cops," said the girl, leading them between two Dumpsters. They took another turn. "It's just up there."

Outside of the L.A.I.R. and his own family, Simon had never met an Animalgam before, not like this. He wasn't sure what he'd been expecting, but with her choppy hair, big boots, and the row of earrings running up the curve of her ear, Bonnie wasn't it.

She pushed aside a piece of plywood, revealing a hole in the wall of a crumbling brick building. "Home sweet home. Watch your head."

One by one, they bent down to fit through the hole and emerged in a dark hallway. Simon blinked, trying to get his bearings. "This is where you live?"

"You don't have to sound so judgmental about it," said Bonnie.

"I—I'm not," said Simon. His ears burned with embarrassment. "I didn't mean it like—"

"Calm down. I know what you meant. It's actually pretty cool once you see the inside." She pulled the plywood over the hole again and, after flipping on a flashlight, led them down the hallway and through a heavy door that squealed as she opened it. "Our security system. You can hear that anywhere in the theater."

Bonnie's flashlight didn't provide much of a view, but in the beam of weak light, Simon spotted a row of plush red velvet seats. She headed over to the foot of an old wooden stage, where she flipped on a lantern.

"It isn't much," said Bonnie, "but it's dry in the winter and there are plenty of places to sleep."

Simon's mouth dropped open. They stood at the front of an old theater complete with hundreds of seats and a balcony that must have held even more. Moth-eaten velvet curtains that matched the chairs hung from the rafters, and the room was dusty and crumbling from what must have been decades of disuse, but when Simon squinted into the darkness, he spotted a mural on the ceiling of a swirling sky and faded angels. Growing up in New York City, he'd been to his fair share of museums and seen enough artwork to fill thousands of theaters. But there was something surreal about seeing it like this, in the middle of a run-down building.

"Told you it's pretty cool," said Bonnie, perching on the

edge of the stage. "Don't go up to the balcony. You'll fall through, and I'm not dragging any of you to the hospital."

Speaking of the hospital, Simon set the cottonmouth down on one of the plush cushions, and Winter shifted back. Her hair was a mess, and Simon could already see bruises forming on the side of her face where she must have hit the wall, but instead of complaining, she glared at him.

"Don't you ever question my loyalty to you again," she said with enough venom to convince him that she would probably be all right. He slumped into the chair next to her, relieved.

"You need to stop trying to save me from Perrin," he said. "One of these times, he's going to kill you."

"Then maybe you should start saving yourself," said Winter.

"She has a point," said Ariana, her heavy boots echoing as she walked up and down the aisles, surveying the theater. "Hasn't Malcolm been teaching you anything?"

"A little," said Simon. But he was so far behind the other students, who'd grown up in the Animalgam kingdoms and had been training to defend themselves their whole lives, that it was almost hopeless. The most he could really do was run fast, and because he was so short, he couldn't even do that right.

"Here." Jam offered Winter her purse, and she snatched it from him. "We're only a couple of blocks from the station. It shouldn't take us long to get there in the morning."

"If we go while it's still dark, we might be able to dodge any lookouts the flock's posted in the area," said Ariana, frowning as she peered into a dusty corner. "This place is crawling with spiders."

"They're nice, for the most part. As nice as spiders can be, that is," said Bonnie as she pulled out a pot and lit a camping stove.

"Oh?" Ariana paused, turning toward Bonnie. "And how nice, exactly, can a spider be?"

Bonnie must have realized her mistake, because her grip on the pot tightened, and her voice went up a few notches. "Pretty nice sometimes. So, if you're all Animalgams, too, then what kingdom do you belong to? Other than the snake, of course. Unless you're all snakes, but I've never heard of so many traveling together before."

"We're—" started Simon, eager to turn the conversation back to something more neutral, but Ariana shot him a look, and he fell silent.

"Wouldn't want to ruin the surprise," she said, resuming her walk around the theater. "What's for dinner?"

Suddenly the door opened, filling the space with the hair-raising squeal of rusted metal, and two boys who looked close to Simon's age spilled through, laughing and trying to pull each other back. "I win!" shouted the first, who had dark hair and a thin cut over his brow. He didn't seem to mind the blood dripping into his eye, however, and he wiped it with the back of his hand.

"You cheated," said the second, who was identical to the first boy, save for the cut. "You started running on 'two.'"

"You did the same thing," said the first, grinning and basking in his win. "Oh, hey. You brought them back with you."

Bonnie's mouth puckered in annoyance. "What else was I supposed to do? Leave them on the streets to freeze?" She poured the contents of a tin can into the pot. "These are my brothers, Billy and Butch. Billy and Butch, these are—" She paused. "I didn't catch your names."

"Simon," he said, raising his hand. "And that's Jam, Ariana, and Winter. You're twins?"

Billy and Butch exchanged a look. "No, we just look exactly alike," said the one with the cut.

"Not anymore. You're bleeding," said the other as he started to dig through a cardboard box on the side of the stage.

Bonnie rolled her eyes. "Yes, they're twins. They're my brothers. And they're obnoxious."

"You haven't ditched us yet," said the one with blood now smeared across his brow.

"Keep this up, and one day I will. Then you'll have no one to cook for you," said Bonnie, waving her spatula around.

"I have a twin brother, too," said Simon. Billy and Butch were the first pair of identical twins he'd met since discovering Nolan existed, and he studied them, curious. What would it have been like to grow up with his brother—with an exact copy of himself running around? They would have been friends, Simon figured. Neither of them would have ever been lonely or felt like an outcast, not when they had each other. Jealousy flared up inside him, even though he knew it was irrational. It wasn't Billy and Butch's fault he hadn't grown up with his brother.

"Why isn't he with you?" asked the twin with the cut. The other produced an old bandage from the cardboard box and ripped it open, sticking it onto his brother's forehead haphazardly.

"He—wanted to stay back," said Simon. He couldn't feel bad about leaving Nolan behind, not when they had run into so much trouble already.

"Are you identical?" said the other boy, and Simon nodded. "We have different haircuts, though."

From the row of ragged seats, Winter made a gagging sound and waved her hand in front of her face. "Are you cooking rotten soy sauce? It smells *disgusting*."

"No, you're just sitting in the chair Billy threw up on when he had some bad stir-fry last month," said Bonnie breezily. Winter yelped and jumped out of her seat, tripping as she scrambled away.

"I'm pretty sure Bonnie was kidding," said Simon.

"Don't care," said Winter, eyeing the cushion like it was still covered in vomit. In a nasty voice Simon recognized as the one she used when she was upset, she added, "Why don't you have parents, anyway?"

"Usual reason. They had the audacity to die before we grew up," said Bonnie, unfazed by Winter's rudeness as she stirred whatever was in the pot. It smelled like baked beans, but Simon couldn't be sure.

"I'm sorry," he said. "Isn't there somewhere you can go? Someplace with—beds?"

"Are *you* going to take us in?" said Bonnie, her voice cracking like a whip. "We don't have any relatives, and the foster system would split us up. We're fine here." She dug around in her bag and pulled out a few apples. "That's the nice thing about being raccoons. If we can't find food, we can forage for it."

Simon wasn't convinced. But Bonnie didn't look bothered by it, and the boys were shouting and racing each other around the theater now. If being with his mom and Darryl again meant living on the streets, Simon would've done it, too.

They ate dinner off paper plates while sitting cross-legged on the stage. Even Winter joined them, and while she wrinkled her nose at the baked beans and kept her distance from the raccoon siblings, she ate without complaint. It was a nice change of pace, Simon thought.

"What about the L.A.I.R.?" he said as he scooped up the last of the beans on his plate. "Can't you go there?"

"The what?" said Bonnie, while one twin tried to steal an extra piece of apple off the other's plate.

"The Leading Animalgam Institute for the Remarkable," said Simon. "It's where we go to school. I bet there's room for the three of you."

"Simon . . ." A pained look crossed Ariana's face. "The L.A.I.R. is really hard to get into. There are only so many spots for each kingdom. And they're selective about which—*kinds* of Animalgams they let in. Usually they only invite predators. Like bears and sharks and venomous spiders."

"We could take on a bear," said the injured twin—Billy, as far as Simon could tell—with his mouth full of stolen apple. "Wouldn't know what hit him."

"I don't doubt it, but the L.A.I.R. is still selective," said Ariana. "Besides, it's November. We're nearly halfway through the first semester."

"There has to be something," insisted Simon, while Bonnie stood and collected everyone's empty plates.

"There are other schools," said Jam, holding open a dingy trash bag streaked with old gravy. "The L.A.I.R. is the only place that accepts Animalgam students from different kingdoms, but the mammal kingdom has schools all over the place. If we can find the nearest group of mammals—"

"Did you or did you not hear the part where we're fine?" said Bonnie, shoving the paper plates one by one into the bag. "We've been on our own for two years, and we don't need anybody else. I'm sorry we're not good enough for you or your precious school, but *we* like it here."

Awkward silence permeated the air, lingering with the stale smell of old food, and Simon slouched. "I'm sorry," he said at last. "I was just trying to help."

"Go help someone who needs it," said Bonnie. "We're fine out here on our own. And even if we weren't, the instant we start trusting adults again, they'll split us up, and I'm not interested. End of story." She nodded toward the velvet chairs. "If you want to leave before dawn, you should get some sleep. We don't have any spare blankets, so tough luck. I'm sure you'll find some way to survive." Snatching the garbage bag from Jam, she tied it shut. "Good night."

Simon climbed off the stage and headed to the chairs, finding one with most of the stuffing still inside the cushions. He made himself as comfortable as he could with the armrests in the way, and as Ariana passed him, she gave him a small, sympathetic smile. He tried to return it as he propped his head up on his backpack, Felix settling in beside his ear, but it felt more like a grimace.

The others curled up in the chairs as well, and soon enough, Bonnie turned off the lantern. Simon closed his eyes and tried to sleep, but all he could see was Perrin's face lingering an inch in front of him, and despite Jam's soft snores, he could still hear the sickening crunch of a cottonmouth hitting a brick wall. Sliding his hand into the pocket of his sweatshirt, he ran his fingertips over the slight indent his mother's handwriting had made in the postcard. A million things could've gone wrong today, and a million things could go wrong tomorrow. But he was doing this for the right reason. Bonnie might not have thought he understood the lengths she would go to in order to keep her family together, but he did. Maybe more than anyone else in that theater.

He wasn't sure when his thoughts turned to dreams, but a piercing shriek jolted him awake, and he sat up, his heart racing. "Winter?"

"Where is it?" Somewhere behind him, he could hear her frantically searching. "It was here when I went to sleep, and now it's gone."

"Where's what?" Simon tried to climb over the rows of seats to get to her, but in the darkness, he stumbled and fell to the floor, knocking his knee against worn-out rug and concrete.

"My purse," sobbed Winter. "It's gone."

10

RACCOON BANDITS

Light flooded the theater, and Ariana stood beside the lantern. "That's not the only thing that's disappeared," she said. "The raccoons are gone, too."

"And my shoes," said Jam in a sleepy voice. He popped his head out from another row, his glasses askew and his blond hair sticking up at all angles. "That wasn't very nice of them."

"Forget about your stupid shoes," snapped Winter, who was tearing down the aisles in a panic, ripping off tattered cushions and checking underneath the seats. "Orion gave me my purse. He made me swear I'd never lose it, and—" She choked on another sob. "It has *everything* in it. My pictures, my books, my credit card—"

"Of *course*." Ariana pulled herself onto the stage while Simon joined Winter to help her look. "Orion gave you that credit card, too, didn't he?"

"Y-yes."

"Then it's a good thing the raccoons stole it," she said. "That's how Orion followed us here. All he had to do was look up the records, and he'd know you bought four tickets to Chicago."

Simon straightened from his spot halfway down an aisle. If Ariana was right, then he owed Winter a huge apology. "Winter—"

"Don't," she said through her tears, searching another row. "I just want to find my purse."

"We need to get to the train station. It's almost dawn," said Jam as he gingerly walked down to the stage in his socks.

"I'm not leaving until I find it," said Winter, wiping her cheeks. "Will you two please *help us*?"

"It's not here," said Simon, ducking down to look underneath another seat. "And the raccoons won't be back until they know we're gone. We have to go, Winter. We need to make that train."

She shook her head and wandered up and down the rows, looking more lost than Simon had ever seen her before. Her face grew splotchy and her hands trembled as she knelt down. The Winter he knew would have never touched the dirty floor, but she barely seemed to notice.

Simon stepped between her and the row of seats, blocking her view. "Winter. It's not here," he said as gently as he could.

"If they'd taken your precious postcards, we'd all be looking," she said through her tears. "But because you don't think my purse is important—"

"It's not important," said Simon. "The fact that Orion gave it to you—*that's* important. And your pictures, and your books, and what they mean to you. That's all important, too. I get that. But holding on to that purse was never going to bring Orion back."

Winter's lower lip trembled, and she sat back against her heels, her shoulders slumping. "It's the only thing I have left of him," she whispered, her eyes spilling over with tears.

"I'm sorry." Simon knelt down and wrapped his arms around her. He would have been destroyed if he'd lost his postcards or his pocket watch, and he wanted nothing more than to hunt down the raccoons and get Winter's things back. But the three siblings were long gone. He knew that, Winter knew that, and all they could do now was get on the train and keep going.

Their trip to the station didn't take long, even with Jam walking around without his shoes. They all kept an eye out for Perrin, but either he was lying low or looking for them elsewhere. Simon hoped with all his might that that was the case.

While he purchased tickets to Arizona with the money he and Ariana had left, she disappeared, returning fifteen minutes later with a brand-new pair of sneakers. "Don't ask," she said, handing them to Jam, and he put them on without a word.

By the time they boarded the train, Simon still hadn't spotted Perrin, and he began to breathe easier. With their new tickets bought with cash and the raccoons undoubtedly using the credit card in Chicago, they might gain a day or two on the flock. It wasn't much, but it was better than nothing.

This time they didn't have enough money for a room, so they found four seats facing each other and settled in for a long trip. While Jam played with the lock picks and Ariana napped on his shoulder in spider form, Winter stared out the window. More than once, Simon thought about trying to talk to her, but he knew nothing he said would make her feel better. So for now, he stayed quiet.

The train stopped every now and then, but for the most part, they kept moving southwest through the country. As soon as they reached Kansas, the trees and hills disappeared, replaced with flat plains that stretched as far as Simon could see. All that empty space made his insides squirm, and he busied himself by making sure Felix was comfortable in his backpack.

Simon spent most of the day thumbing through his mother's notebook and reading up on Arizona, but even that didn't help calm his nerves much. The closer they got, the heavier the weight on his chest felt. He had no idea what he was doing. His mother was depending on him, and he couldn't even outrun a single Animalgam without help. How was he supposed to rescue her?

He would find a way. He had the Beast King's powers, and no matter how badly he wanted to keep it a secret, he knew that if it became a choice between remaining quiet or rescuing his mother, he would choose his mother.

By the time the sun was setting, Jam disappeared into the dining car, returning a little while later with several wrapped sandwiches. Winter was fast asleep opposite Simon, so instead Jam sat down next to him.

"Turkey or tuna?" he offered to Simon. Simon chose turkey, and after dropping a piece into his backpack for Felix, he noticed Ariana was still sleeping on Jam's sweater.

"Aren't you tired, too?" said Simon. After their night in that musty old theater, Simon had been fighting exhaustion for hours, but he couldn't bring himself to nap. There was too much to think about and too much that could go wrong.

Jam shrugged. "I'll sleep when we reach Colorado. We're not far—fifty miles away, maybe."

Simon shook his head, amazed. "How do you *do* that?"

"Do what?" said Jam through a mouthful of tuna and bread.

"Know exactly where we are all the time."

Jam's cheeks flushed, and he swallowed. "I don't know. I just do."

Simon let it drop for now, focusing on his sandwich instead. Eating helped ease the fatigue from his body, and he peered out the window as the sun dipped below the endless horizon, leaving a smear of pink behind. "I don't know what I'm doing."

Jam balled up the wrapper of his now-eaten sandwich and said slowly, "That's all right. You don't have to know."

"But what if Orion isn't in Arizona?" said Simon, and he glanced at the bruises on the side of Winter's face. "Or what if someone gets hurt again?"

"We all know what could happen. We're here because we want to help you find your mom, not because we think you have a foolproof plan." Jam gave him a wry half grin, his glasses falling down the bridge of his nose. "Besides, it's more exciting this way. I never got to be spontaneous before I met you."

Simon sighed. "I just . . . after what happened to my uncle . . ."

"That wasn't your fault," said Jam. "And that kind of thing isn't going to happen this time. We're in this together, and you can trust us, Simon. We'll watch your back."

"That's kind of what I'm afraid of," he said miserably.

Jam straightened and pulled his padlock from the pocket in his jeans, fiddling with the lock pick still stuck inside. "The general planned my whole life for me," he said. "I've had a daily schedule since I could walk. That's just how we do things underwater—if you leave no room for error, there won't be any. But there's no room for fun, either, or figuring things out on your own, and that's what I like to do. I like swimming off in the wrong direction to explore a cave I've never seen before, and I like having an hour or two where I can do anything I want. But our kingdom is so big that if everyone did their own thing, nothing would ever get done, so I always feel like I'm stuck in a routine I can't stand."

From what he had seen of the underwater section at the Den, Simon had always had the impression that Jam didn't fit in with the rest of his kingdom. Hearing him talk now only confirmed it, and he frowned. "It's okay to be different. It's *good* to be different."

"I know it is," said Jam. "But when you're supposed to be the leader of the whole kingdom one day . . ."

"Maybe it's time you shake things up," said Simon. "Change isn't always a bad thing."

"I know. I like change. I like being different. And I like not always knowing what's going to happen, even if that means I get into trouble more than I should. But the general hates it when I'm someone he doesn't think I should be."

"I like who you are," said Simon firmly. "And I'll explore as many caves with you as you want."

Jam turned pink and tugged on the padlock, but it refused to open. "Thanks, Simon. You'd be surprised what sort of stuff you can find. Plus, knowing our way around the caves will come in handy if we ever have to hide from a hungry shark, right?"

Simon didn't want to think about being chased by any creature with that many teeth, but he nodded. "It's good to be prepared."

"The general does always say preparation is the key to success," said Jam with a small grin. "That's why I'm trying to learn how to pick this stupid lock. Because maybe one day, I'll be stuck in a cage, and this will be my only way out." He offered it to Simon. "Do you want to try? I have an extra set of lock picks you can keep, if you want. Ariana gave me two just in case I lost one."

Simon took the lock and studied it. Right now, he had to prepare himself for a lot of things. He had no idea what they would be facing in Arizona, and he needed to be ready for the possibility that his mother wouldn't be there. For the possibility that Orion and the flock would capture him. For the possibility that, despite his best efforts, he would fail miserably and never see his brother or Malcolm again.

There was a possibility he would succeed, too. That was the whole reason they were doing this, after all—because if there was even a chance Simon could save his mother, he had to give it everything he had.

For the next hour, Jam showed him how to jiggle the two long metal tools in order to trick the mechanism into opening. It wasn't too difficult once Simon got the hang of it, and after he and Jam had opened the lock several times, Simon slid the second set of lock picks into his pocket beside his father's watch, and they settled into their chairs for the night. Jam's soft snores began almost immediately, but with the way Simon's thoughts raced now that he had nothing to hold them at bay, he was sure he would never fall asleep.

He must have at some point, however, because later—much later, judging by the quiet of the train car—his eyes snapped open. His forehead was pressed against the cold window, and he could feel a small trail of drool down the corner of his mouth. Wiping his face with his sleeve, he glanced at the others, but they were all sleeping, too.

Annoyed at himself for waking up, he shut his eyes again and tried to fall back asleep, but after a minute of this, he gave up and made his way to the bathroom instead. After he had done his business, he stared at his reflection in the mirror as he washed his hands. The harsh fluorescent light overhead made him look paler than usual, and there were dark circles beneath his eyes that he had never seen before. It was no wonder—they had been on the run for more than two days now, but it felt much longer.

He braced himself as the train pulled to a stop at one of the many smaller stations between Chicago and Arizona. After drying his hands, he slipped out of the bathroom and closed the door quietly, not wanting to wake any of the sleeping passengers. The car was dark and quiet, and

Simon hoped the lull of the train would help him get back to sleep.

As he took a step toward his seat, however, a hand clamped over his mouth. Simon's eyes widened, but before he could protest, he was pulled through the door and off the train, spilling out onto the cold, dark platform.

11

STONE FOX

Simon fought his abductor with all his might, kicking and yelling into the warm palm stifling his cries for help. He struggled against the unyielding grip that held him in place on the platform, but it was no use. Whoever had him was much stronger than he was, and despair filled him as he watched the train start to move once more. His friends wouldn't realize he was missing until morning, and by then—

"Would you hold *still*?" his captor demanded in a deep, unfamiliar voice, but Simon wasn't about to let him win that easily. He tried to yank his arm from the man's grip, and a shot of pain ran through his shoulder.

"You're going to hurt yourself," said another voice. A

young woman stepped into the light, her copper hair flaming. She looked Simon up and down, as if deciding whether he was big enough to serve as an entrée, or if he would have to do as an appetizer. "You can let him go now, Keval. He has nowhere to run."

The meaty hand over his mouth disappeared, as did the arm holding him upright. Simon stumbled forward, and the woman held out a hand to stop him from plowing into her. "I need to get back on the train," he sputtered. "My friends—"

"Which friends? Those friends?" The woman pointed across the train tracks. Simon whipped around. On the other side of the platform stood Jam and Winter with their bags at their feet. More goons crowded around them, blocking any chance they had to escape, and one held a plastic container half the size of a shoebox.

"Jam! Winter!" he called. Neither of them struggled against their kidnappers, but Winter looked especially pale, while Jam's glasses were askew and he kept glancing nervously at the box.

"Simon, we're okay," he called. "They trapped Ariana."

"She's fine," said the copper-haired woman. "We'll take good care of her, don't worry."

Simon shivered in the cold night air, and he wrapped his arms around himself. "You have to let us go. We don't have any money—"

"I don't want your money." She started to walk the

length of the platform toward a staircase, and the man—Keval—nudged Simon forward, forcing him to follow. Simon dragged his feet, keeping an eye on his friends on the other side of the tracks.

"Then what do you want?" said Simon.

"A vintage motorcycle. World peace. A decent partner in crime." She turned back to look him up and down once more. "Admittedly I wouldn't say no to a billion dollars, either, but you'll do for now, Simon Thorn."

In that moment, as his pulse raced and the world around him tilted, it took everything Simon had not to shift and fly away. Of course the flock wouldn't be the only birds after them. Orion had agents all around the country. It was only a matter of time before others tracked him down, too.

Once they were all at the bottom of the platform, the two groups merged, and Simon snatched his backpack from one of the goons that surrounded them as they marched down a dusty sidewalk. He wasn't sure where they were headed—from the few streetlights nearby, the town didn't look very big at all.

"You don't have to do this," he said. "Whatever Orion told you—"

"Orion?" The woman laughed. "You think we have anything to do with that molted birdbrain?"

Simon frowned. "But—"

"We're the good guys, Simon," she said, twisting around to grin at him.

"Yeah?" said Winter in a shaking voice. "Last time I checked, good guys don't kidnap people."

"And last time *I* checked, children aren't allowed to travel across the country without parental approval," she said easily. "I take it you're Winter Rivera."

The loss of her anonymity seemed to startle Winter into silence, and she sniffed, neither confirming nor denying.

"And you . . ." The woman looked at Jam. "You're Benjamin Fluke, son of General Fluke. The spider in the box is Ariana Webster, daughter of the Black Widow Queen. If we weren't on your side, we could make a good chunk of that billion off the ransom alone."

"Lucky us," muttered Simon. None of this was making him feel any better. "How do you know who we are?"

"I know everything," she deadpanned. "And the Alpha offered a reward for your safe return. I'm surprised you got this far, considering every mammal community in the country is keeping an eye out for you."

So Malcolm was looking for them. This shouldn't have surprised Simon, but for some reason, it did. He hadn't thought about what his uncle would do once they escaped from the Den. Then again, he hadn't thought much of this through at all.

"Hold up," said the burly man who had snatched Simon from the train. "We have company."

On instinct, Simon looked up toward the twinkling night sky. A pair of hawks circled overhead, and soon several more raptors joined them. Simon stiffened, ready to run, but the woman stood her ground.

"Really? That's all you brought?" she called. "I thought your kind was supposed to be smart."

"You will release the boy into my custody, or you will face the consequences," said an all-too-familiar voice. Simon blanched. So Perrin had managed to follow them after all. But if the flock had known where they were the whole time, why hadn't they tried to grab them?

Because they were on a train headed to Arizona anyway, Simon realized. Why would they risk losing them again when Simon was running straight for Orion?

"This is my territory, and in case you haven't heard, birds aren't welcome," said the copper-haired woman as the flock circled lower. She was thin and didn't look very strong, but she moved like a predator—like she was *enjoying* the challenge of facing down a dozen birds. "So unless you're in the mood to die, I'd recommend leaving."

The hawk puffed up, and Simon could practically feel the indignation radiating from him. "You have no idea who you're threatening."

"Oh, I have some," she said with a wicked smile. Around her, the others elbowed one another and seemed to position themselves in some sort of formation, and the birds flew close enough for Simon to see their sharp talons.

"I will give you one last chance," said Perrin. "Release the boy, and we will leave you to your fleas. If you do not do as I command, I will slaughter every last member of your pack and wear your furs as trophies."

The woman sighed theatrically. "Is that how it's going to be?" she said, her eyes dancing. "All right, if you insist. I could use a good fight, and it *has* been a while since I've had chicken for dinner."

A hair-raising screech filled the empty street, and a chorus of cries followed. Before the flock could attack, however, the humans formed a ring around Simon and his friends, and the adults began to shift. One man turned into an opossum; another shifted into an armadillo. Dogs, gophers, beavers, even a donkey—Simon could barely keep track.

The birds dived toward the mammals, screaming threats and curses. Winter shrieked while Jam ducked his head, and the three of them huddled together in the center of the melee. Talons clawed at fur, teeth ripped out feathers, and in the midst of it all, Simon saw the woman leap from the dusty street toward Perrin, shifting into a red fox midair.

The hawk was too quick for her, though, and by the time she had shifted completely, Perrin had already flown far out of reach. The fox snarled and weaved between the legs of a coyote, darting toward them.

"Come on, while they're distracted," she said, nodding toward an opening in the circle. Simon hesitated for a fraction of a second. The mammals *had* kidnapped them, after all, but he hastily shook off his doubts and followed her.

As they hurried through the fighting Animalgams, Simon bent down to snatch the discarded plastic box. "Are you okay?" he said to the spider inside. If Ariana responded, he couldn't hear her, but she managed a wave with one of her legs.

"Catch them!" cried Perrin from above, and the few birds that weren't tangled up with the mammals soared toward them. Simon raced after the others, tucking the box underneath his arm.

The fox swore. "If you could all run a little faster, now would be the time to do it."

"Sorry we don't all have four legs," shot Winter as they raced down the street toward the darkness. "Please tell me there are more of you somewhere."

"If it'll make you run faster, sure," said the fox. Simon broke out in a sprint.

"Where are we going? There's nothing out there," said Jam, already breathless. "It's just desert."

The fox dropped back behind them and snapped at his heels. "You can either trust me, or you can get abducted by birds. Your choice."

If Jam was right and they were heading toward nothing, then Simon wasn't so sure it was much of a choice at all. He searched the sky. Three members of the flock, Perrin included, still followed them.

"Keep going," he said to the others, skidding to a stop and setting the box and his backpack down. By the time their protests reached his ears, he had already shifted into a golden eagle and was climbing through the air toward the flock. Maybe it was stupid—maybe it was reckless. But they were only chasing his friends because of him. This way, they might have a chance to escape.

He swooped toward Perrin and the falcons that had followed them. The only bird of prey Simon had ever gone up against was his grandfather, Orion, who was also a golden eagle, so he expected that the members of the flock would be as big as he was. But immediately he realized how wrong he was.

Simon, despite being young, was already twice Perrin's size. His wingspan dwarfed the hawk's, and as he barreled toward Perrin, the other members of the flock screeched and fled back toward the fight on the ground.

"Leave us *alone*," shouted Simon, and with his outstretched talons, he caught Perrin's wing and dragged him back toward the brawl in town. "If you ever lay a feather on one of my friends, I'll make sure you never fly again."

With strength he hadn't known he possessed, he flung Perrin's delicate bird body toward a waiting coyote. The older hawk spiraled toward the ground, and for one heart-stopping second, Simon thought he'd accidentally snapped his neck. But at last Perrin spread his wings, catching a current before the coyote could take a bite out of him.

"Brothers!" he shouted, tumbling through the air toward Simon once more. "With me!"

But no one joined him. The rest of the birds were too busy battling the mammals, and the feathers that littered the ground made it clear who was winning the fight. Somehow, despite being nowhere as big as the wolves and bears that populated the L.A.I.R., this ragtag bunch of mammals was holding its own against the flock.

Perrin was halfway to Simon when he realized he was alone. With a furious shriek, he flashed his talons at Simon. "This isn't over," he cried, and at last he circled back toward the skirmish. "Retreat!"

The remaining members of the flock soared upward to join him, leaving the growling mammals behind. Simon stayed in the air as he watched them turn sharply to follow the train tracks, disappearing into the darkness.

He'd done it. He'd really scared Perrin off. Dazed and amazed, he flew back toward his friends, diving through the air until he reached them.

"The flock's gone," he shouted. "You don't have to run anymore."

Simon landed beside his discarded backpack, and as soon as he shifted back into a human, he opened the box that held Ariana. She crawled onto the ground and shuddered. "That was fun," she muttered.

"Sorry," said Simon, kneeling on the crumbling dirt. It wasn't quite a desert, but it wasn't exactly grass, either. "Are you okay?"

"I'm fine." In a split second, her human form reappeared. "I guess we'll have to find another way to Arizona."

"Guess so," said Simon as Jam and Winter joined them, trailed by the red fox.

"Why did he fly away?" said Jam, staring up at the starry sky with his mouth hanging open. "The flock never gives up like that."

"I don't know," said Simon, still shocked. "I guess I'm bigger than he is."

"Or he didn't expect you to attack him head-on," said the fox. She shifted back into a human and examined a shallow cut on her forearm. "Nothing like a good brawl to get the blood flowing. Good work, Simon." She stuck her hand out, and Simon noticed it was decorated with smaller battle scars. "I'm Zia Stone, by the way. Thanks for your help. That was brave of you, attacking Perrin like that. If you were older, I'd buy you a drink."

He shook her hand hesitantly. She wasn't an enemy, not like the flock was, but she wasn't exactly an ally right now, either. "We're not going back to New York. We left for a reason."

"I'm sure you did, kid, but you're practically an infant. And infants shouldn't be traveling the country alone."

Simon bristled. "I'm twelve—"

"You're not helping your case." Zia began to climb a hill, but Simon refused to follow her. Beside him, his friends stood their ground, too.

"The flock's gone," said Simon firmly. "We can take it from here."

Zia stopped halfway up the hill, her head tilted curiously as she studied them. "Bravery without brains doesn't amount to much, kid. You do realize it's dark out, you're in the middle of nowhere, and you're surrounded, right?"

Simon looked around. A dozen other mammals had rejoined them now, some human and others still in their Animalgam forms. The lights from the town glowed in the distance, too far away to be a beacon of escape now. "You can't hold us hostage."

"I'm not holding you hostage. I'm protecting you," said Zia. "The Alpha wants you back safely, and we do our best not to upset him, so come on. You might be able to fly away, but I doubt your friends can."

Simon scowled as he tried to come up with a way out of this. He wasn't sure which was worse—being captured by Perrin and brought straight to Orion, where at least he'd have the chance to see his mother again, or being kidnapped by a group of mammals who had every intention of sending him back to Malcolm.

"Might as well," said Ariana quietly. "Once the Alpha's here, maybe he'll help us."

Getting his uncle involved was the last thing Simon wanted. But the mammals behind them pressed closer, and at last he wordlessly led his friends up the hill. Zia stopped at the very top, near a sloping rock face that was oddly smooth.

"Normally we don't allow members of other kingdoms

to join us, so consider yourselves lucky." As she spoke, she pulled on a piece of vine, and a cleverly camouflaged door opened from the rock, revealing a well-lit tunnel.

"No way," said Winter, taking a step backward. "I've heard about how disgusting mammal dens are. I'm not going in there."

"Then don't," said Zia. "Spend the night up here instead. I'm sure the coyotes won't bother you. Or the rattlesnakes. I can't promise the vultures won't keep you up, though. They enjoy live company more than you'd expect. The ones around here think they're comedians."

Simon gave Winter a beseeching look. "If you survived the theater, you'll survive this," he promised.

Her expression tightened, but she didn't argue any further. With a grumble, she trailed after Jam as they entered the tunnel. Lights hung every few feet, making it brighter inside than it had been out in the open, and soon the tunnel opened up into a large cavern.

Simon had never seen anything like it in his life. Unlike the Den, which was an underground building surrounded by a moat, this looked like a small community. A secure staircase zigzagged down the cavern wall, and he spotted at least half a dozen levels of doors carved out of the rock itself. Below them, in the center of the atrium, was a garden with several picnic tables scattered around.

"What is this place?" he said to Zia as they descended to the third floor.

"It's called Stonehaven, after my family," she said. "It's a safe place for mammal Animalgams. This town—it was built on the edge of the reptile territory to the south and the bird territory to the west. This is still mammal terrain, of course, but we get pushback from both sides regularly. They can't get us down here, though," she added as she stopped at a door that blended in with the rest of them. "Not without heavy losses on their side. We've won enough fights that they leave us alone now, for the most part."

Pushing open the door, she gestured for them to enter. Simon went first. He wasn't sure what he expected—a cave, maybe, with stalactites hanging from the ceiling and water trickling down the wall. Instead he walked into what could have been any living room in any home across the country, complete with a couch, wallpaper, carpet, and even—

"Hey, Felix, look," he said, unzipping his backpack. "A TV."

Felix crawled out faster than Simon had ever seen him move before. "It's about time," he said, and he leaped onto the arm of the sofa. "Where's the remote?"

Zia didn't seem the least bit bothered by the fact that Simon had been keeping a mouse in his backpack. On the contrary, she found the remote and set it on the couch for him. "Don't crank the volume up too high. It's after midnight."

With Felix content to watch reruns of an old sitcom, Simon and his friends followed Zia deeper into the apartment. She led them into a tiny kitchen. "Thirsty? Hungry?"

she said. All four of them shook their heads. "If any of you change your mind, glasses are in the cabinet and food's in the fridge. Bedrooms are through here," she added. "There are only two, so you'll have to share."

"You mean this isn't your home?" said Simon. He wasn't sure why he'd assumed it was, but now that he'd guessed otherwise, it was obvious. There were no pictures hanging on the walls, no normal clutter lying around—if anything, it looked like a hotel room. A big hotel room, but still comfortable and welcoming without any personal touches.

"This is one of our transitory dwellings," said Zia. "We get plenty of people who are traveling through and need a place to stay the night."

"So you're like a hotel for Animalgams," said Ariana.

"More like a motel. What's that smell?" muttered Winter, wrinkling her nose as she peered into one of the bedrooms. Simon elbowed her in the side, and she elbowed right back. "What? They're the ones who kidnapped us."

"Still not a kidnapping," said Zia, pushing open the door to the second bedroom. Ariana waltzed inside, and Winter reluctantly followed. "Someone has to make sure you don't get turned into bird feed."

"We can look after ourselves," said Simon.

"Yeah, I can see that." Zia leaned against the wall in the hallway, arms crossed. Simon refused to look away. There was something about her he didn't trust—something underneath the surface that made him think this was about more than babysitting them.

"How long until my uncle gets here?" he said.

"Keval's calling him now. If he can catch an early flight, he'll be here before noon."

That didn't give Simon a lot of time to figure out a way to escape. And as soon as he thought it, he realized that was exactly what he needed to do. Malcolm would return them to the safety of the Den as soon as possible, and if he *was* willing to risk sending someone to rescue Simon's mother, it wouldn't be a twelve-year-old who had only been shifting for a couple of months. It would be the pack.

Simon considered his options. He could shift into an ant and sneak back onto the surface. From there, he could fly to Paradise Valley on his own. It would take a while, and he didn't know the way, but he could figure it out. Then, his friends would be safe, and he could still find his mother.

"Hot chocolate?" said Zia suddenly, and Simon blinked. He'd gotten so lost in his thoughts that he hadn't realized she'd moved back into the kitchen. Simon stood alone in the hallway.

"Uh, I should probably . . ." He glanced into the bedroom, where Jam was sorting through his own backpack.

"You'll have plenty of time to sleep in," said Zia, already pulling out two mugs. "Go join your mouse friend while I make this. I want to hear how you managed to get all the way to Colorado without getting caught."

"Dumb luck," he mumbled as he trudged past her and into the living room, where Felix was captivated by the television. Not wanting to disturb him, Simon sat in an armchair nearby and pulled off his shoes. His feet were sore from running so much, and he flexed his toes as he watched a man and woman argue about where to eat dinner. It didn't sound very funny to Simon, but Felix squeaked with laughter.

"Mice always have the strangest sense of humor," said Zia as she joined them. Felix's expression instantly darkened.

"Just because you don't have the sophisticated tastes that come from living in a big city doesn't mean *I* have to endure your insults," he said.

"I've been to plenty of big cities," said Zia as she handed a mug of hot chocolate to Simon and sat down on the edge of the sofa. "And I've met plenty of mice who wouldn't know a good joke if it hit them over the head and left a lump."

"Couldn't be a very good joke if it hurts," said Simon.

"Humor and pain aren't mutually exclusive. Drink your hot chocolate. It's good, I promise."

Though he was growing more and more wary of Zia, he sipped his hot chocolate. It had a kick to it he hadn't expected, and warmth spread through him as he drank more.

Felix huffed and turned back to the television, while Zia focused on Simon, her gaze settling over him heavily. Simon was growing used to people staring at him, especially when he and Nolan were together, but the way she watched him made him feel like she could see through his skin to all the secrets underneath. He fidgeted uncomfortably.

"Is there something else in here?" he said, glancing into his drink. "Cinnamon or something?"

"Secret family recipe," she said, her fingertips drumming against her porcelain mug. "The Alpha didn't say why you'd run off. Care to enlighten me?"

"No," said Simon before he could stop himself, and Zia snorted with laughter.

"I like you, Simon. It takes a whole lot of something to lead your friends out here without any backup. Whatever it is you're after, it must be important."

He fell silent. It *was* important. It was the most important thing in the world to him.

"I get why you don't want to tell me," she said, leaning forward with her elbows on her knees. "I wouldn't trust me, either. But it's okay to ask for help sometimes, especially for the important stuff. We need each other, and it isn't a bad thing. Like this community, for instance. The birds would've taken out countless mammals if this place didn't exist. Refugees need us in order to make it through to the other side, and there's no shame in that. There's no shame in not being able to do everything by ourselves."

"And you're going to help me?" said Simon. "Just because I'm here and you have nothing better to do?"

"Like I said, whatever you're doing must be important. The instant the Alpha arrives tomorrow, he's going to take you back to New York, and I'm pretty sure whatever you're after isn't in the city." Zia's eyes locked on his, and Simon had to fight the urge to look away. "Tell me what's going on, and I will do everything I can to help you."

Simon faltered. He wanted to believe her, but what was she going to do, come to Arizona with him? In the back of his mind, a voice that sounded an awful lot like Darryl's whispered a warning. *Trust no one.*

Even if his mission in Arizona worked out perfectly, he wasn't just after his mother and the reptile kingdom's piece of the Predator. Destroying the weapon was the only way to make sure Orion and Celeste didn't use it to try to kill his brother and gain the Beast King's powers, and Simon had learned months ago that the Predator could only be damaged when it was fully assembled. That meant if Simon wanted any chance of protecting Nolan, he had to track down all five pieces before Orion could find them first. And no matter what help Zia thought she could offer, he couldn't risk telling her. He had to keep his mouth shut.

"Simon? Is everything okay?" Jam stood in the archway between the living room and the kitchen, already dressed in pajamas.

Relieved to have an excuse to break away from Zia,

Simon set his hot chocolate on an end table and scooped Felix up. "Yeah, everything's fine. I'm tired. We should go to bed now."

"I'm not tired," said Felix indignantly, trying to leap back onto the sofa, but Simon caught him.

"You can watch as much TV as you want in the morning," he said as he joined Jam. The last thing he needed was Zia trying to interrogate Felix while he was absorbed in an episode and not paying attention to what he was telling her.

"I'll be out here if you need anything," said Zia easily, but once again, there was an undercurrent to her words Simon didn't entirely trust. "Get some rest. Busy day tomorrow. You'll be back in the city before you know it."

Jam gave her a weak wave good night, but Simon marched down the hallway without a word. She was wrong. He didn't need her help, and no one—not Malcolm, not Zia, not even a town full of Animalgams—was going to stop him from getting to Paradise Valley and finding his mother.

FOX IN THE HENHOUSE

Simon had every intention of staying awake and sneaking out once Jam fell asleep, but as soon as he lay down in that soft bed, he couldn't resist the heavy drowsiness that spread through him. As he drifted off into a deep sleep, his last thought was of the hot chocolate on his tongue, and how it hadn't tasted quite right.

He woke up confused and feeling as if his head were stuffed with cotton. Though the illuminated numbers on the clock said it was well after ten in the morning, without any windows, the bedroom was as dark as ever.

"Jam?" he said, rubbing his eyes. The other bed was empty, and there was no sign of Felix, either. But a low, rumbling voice through the wall caught his attention, and Simon sat straight up.

Malcolm was there.

Simon bolted out of bed and rushed to get dressed. He had been an idiot lying down the night before. He should've waited until everyone else was asleep, and then he should've taken his only remaining chance to leave on his own. Malcolm would never let him out of his sight again. Simon had to get out of there before—

"I see you're finally awake."

Malcolm stood in the doorway. Simon froze in the middle of pulling on his sweatshirt, but before he could say anything, his uncle crossed the room in three long strides and pulled Simon into a tight hug.

"Don't you ever do that to me again," he said, his voice breaking. Simon stood perfectly still, stunned. He'd expected anger and rage, not this. "Are you all right? Stone told me what happened. Did the flock hurt you?"

It took Simon a full five seconds to remember that *Stone* was Zia. "I'm fine. Everyone's fine." He tightened his jaw. "I can't go back, Malcolm. Not yet."

Malcolm pulled away, his hands on Simon's shoulders as if he were afraid Simon would disappear if he let go. "What's going on? Why did you leave in the first place?"

"I—didn't the others tell you?"

His uncle shook his head. "I wanted to hear it from you."

Simon hesitated. He couldn't tell him, not when it meant Malcolm might risk his life to go after Orion himself. "I just . . . I was worried about Winter. She isn't happy in New York, and we decided to bring her to her family instead."

Even as Simon said it, he knew it was an obvious lie, and the skeptical look on Malcolm's face made it clear his uncle hadn't bought it, either. But what was he supposed to do? Admit he was trying to save his mother from one of the most vicious rulers in the Animalgam kingdoms, with only his friends to help?

"We'll talk about how to help Winter when we get back to the L.A.I.R.," said Malcolm. "But that isn't your job, Simon. It's mine. If Winter wanted to see her family, you should've asked me. I would've helped her. I *will* help her, any way I can."

Simon averted his eyes. "I can't go back, Malcolm, not before—"

"I know you're miserable." Malcolm's voice was quiet, but the heaviness in his words drew Simon up short. "It's been hard for you lately, probably harder than I can under-stand. But I do know Nolan hasn't been the best brother he could be. I know you miss your mom, I know you miss Darryl, and I know your life now is never going to live up to your memories of how everything used to be no matter how much all of us try. But sometimes . . . sometimes that's just how it goes. Life is hard, and it changes in ways we don't want or expect. Running away isn't the answer. We have to find the good in what we have, and we have to appreciate it. Otherwise you're never going to be happy no matter where you are, Simon. And that goes for Winter, too."

Simon said nothing. Maybe finding his mother wouldn't

bring back Darryl or his old life, but at least they would be a family again. Maybe Nolan wouldn't hate him so much then. Maybe Malcolm wouldn't be so disappointed in him. But no matter how tempting it was, he still couldn't tell his uncle what was really going on.

When it became clear Simon wasn't going to reply, Malcolm leaned in closer, his grip on Simon's shoulders tightening. "I'm sorry I'm not Darryl. I wish he were here, too. More than I can say." Malcolm cleared his throat. "But he isn't anymore, and we're both going to have to find a way to accept that. He would want you to be happy, Simon. Him and your mom."

"I know," mumbled Simon.

"Then let's try this, all right? You and me and Nolan, when he isn't being—Nolan."

That got a ghost of a smile out of Simon, which seemed to encourage his uncle. He patted Simon on the back and straightened, finally letting him go.

"Our flight leaves in a couple of hours," he said, checking his watch. "We should get moving if we're going to make it."

That was the last thing Simon wanted to do, but arguing wouldn't help, so he reluctantly packed his things and followed his uncle into the living room. Jam and Ariana sat together, and both of them glanced nervously at Simon when he arrived. Winter was curled up in an armchair as far away from them as she could get, while Zia leaned against the couch. Naturally, Felix was absorbed in another television show, seemingly oblivious to the tension in the air. Simon hadn't seen him this happy since before they'd arrived at the L.A.I.R. months ago.

"Do you want to stay here?" he said to the mouse, who was perched on his hind legs, clutching his tail.

"What?" Felix tore himself away from the screen. "You're leaving me behind?"

"No, I just thought—" Simon gestured to the television. "I thought you'd want to stay, since the L.A.I.R. doesn't have a TV."

Immediately Felix climbed up the sofa and leaped toward him, grabbing hold of Simon's sweatshirt and scrambling into his backpack. "I'd rather have you. Wake me up when we're in New York."

To his credit, Malcolm didn't object, even though Simon was positive he would've preferred the little mouse stay with Zia Stone. Instead his uncle nodded to the door. "All right— the rest of you, come on. We've got a plane to catch."

One by one, the others stood and followed Malcolm out of the apartment. As Simon passed Zia, their eyes met, and that spark of interest made a shiver run down his spine.

"Did you put something in my hot chocolate last night? Something to make me sleep?" he blurted in the doorway. She tilted her head curiously.

"Why do you think that?" she said.

"Because—" Because he had fallen asleep so quickly

when he'd planned on staying up to give himself time to escape. "Because it tasted funny, and you didn't drink any of yours."

Rolling her eyes, she ushered him into the hallway as she pulled the door shut. "It tasted funny because I put nutmeg in it. Family recipe, remember? And I drank mine once you went to bed. You were exhausted, Simon. You could barely keep your eyes open. I didn't have to give you anything to help you sleep."

Grudgingly he admitted she was probably right, but he still kept his distance as they joined the others in the corridor. She had no reason to give him anything to make him sleep, anyway. As far as she knew, he was a golden eagle. If she'd kept watch over them like he suspected, there was no way a bird that big could have sneaked past her.

The enormous cavern was much busier now than it had been the night before. There must have been an opening in the rock above them, because sunlight streamed down into the atrium, where humans and animals milled about. Simon spotted two dogs tossing a Frisbee back and forth, and he watched them wistfully. While he didn't resent the way Darryl had raised him, he couldn't help but wonder what it would have been like to grow up with other Animalgams, even if he was a Hybred.

Zia led them down the zigzag staircase to the lower level. "There's a garage through here," she said, opening one of the doors that led into a hallway with white plaster walls. "I'll drive you to the airport."

A man Simon recognized from the night before followed them into the corridor. "Stone, got a minute?"

"Does it look like I have a minute, Keval?" she said. "Walk and talk if it's important."

Keval grimaced. "We've got incoming from the west," he said, stepping between her and Simon. "Don't look too good, and they've got kids with them. Thought you might like to handle it yourself."

"Why? You're more than capable," she said, jangling a set of keys in her hand. "I'll meet with them when I get back."

"But—"

"*What*, Keval?" Zia reached the doorway at the end of the corridor and spun around to face him. "Did you suddenly forget how to do your job? I'll be back once I've dropped the Alpha and the kids at the airport. If this really can't wait an hour, then maybe I ought to find a second-in-command who knows what they're doing."

As she pushed open the door that led into a large garage, a low growl emanated from Keval's throat. Malcolm grabbed the back of Simon's sweatshirt and yanked him away, but it was too late. Inside the garage, a dozen other men and women waited, leaving no room for them to pass.

"What the—" began Zia, but Keval interrupted her.

"He may be your Alpha, but he isn't ours."

At once, several of the waiting men and women shifted into their mammal forms—all smaller than the predators at the L.A.I.R., but they still had teeth. Malcolm roared, and his grip on Simon disappeared as he shifted into a hulking wolf. Keval remained human, but from the waistband of his pants, he pulled out a gun.

Out of all the things Simon had faced so far, he'd managed to avoid firearms, and his blood turned to ice at the sight of it. He knew instantly Keval's first target would be his uncle, and Simon wasn't losing Malcolm. Not like this.

The door to the garage slammed shut, cutting them off from the other mammals. Simon heard Zia's muffled cry of outrage from the other side, but he was focused wholly on Keval. Malcolm snarled, and Simon's ears rang as every part of him turned to lava. He didn't care that he was about to shift in front of his uncle and friends. He didn't care that it would expose him as the Beast King's heir. All he cared about was making sure his uncle got out of there alive, and this time he wasn't going to fail.

But before his fingers could curl into claws, Jam appeared behind Keval and kicked him between the legs. Hard. Keval cried out and dropped the gun, and it skittered across the floor toward Simon.

He scrambled for it, his fingers closing around the metal handle. As he raised the weapon, however, a cottonmouth snake struck Keval's exposed ankle with a hiss, and a shiny black spider appeared on his collar and sank her fangs into his neck. Simon had never seen both Winter and Ariana strike at the same time, and Keval's eyes rolled back into his head as he collapsed on the floor.

"Uh, Simon? I think we got him," said Jam.

Simon let go of the gun, his hands trembling. The wolf nudged his hip.

"Stay here," growled Malcolm, and before Simon could protest, he pushed open the door once more and leaped inside the garage, where the red fox snarled and jumped from one small mammal to the next.

A knot formed in Simon's throat as he watched his uncle take on three mangy coyotes at once. The wolf was bigger, but what if someone else had a weapon? Or what if his uncle couldn't handle fighting against so many at once?

Ariana appeared beside him and picked up the gun, handling it like a favorite toy as she checked the chamber for bullets. "We might need this to get out."

Winter shifted back into a human as well, shuddering. "We can't go back the way we came. There might be others waiting for us in the atrium."

"I think there's an exit through here," called Jam, pushing open another door halfway down the hall.

Winter scoffed. "How could you possibly know that?"

"The same way I knew how to get around in Chicago," said Jam. "Just trust me."

Simon grabbed Winter's arm and led her into the dark room, while Ariana brought up the rear. With light from the hallway spilling in, Simon could make out shelves covered in paint cans, rusting tools, and old tires.

Jam hurried through the narrow storage room and out another door. They burst into the garage only feet away from the edge of the fight, and as the others bolted toward the collection of cars, Simon skidded to a stop. Malcolm was holding his own against the mammals, but there were too many of them. One wrong move, and they could easily overpower him.

"Hey!" Zia's voice rang above the others, and she appeared in the middle of the crowd, with several opossums and squirrels clinging to her clothes. She tossed a set of car keys toward him, and Simon managed to catch it. "Get in the car. We'll be right there."

Simon paused, torn between helping his uncle and getting his friends to safety. Before he could decide, Ariana seized his elbow and dragged him away from the fight.

"Malcolm can handle himself. And I'll take those." She snatched the keys from him and pressed a button. A red Mustang beeped, and a wicked grin spread across her face. "Excellent."

She hopped into the driver's seat, and Jam and Winter climbed into the back. Simon stopped, glancing at the fight once more.

"If we wait for them, we'll be in New York in time for dinner," said Ariana, starting the engine. "If we leave now, we might actually make it to Paradise Valley. It's your choice."

She was right. A howl echoed through the garage, and sucking in a breath, Simon jumped into the passenger seat. They'd come this far. He couldn't give up now.

"Leave the gun," said Simon.

"But—" began Ariana.

"We're not taking it with us."

Grumbling, Ariana swiftly removed the bullets and tossed the empty firearm into a nearby convertible. "Spoilsport."

She could call him any name she wanted. Simon didn't want to be anywhere near that thing.

"You know how to drive?" said Winter dubiously from the backseat.

"My mother taught me as soon as I could reach the pedals. It's come in handy a few times," said Ariana, pulling on a pair of sunglasses from the center console. "Buckle up."

She slammed on the accelerator, and Simon flew back against the seat. He managed to pull his seat belt on as they sped out of the garage, leaving the snarls and growls of the fight behind. The car flew across the dusty path as Ariana steered them toward the nearest road.

Simon twisted around and tried to get one last look at what was happening inside the garage, but all he could see was rock and dirt. He must have looked as nauseated as he felt, because Ariana patted his arm awkwardly. "Nothing's going to happen to your uncle. They're a bunch of squirrels and rabbits. They might try to gnaw him, but they won't get very far. He's the Alpha for a reason."

"Darryl was bigger and stronger than he was," said Simon.

"Darryl was on a glass roof forty stories above the city," she countered. "And he was injured. Malcolm's perfectly healthy and furious. He'll be fine."

Ariana may have been right, but that didn't stop yet another round of guilt from coursing through him. After checking to make sure Felix was still in one piece, he secured his backpack between his knees and settled against the seat, closing his eyes and trying not to picture his uncle with animals dangling off him. Simon knew all too well that a lot of anything, no matter how small, could kill.

DOLPHIN IN THE DESERT

Simon's worry only grew the farther away from Stonehaven they got. Over and over, he wondered if that had been the last time he'd see Malcolm alive, and the image of Darryl as he lay dying haunted him until he had no choice but to open his eyes and pay attention to the road instead. All that surrounded them was dust and scraggly trees, with a mountain range looming in the distance, but it was better than remembering that horrible night on the roof of Sky Tower.

It took them twenty miles to reach the first stoplight, and as Ariana braked, she said, "Which way, Jam?"

"What do you mean, which way? Don't you have a map?" said Jam.

"Yes. You."

"But what if I'm wrong? Wouldn't it be better to make sure—"

"*Which way,* Jam?" said Ariana with such force that Simon couldn't stay silent any longer.

"Just because Jam can sometimes tell where we are doesn't mean he has a compass in his brain," he said testily. "If he doesn't know, he doesn't know."

"But he does know," said Ariana, annoyed, as her fingers tapped the leather steering wheel. Even with the seat as high as it would go, she had to crane her neck to see over the dash. "It must be a dolphin thing."

"What do you mean, a dolphin thing?" said Simon.

"Dolphins can always tell where they are in the ocean," chimed in Winter. "What's it called? Echolocation?"

"Yeah," admitted Jam. "It's not GPS, but it's better than nothing."

"Right. That's why Jam has a better sense of direction than most people," said Winter, her eyes meeting Simon's through the rearview mirror. "Like how I have a really good sense of smell. It's been getting stronger the more I shift."

"See? There are advantages to being a snake," said Ariana. Winter made a face.

"Yeah, until you have to smell everyone's body odor and dirty laundry," she muttered. "Anyway, that's probably why Jam is so good at finding his way around places he's never been before."

"Exactly," said Ariana as the light turned green. "So which way are we going, JPS?"

He sighed. "Straight. Just keep going straight until New Mexico. Then turn right."

"That wasn't so hard, was it?" said Ariana, and she slammed on the accelerator again, knocking Simon back into his seat.

He was quiet for several miles while his friends speculated over Animalgams' enhanced abilities—though twice he had to tell them his eyesight hadn't gotten any better after shifting into an eagle—and it wasn't until they reached a sign welcoming them to New Mexico that the question he had been mulling over in his mind formed into words.

"Why did the mammals attack us?" he said. "If Malcolm's their Alpha, don't they follow his rules?"

"Isn't it obvious?" said Winter, rubbing coconut-scented sunscreen into her skin. Where she'd gotten it, Simon had no idea. "Keval said Malcolm wasn't his Alpha."

"It's not that weird for a kingdom to be divided when the old leader is still alive," said Ariana. "Malcolm should have killed her when he had the chance."

The thought of Malcolm killing his own mother, even if she was horrible and bloodthirsty, made Simon cringe. "He wouldn't do that."

"Then there will always be members of the mammal kingdom who think she's still the Alpha," said Ariana.

"That's just how it works. In my kingdom, we die as queens. No one ever steals the throne and lets the other live."

Simon wasn't sure how he felt about that. The mammal kingdom was ruthless enough for him; the thought of the insects being even worse made him shudder.

"I don't think there's ever been a revolution like that in my kingdom," said Jam. "My sisters keep trying to talk my father into making one of them the general instead. Take the right fork up here."

Through the rearview mirror, Simon could see Winter giving Jam a long, hard look. "I can't believe *you're* going to be leading an Animalgam kingdom someday."

"Join the club," said Jam with a sigh.

Simon remained mostly quiet throughout the ten-hour trip across the desert. It was a small miracle Ariana didn't get pulled over, but the aviator sunglasses she wore must have made her look old enough to get away with driving. Twice they had to stop for gas, and both times Ariana paid with the cash they had left. Simon could tell by her pinched expression that they were running low, and when she came out of the second gas station with snacks hidden underneath the sweatshirt she'd borrowed from him, he didn't ask any questions.

By the time they neared Paradise Valley, it was hours after sunset. As he watched the lights of the city surrounding the tiny suburb grow brighter, the knot in Simon's chest tightened. It had been easy to ignore the fact that he didn't have a plan when they had been safe on the train, a thousand miles from their destination, but now that they were rapidly approaching, it felt like an impossible mission: somehow, someway, not only did they have to free his mother, but they also had to find the reptiles' piece of the Predator before Orion could.

"We need a plan," he blurted. "I know you said it's fine that we don't have one, Jam, but it isn't, not anymore."

"*Jam* said it was fine not to have a plan?" said Winter. "I've met the general twice, and both times I got a lecture in how 'the key to a successful mission is a well-organized strategy.' "

Through the rearview mirror, Simon saw Jam blush. "The general isn't always right. We have no idea what we're walking into."

"We have some idea," argued Simon. "We know it's a hotel."

"Yeah, but we don't know where the piece is hidden *or* where Orion is keeping your mother," said Ariana. "Once we know what we're up against, we'll figure out the best way to find both. Right now, the most you can do is decide what you want more, Simon—to save your mom or to find the reptiles' piece of the Predator."

To Simon, there was no choice. "My mother," he said immediately. "But we have to find both. Orion already has the bird kingdom's piece. If he finds all five and assembles the Predator—"

"He'll go after Nolan and try to kill him so he can steal his powers. We know," said Winter, and Simon could practically hear her rolling her eyes.

"The point is, if something goes wrong, you might have to choose," said Ariana. "And normally—"

"Normally the strategic thing to do is to go after the best bet," said Jam hesitantly. "If we know where the piece is, but not your mom . . ."

"I'm not leaving her behind," said Simon.

"But what if it means Orion gets the piece?" said Ariana. "Is that a risk you're willing to take?"

"Ariana's right." Jam's tone was apologetic, and he leaned closer to Simon. "Saving your mom is important, but Orion's trying to seize control of the whole Animalgam world. My father's the General of the Seas, and Ariana's mom is the Black Widow Queen, and your uncle's the Alpha—" Jam swallowed hard. "He'll kill our families, Simon."

"That won't happen," said Simon, bristling. "It's only the second piece. There are three others out there he has to find first."

"Maybe," said Ariana. "Or maybe in the past two months, he's found them, too."

"If he had, we would have heard about it from your parents," snapped Simon, crossing his arms. "If you only want to go after the reptiles' piece, fine. But I'm finding my mom."

For the rest of the ride to Paradise Valley, Simon stewed silently in the passenger seat. The logical part of his brain knew his friends had a point, but after all Simon had been through, he couldn't choose anything—even the fate of the Animalgam world—over rescuing his mother.

Using the guidebook, Jam directed Ariana to the hotel. Mountains rose up from the sprawling suburban neighborhoods around them, and Simon craned his neck, searching for any sign of birds of prey. It was too dark to see beyond the lights of the city, however, and by the time they reached the long drive of the Stilio Resort and Spa, he had resigned himself to waiting until morning.

The hotel sat at the base of one of the smaller mountains, and the winding road was lined with cacti and exotic trees. Rather than drive up to the front entrance, Ariana parked the car in one of the shaded corners, and the four of them piled out.

"Hotel valets are supposed to park for us," said Winter as she tested the gravel drive.

"Yeah, but how do you think they're going to react when they see me behind the wheel instead of an adult?" said Ariana. "Gas station attendants might not pay much attention, but the hotel staff will. Now stop whining and start walking. It isn't far."

Together they headed up the path to the glowing entrance, and Simon swallowed his anger and nerves. His friends were only looking out for their loved ones, and he couldn't blame them for that. He glanced around, taking in the strange flora around them. Even though the sun had already set, it was too warm for a sweatshirt, and as they passed a fountain in the middle of the circular drive, Simon dropped his backpack and paused long enough to pull his hoodie off. As he ran his fingers through his hair to comb it back into place, his gaze fell on the statue.

The statue looked back.

"Whoa." Simon jumped, nearly tripping over Jam in the process.

"What?" he said, catching Simon with surprising strength. "Did you see something?"

Simon took a tentative step closer to the fountain. Two stone snakes wrapped around a flowering cactus, and water spouted from their mouths. But that wasn't what had startled Simon. Instead, a lizard perched on the end of one of the stone snakes, the light reflecting in its tiny black eyes.

"Here to see the council?" said the lizard in a funny accent. Australian, Simon thought.

"Uh—yeah," he said. "How did you know?"

"Because you're talking back." The lizard flashed him a grin. "I'm Ronnie. Ronnie the dragon."

"You don't look like much of a dragon," said Winter, eyeing him. Ronnie sniffed indignantly, and Simon could've sworn the underside of his throat turned black.

"And you don't look like much of a human," he said. "I'm a bearded dragon. Much better than an imaginary one. Room for four? Animalgams get discounts."

Simon looked at Ariana, who shook her head. They didn't have enough money left to afford a room at this place, even with a discount.

"That won't be necessary," said Winter, who looked down her nose at the dragon, clearly not impressed with him. "I'm Councilman Rivera's granddaughter. He's not expecting me, but I'm sure if you let him know I'm here—"

"Rivera?" Ronnie scoffed. "Rivera doesn't have any grandchildren."

Winter leaned in. "Are you sure about that? Do I need to prove how venomous I am?"

The pupils in her green eyes turned to slits, and she hissed threateningly. Ronnie leaped backward, falling into the fountain and splashing around.

"R-right—Rivera—of course. I see the resemblance now." Ronnie gulped as he scrambled out of the water. "If—if you'll follow me—"

Winter straightened. "Thank you, Ronnie. I'm sure my grandfather will be extremely grateful."

The dragon hopped off the fountain and led them toward a door to the left of the main entrance. It blended in with the wall and, as they grew closer, Simon saw it was marked private.

"The hotel is of course open to guests of all backgrounds,"

said Ronnie, his voice trembling as he nosed a button nearly hidden among the brush, and the door swung open. "But this is the council's private wing, reserved for family and members of the kingdom. You *are* members of the kingdom, aren't you?" Suddenly the tremor in his voice was gone as he looked Simon, Ariana, and Jam up and down.

"They're my friends," said Winter. "That should be more than enough."

Ronnie grumbled, but he darted through the doorway and led them inside without further comment. Simon only hoped Winter was right; he had never considered the possibility that Rivera might kick them out for being the wrong kind of Animalgam.

The inside of the hotel was more magnificent than Simon could've imagined. The walls of the private lobby were covered by artwork in lavish gold frames, crystal chandeliers hung from the ceiling, and overstuffed leather armchairs and sofas sat every few feet. Soft classical music played over the speakers, and the handful of people loitering around, speaking quietly in groups or admiring the paintings, all seemed relaxed and at ease. It was nothing like the bustle of New York.

None of the other guests paid any attention to Simon and his friends following a bearded dragon across the gleaming hardwood floor. In fact, when Simon peeked over his shoulder, he spotted a trio of iguanas on the sofa, their heads bent in whispered conversation.

"The official tour will have to wait, but this is where you'll find the spa, the music gallery, and of course the sunroom," said Ronnie as he led the way past the elevators and down a long hallway covered in even more artwork.

"Whoa, is that real?" said Jam, stopping in front of a painting of a woman holding a baby.

"Every piece in our collection is the original, though some have been painstakingly restored," said Ronnie proudly. "Down here, you have our library—it's the biggest room in the wing."

Simon couldn't resist cracking open the door and poking his head inside. His mouth formed an O. The library rose five stories, with row after row full of books he was itching to explore, and a large window looked out on the starry sky.

"You're welcome to browse when we're not in a rush," called Ronnie, and Simon reluctantly closed the door and hurried to catch up with them. "We have a theater in the wing as well, complete with a variety of nightly performances."

As they headed down the hallway, Winter's expression remained blank. Simon knew it was all a front. He might not have known Winter very long, but he was absolutely certain that this place was nothing short of paradise to her. He didn't understand why she was pretending she didn't love it, but judging by the way Ariana was also watching Winter suspiciously, she wasn't fooled, either.

Finally they reached another doorway at the end of the corridor, and Ronnie cleared his throat. "If one of you wouldn't mind . . . short legs, you see . . ."

Simon pushed open the double wooden doors, revealing a large room with mirrors for walls, making it look like it reflected in on itself again and again. A blast of sweltering heat hit Simon, and he pushed his hair from his forehead, grateful he'd taken off his sweatshirt earlier. In the center of the room, a white marble serpent rose at least ten feet, and smaller marble vipers gathered at the base almost reverently. Focused on the glinting black eyes of the statue, Simon started forward, but before he could take more than a step, Ariana said, "Watch it!"

Simon looked down. A moat of sorts surrounded the room, with a short glass bridge the only way across. But the moat wasn't filled with water. Instead, hundreds of snakes slithered over one another, their low voices joining together to form an almost hypnotic murmur. Vipers, cobras, coral snakes—every species Simon could name, and dozens more he couldn't.

"They won't bite so long as you don't," said Ronnie as he meandered across the bridge toward the statue. "Our snake pit is decorative, for the most part, but it serves as security to the council, too. Can't be too careful, can you, mate?"

Simon followed, beads of sweat already forming at his temples. The bridge felt sturdy enough, but as Ariana and

Jam walked across, Simon noticed both of them took very big steps. Winter, on the other hand, continued to look distinctly unimpressed.

"If you'll wait here, I'll let Councilman Rivera know he has—visitors," said Ronnie, and he scampered away, leaving the four of them alone.

"If he's an Animalgam, why doesn't he just shift into a human to open doors? Wouldn't that be easier?" said Simon.

"Plenty of Animalgams choose to live their lives as animals instead of humans," said Jam, inspecting the statue. Ariana, in the meantime, got as far from the pit of vipers as possible.

"Why would they do that?" said Simon, shoving his hands in his pockets. His fingers brushed up against the pocket watch that had once belonged to his father. It felt warmer than usual, though the room *was* boiling.

"They prefer their Animalgam form to their human one," said Ariana with a shrug. "Just because you'd rather have two legs doesn't mean everyone would."

Before Simon could reply, the zipper of his backpack opened, and Felix climbed onto his shoulder. "That's the ugliest statue I've ever seen," said the mouse.

"Get back in my bag," said Simon. "It isn't safe."

"If I wanted to be safe, I'd still be in front of that TV," said Felix, and though he tried to sound tough about it, Simon could hear the wistfulness in his voice. He straightened his whiskers as he peered up at the marble. "Do you think that thing has any idea how hideous it is?"

"That 'thing' is the Kingsnake, the most feared and revered figure in our kingdom's history." A tall man stepped into the room. His black hair was tied into a short ponytail at the nape of his neck, and he moved gracefully, his hands clasped behind his back. "Though the Beast King hunted the Kingsnake Animalgams to extinction, we continue to honor our royal line's legacy. Now, unless you are here to offer yourself as an evening snack to one of our honored guards, I must inform you we do not allow nonhuman mammals on our premises."

"I'll show you who the real snack is," muttered Felix, the challenge in his voice at odds with the way he dived back into the bag.

Simon swung it around so he could pull the zipper closed. "He's my friend, not a snack."

"I'm afraid I see no real difference," said the man. He eyed them all, his narrowed gaze lingering on Ariana's purple hair.

Winter stepped between them, flipping her dark braid over her shoulder. "He's *my* friend, so does that make a difference to you?"

Friend was a generous term to describe her prickly relationship with Felix, but Simon shot her a grateful look. She ignored him.

"That depends on who you are," said the man, looking

down his nose at her. If Simon hadn't been sure who the man was before, he was now. The resemblance was uncanny.

Winter must have been certain, too, because she crossed her arms and glared at him. "I'm Winter. Your granddaughter."

14

THE REPTILE COUNCIL

The change in Robert Rivera's expression was immediate. His jaw went slack, and every trace of snobbery vanished. Moving forward with urgency he hadn't shown before, he stopped inches in front of Winter, kneeling down to look her in the eye. "It can't be."

"Why not?" said Winter, annoyed. "You've been writing to me for years."

"I thought—I thought Orion . . ." Rivera's voice hitched, and tears sprang in his eyes. Wordlessly he embraced Winter, and much to Simon's surprise, Winter hugged him back.

The seconds passed, and finally Winter said, "You don't have to hold on so tight. I'm not going to disappear when you let go."

Rivera reluctantly released her, though he set both hands on her cheeks and gazed into her eyes. "You look so much like your mother. I have missed her every day."

"Me, too," said Winter, quieter this time. She cleared her throat. "These are my friends. You've already met Felix, and this is Jam, Ariana, and—"

"Simon Thorn." Rivera stood, setting his hand on Winter's shoulder.

"How come everyone's always heard of you?" said Jam, pushing his glasses up his nose. Simon shrugged.

"Just lucky, I guess."

"Luck has nothing to do with it," said Rivera. "Half the Animalgam world is on the hunt for you children. Malcolm Thorn mentioned you were heading this way, and he asked us to keep an eye open."

Hope fluttered inside Simon. "You talked to Malcolm? When?"

"Earlier this afternoon," said Rivera, and Simon exhaled sharply. So Malcolm was all right. He hadn't been killed in the garage after all. "And you two . . ." Rivera turned to Jam and Ariana. "Your parents certainly aren't happy with either of you for running away."

Jam wrung his hands nervously. "The general's probably furious. And your mother—"

"My mother knows I can handle myself," muttered Ariana, inspecting the base of the statue. Rivera ignored them.

"I will inform the Alpha immediately," he said with a flourish of his hand. "You will be safe here. In the meantime, I must call a council meeting—Ronnie."

Ronnie the dragon plodded in front of him. "Yes, Your Honor?"

"Gather the others. We must discuss what to do at once."

While Ronnie scurried off to gather the rest of the council, Rivera ushered them toward another doorway beyond the statue. "Come—the council won't take long to arrive. Few of us ever go far beyond the hotel, and now even fewer still, with tensions being as they are."

"Tensions?" said Simon as he followed Rivera and his friends into a smaller lavish chamber, complete with overflowing bookcases lining the walls and a round mahogany table with twelve seats that, to Simon, looked more like thrones than chairs.

"Oh, yes—nothing to worry about, always little spats going on between the kingdoms." Rivera guided them to a row of plush sofas near the wall, close enough to hear what was going on at the table, but not close enough to distract or get involved. "Please, make yourselves comfortable. The council should be here shortly."

While Simon, Jam, and Ariana sat together, Rivera steered Winter into another corner of the room and spoke to her in a low voice. From a distance, Simon couldn't spot any trace of haughtiness or snobbery—instead, Rivera looked every inch the warm, doting grandfather. Winter, for her part, looked genuinely interested in her newfound family, but she held herself with the same stiffness that Simon recognized as uncertainty.

Soon enough, the rest of the council began to trickle in: men dressed in suits and women wrapped in silks, some as young as Simon's mother, but most old enough to be his great-grandparents. Few of them spared Simon and his friends much more than a glance. Instead, they nearly all seemed focused on Rivera and Winter's quiet conversation in the corner.

"Are we getting on with it or not? I've got an opera to catch," said a man with a smattering of white hair left on his shiny scalp. He wore thick tortoiseshell glasses and leaned heavily on a cane, and the woman beside him pulled his seat out for him.

It was only because Simon looked immediately at Rivera that he spotted a flicker of annoyance crossing his face. When Simon blinked, it was gone. "Of course, Crocker," said Rivera, and as the others took their seats, he led Winter to the council. "I would like to introduce you all to my granddaughter."

The man with the cane—Crocker—peered at Winter. "You mean the mutt your daughter left with the birds?"

Simon bristled at the insult. *Mutt* was a terrible thing to call an Animalgam. He opened his mouth to protest, but Ariana wrapped her fingers around his wrist in a warning.

"Don't," she whispered, and Simon's retort died on his

tongue. She was right. They couldn't afford to get kicked out now.

To his credit, Rivera scowled. "She is my *Hybred* granddaughter, yes. And she had the misfortune of being raised by a tyrant with feathers, but she has assured me—"

"I like Orion about as much as you do," said Winter, raising her chin as if daring any of the men and women watching to question her. "He abandoned me when he found out I was a cottonmouth, and as soon as I could get away, I headed here. To my real home, to be with my real family."

If Simon hadn't spent the past two months witnessing firsthand exactly how much Winter loathed the idea of belonging to the reptile kingdom, he would have believed her. As it was, a murmur rippled through the council, but Crocker stood and fumbled with his cane. "If the only reason you interrupted my perfectly lovely evening was to flaunt your deviant gene pool, Rivera, then I have better places to be."

Several other members began to join him on their feet, one by one turning their attention away from Winter. Rivera's jaw set, and the haughtiness he'd lost when it had been only the two of them came back full force, forming a smooth mask over any true emotions he might have had.

"That isn't all," he said, his voice rising above the hum of restarted conversations. "It seems my granddaughter brought her friends along with her—including Simon Thorn."

The room went silent. Suddenly all eyes turned to the couch, and Simon clasped his hands together, his heart thundering at the unexpected attention.

"He's the one without glasses," said Rivera drolly. "I will be alerting the Alpha as soon as we adjourn."

"Simon Thorn?" Crocker sat back down heavily, and others followed suit. "Son of Isabel and Luke Thorn?"

Nodding numbly, Simon said, "You know my mom?"

"We have become great friends over the years," said Crocker. "She spoke of your brother often. I'm afraid she didn't mention you, but considering we didn't know you existed until September . . . well. What are you doing in Paradise Valley without her?"

Simon hesitated. He couldn't tell the council the whole truth, not when news of Orion's plans would undoubtedly spread throughout the five kingdoms and cause panic, but Simon couldn't rescue his mother *and* find the piece of the Predator before Malcolm caught up with them. And if Crocker was a friend of his mother's, then maybe that would be enough for the council to help without asking too many questions.

Climbing to his feet, Simon cleared his throat. "Orion kidnapped my mother, and they're somewhere in Paradise Valley," he said. "We knew Winter wanted to—come home, so we all decided to go together to try to find my mom."

Shock spread through the room, and several members

ducked their heads together in worried whispers. Even Rivera paled, but Crocker held Simon's gaze, his expression never wavering. "You're sure Orion has your mother?"

Simon nodded. "Positive. She's been gone for two months."

The entire council broke out into frantic discussion, and Simon could only catch snippets. "Two months?" said one council member.

"And no one told us?"

"That's long enough for—"

"Do you think he's—"

"—why else would he—"

"Perhaps he's only protecting his line—"

"Don't be naive—"

"Should we—"

"—hidden for a decade—"

"Enough." Crocker's deep voice echoed throughout the room, and the council fell silent. "Have there been reports of increased activity from the bird kingdom in the past two months?"

Rivera cleared his throat. "No increase, no, and no sign of the flock on Beak Peak." His lip curled with disdain.

Crocker refocused on Simon. "How did you discover Orion had taken your mother here?"

"A—a friend tipped me off."

"And you didn't think the information credible enough to bring the pack with you?"

Winter jumped in, breaking Rivera's hold on her arm. "I thought the pack would never let me leave the L.A.I.R., so I asked my friends not to tell the mammals."

Crocker harrumphed. "And instead you sent them on a wild-goose chase across the country."

Simon shrugged. "We—we just wanted to make sure Winter could return to her family."

"And so you did," said Rivera, joining Winter once more. "As joyful as this news is, we must focus on the problem that comes with it. Isabel Thorn is the only one outside this room who knows where—" Rivera glanced at Simon, Jam, and Ariana. "—where *it* is hidden. If she's under Orion's thumb—"

"We have no proof of this, nor do we have any reason to doubt Isabel's trustworthiness," said Crocker.

"Trustworthiness has nothing to do with whether she'll sing like a canary if Orion finds something to hold over her," said Rivera. "We were fools to allow her access in the first place. Now is the time to remedy that and move it to a location only we know."

"If the boy is correct and the flock is hiding out, they could very well be waiting for that exact plan," said Crocker. "Perhaps this is all a trick to get us to reveal it in the first place."

Simon wasn't an idiot—he knew exactly what they were talking about. His mother was the only person who knew where all five pieces of the Predator were, and when she had secretly made copies for an oblivious Celeste, she must have helped the reptiles hide the real piece again. He couldn't blame the council for not trusting her, not when she was being held captive by the bird kingdom, but the idea that he would ever help Orion made his blood boil.

"Orion killed my uncle," he said. "He kidnapped my mother, and he's—" He was planning on killing his brother, but Simon couldn't say that without revealing Nolan's abilities. "He's holding her hostage," he said instead. "I would never do anything to help him."

"Do you know what he plans on doing with her?" said Crocker, peering at him over the rim of his glasses.

"I—no," said Simon, his heart pounding. Playing dumb was the only option he had right now. If the council knew he was looking for the piece, too, they would definitely move it, and maybe Crocker was right. Maybe that was exactly what Orion was waiting for.

One of the women closest to him hissed. "He smells like fear and lies."

"Everyone smells like fear and lies to you, Lissa," said Crocker tiredly. "Why do you think Orion took your mother, young man?"

Simon's eyes darted toward Ariana, who watched him intently, almost like she was trying to silently communicate with him. Simon wished they had thought to get their cover story straight earlier. "Because she's loyal to the mammals," he said at last. "Because she's his heir, and she's spent years running away from him. Because—because—" He faltered, his shoulders slumping. "I don't know, and I don't really care. I just want her back. I've never had much of a chance to get to know her. She visited a couple times a year, but she never stayed long, and—all I want is a family."

Several long moments passed. Crocker sighed and removed his glasses to pinch the bridge of his nose. "We will not move it."

A cry of protest rang out from several of the others, and Rivera fumed. "I insist on a vote."

"By all means, but you heard the boy," said Crocker. "Isabel has been missing for two months, yet it has remained safe so far. If Orion has gone this long without accomplishing his mission, it is best to stick to the status quo. As it stands, theft would be impossible. There is no safer place in our kingdom regardless of what knowledge may or may not be passed on to Orion. Let that be a comfort to all." He stood and reached for his cane. "You know my vote. Now, if you do not mind, I have an opera to catch. While the rest of you debate the matter, I suggest you see to it that the children are taken care of. They shouldn't be forced to sit around all evening and listen to you yammer on."

"We *are* hungry," said Winter.

"See? Give them a hot meal and a place to sleep, and then you'll be free to argue for as long as you dusty lot like." Crocker tipped Simon an enormous wink, and as he limped out of the room, Ronnie waddled toward them, his beady eyes on Rivera.

"Your Honor, if you'd like me to escort the children upstairs . . ."

"Yes, yes. You'll stay in the family suite, of course," he added to Winter. "Your mother's room has been untouched since she . . . disappeared, and I think you might like it in there."

"I'm sure I will," said Winter, and she added under her breath, "Anything's better than that train."

"And you three—" Rivera looked at Simon again. "Are you a fan of the early Renaissance, or do you prefer post-modernism?"

Simon and Ariana exchanged blank looks. Jam, however, said cheerfully, "I've always liked Impressionism."

"Ah, a boy after my own heart. Yes, I have just the room for you. Ronnie, the Monet suite, if you will."

Leaving Rivera and the rest of the council members behind, Ronnie led the four of them back into the statue room. Simon's pocket watch grew warm once more, and it was then that he realized it had cooled in the council's chambers. The warmth vanished in the hallway, though, and by the time they reached the elevator bay, Simon gave up trying to make sense of it.

"What's Beak Peak?" he said as they waited for an elevator. Ronnie's tail twitched.

"It's our kingdom's clever little nickname for the mountain overlooking the hotel. When the flock's in town, that's where they stay. Like the view, they claim, but really they just like looking down on us." The elevator doors opened, and Ronnie led them inside. "Tenth floor, if you will, mate."

Simon punched the button. "And they're not there right now?"

"There are always some birds hanging about, but no sign of Orion lately."

Simon saw Ariana raise an eyebrow, and he shoved his hands in his pockets and stared at his feet.

As soon as the elevator opened again, a pair of guards cornered them. "Floor's closed to guests," said the taller of the pair.

Ronnie's throat grew dark again. "Rosencrantz. Guildenstern. This is Councilman Rivera's granddaughter, Winter. She'll be staying in the family suite, while her friends stay in the Monet suite. It's all been approved by Rivera himself, I assure you."

The two burly men eyed them up and down. "Go ahead," muttered one, stepping aside to let them pass.

As they turned down another opulent corridor, Winter glanced over her shoulder. "Are those their real names?"

"What? No, of course not," said Ronnie. "Can't be bothered to tell them apart from the other guards, can I? They're all Rosencrantz and Guildenstern to me."

"Other guards?" said Simon, and Ronnie looked back at him.

"Full of questions today, aren't you?"

Simon shrugged. "Just curious."

Ronnie stopped in front of a corner room. "Guards change every six hours, but they're always here to secure the council's private quarters." He nodded to the door. "The Monet suite. Code 4477."

Simon punched the numbers into the keypad above the door handle, and the lock clicked. "What about Rivera's suite?"

"Right down the hall," said Ronnie, using his tail to point. "If you need anything, ask the guards. They'll make sure no one bothers you. And do yourself a favor and don't open the balcony. Birds love dive-bombing us. It's all sport to them, the miserable mongrels."

The suite was exactly what Simon was beginning to expect from the reptile kingdom: luxurious, rich, and covered in art. Stepping inside the sitting room felt more like stepping inside a museum, and Jam let out a low whistle.

"The general would never approve of this waste of treasury funds," he said, but he immediately flopped down on the overstuffed leather sofa anyway.

"Someone will bring you dinner soon," said Ronnie. "Winter, this way."

Despite the emotionless expression she still wore, Simon could see a flicker of fear in her eyes at the thought of leaving them. "You could stay in here, if you want," he offered.

"But—" said Ronnie.

"I'll go with Winter," interrupted Ariana. "I don't want to share a suite with you two anyway. When was the last time either of you showered?"

Once they were alone, both Simon and Jam sniffed their shirts. "Anything?" said Simon, and Jam shook his head. "Me neither."

While Jam looked around the suite, which was big enough to house an entire family comfortably, Simon unzipped his backpack. "If you wander off in this place, a snake will eat you before I know you're gone," he warned as Felix nosed his way out from his socks.

"I'd like to see them try," he said grumpily. Simon shook his head.

"I mean it, Felix. You wanted to come, so you have to follow my rules."

The little mouse scoffed. "Who died and made you Alpha?"

His words hit Simon like a kick to the gut, and he clenched his fists, his breaths suddenly shallow. Felix seemed to realize his mistake as soon as he said it, and he climbed up Simon's side.

"C'mon, you know I didn't mean it like that," he said, perching on his shoulder. "I just meant—"

"I don't want you to die, too, okay?" said Simon thickly, scooping Felix up and setting him down on the sofa in front of the television. Felix's tail drooped. "I don't want anything to happen to you or Malcolm or Nolan or Winter or Jam or Ariana—"

"Nothing's going to happen to us." Jam stood in the doorway to one of the bedrooms, already dressed in a fluffy bathrobe with a towel slung over his shoulder. "Ariana and I can take care of ourselves."

"Darryl could, too. And my mom. Look what happened to them," said Simon, his jaw tightening.

"It won't happen to us," said Felix. "We know who the bad guys are."

Simon raked his fingers through his hair. The problem was, right now everyone was trying to stop them somehow, even the good guys. "Rivera's probably already called Malcolm. He'll be here by morning."

"That gives us . . ." Jam checked his watch. "Twelve hours, maybe. If we're lucky."

"I need to check out Beak Peak," said Simon. "If Orion's here—"

"You can't go alone. What if he *is* there?"

"And what if my mother's there, too? If you had wings, I'd ask you to come, but you don't. Someone needs to stay here anyway, in case Ronnie checks on us."

"I don't have wings, but you can carry me," said Felix, standing on his hind legs. Simon shook his head.

"You're not going anywhere near the flock. They'd eat you for dinner."

Jam took a step toward him. "You can't go, Simon. Not on your own. At least wait until Malcolm arrives—"

"I'm not putting my uncle in danger. Not again," he said firmly, moving toward the balcony. The lights from the city glowed around them, but a mountain rose up behind the hotel, a silent menace now that Simon knew what it held. "I'll be back by morning. Whatever happens, make sure Orion doesn't get the reptiles' piece, all right?"

Jam pursed his lips. "Okay, all right, just—be careful, will you? Don't let them catch you."

"I'll try," said Simon, pushing open the balcony door. The night air was cool against his skin, and he took a deep breath and shifted into a golden eagle.

With a soft cry, he launched himself off the balcony and into the sky, heading straight toward the mountain—and, with any luck, his mother.

15

BEAK PEAK

Simon soared through the air, circling the peak of the mountain. He had never been this high up before, and part of him didn't want to look down. But he had to—because somewhere on that sandy slope had to be a clue about where his mother was. He just needed to find it.

His vision in the dark was terrible, but at last he spotted movement at the very top of the peak, near what looked like a black hole mostly hidden by rocks and trees. Concealed by the night, he swooped down as a pair of hawks disappeared inside. Simon cautiously landed on a scraggly branch the next hill over. He couldn't see anything, but his hearing had sharpened to make up for his impaired vision, and he could detect what sounded like human voices echoing from inside.

He started to spread his wings to fly into the entrance, but he stopped himself. He didn't know if there were any other golden eagles in Orion's flock, and he couldn't risk tipping him off. Stepping into the shadows, Simon closed his eyes and concentrated. He grew smaller, his wingspan shorter, and he could feel his feathers adjusting as he shifted into a hawk.

Swallowing his nerves, he crossed the empty air and ventured into the dark entrance. It was on the side of the peak, where no human would be able to reach it, and the tunnel twisted in on itself, hiding whatever was inside. But as soon as Simon flew around the corner, bright lights flashed in his eyes, and he squinted.

Landing on a rock jutting out from the wall, Simon turned his head to get a good look with his keen hawk sight now that he wasn't immersed in darkness. He was inside a cavern not unlike Zia Stone's mammal haven in Colorado, though this was full of birds. Dozens of hawks, falcons, and even eagles rested on perches across the roomy cave, and several humans lounged at long wooden tables. Most had drinks in front of them, and they spoke loudly, their laughter and conversation all jumbling together.

Simon scanned the crowd, spotting a familiar face. Near the entrance to one of several tunnels leading into deeper parts of the mountain, Perrin sat at an otherwise empty table, hunched over and looking worse for wear.

So Perrin had made it to Arizona, too. Simon studied him, but Perrin did nothing but nurse his drink. As the minutes ticked by, Simon flew from perch to perch impatiently, trying to get closer to Perrin without being noticed. There was no point, though—Perrin was alone, and even if he was talking to someone, the murmur of conversation in the cavern was too loud for Simon to eavesdrop.

At last, when Simon was sure he would have to take a chance and explore the tunnels on his own, Rowan stepped out from an opening nearby. He leaned down to murmur something in his father's ear, and Perrin's expression grew pinched. Pushing aside his bottle, he rose and followed Rowan into the tunnel, and Simon soared through the cave after them. *Finally*.

Simon kept his distance from the pair, neither of whom seemed to notice the hawk following them. But when the tunnel opened up to another cavern, Simon realized sneaking through the shadows hadn't been necessary. Another dozen raptors perched around the room, many with their heads tucked under their wings at this late hour. Trying his best to stay inconspicuous, Simon made himself comfortable on the back of an unused chair in the corner.

Perrin and Rowan moved into the center, where another long table stood, this one covered in maps and books. Simon ruffled his feathers. Maybe he had been wrong. Maybe Orion wasn't here after all.

"It's about time." Orion's voice boomed off the rock walls, and it was through a supreme act of willpower that Simon managed not to startle. Orion strode in, his limp obvious but his gait still powerful. From this angle, Simon had a perfect view of his blind eye, and he forced his racing pulse to slow. Even if Orion could have recognized him as a hawk somehow, he couldn't see him from here. "Did you find them?"

Perrin straightened, his hands clasped behind his back. "We watched them enter the Stilio, Your Majesty. They are now in the reptile council's custody."

Orion tensed. When he finally spoke, his voice was soft and frigid. "You had one job—rescue my grandson. How many times has he slipped past you now?"

Perrin stood still, his expression blank. "As soon as he leaves the hotel—"

"He won't be leaving, not on his own." Orion began to pace. "Malcolm will come for him, no doubt. If we go after him now, before the Alpha arrives—"

"But sir, the reptiles—"

"Would you rather face the reptiles or the mammals?" Orion whirled around, grabbing the edge of the table to remain steady. "All you had to do was capture Simon when he got off the train, and you couldn't even do that much."

"The mammals stole him—"

"A bunch of ragtag misfits who could barely hold off a sparrow. Yet somehow they managed to best you." Orion took a menacing step toward Perrin. "Did I make a mistake, appointing you my lieutenant?"

Perrin's jaw tightened, and his Adam's apple bobbed. "No, Your Majesty."

"Is that so? Because from where I stand, it certainly seems that way."

"If Simon wanted to be here, Father, he would be," said a new voice, and Simon's head twisted around so fast he nearly strained something. His mother stepped through the same entrance Orion had used, her blond braid slung over her shoulder, and she carried a stack of books with her. Simon hadn't seen her in human form since the rat army had kidnapped her two months earlier, and the sight of her whole and healthy made his heart skip a beat.

"He's twelve years old. Someone needs to protect him from the likes of Celeste and the pack," said Orion. "It's only a matter of time before they use Simon against us."

"You mean the way you're planning on using Simon against me?" said his mother. "Or is it me against him? I never quite caught the nuances of your spectacular plan."

Orion's face slowly turned red. "You're my daughter, and he's my grandson. All I want is to protect you both."

"And Nolan?" His mother fixed Orion with a steely glare.

"Nolan is also my grandson," he said slowly, "but you must accept that if . . ." He paused, glancing at the birds perched around him. For one horrible second, Orion's gaze fell on Simon, but before he could panic, Orion looked away. "If his *secret* gets out, his life will be in danger."

"It already is," said Simon's mother. "Or did you have another reason for trying to put the Predator together?"

Orion began to pace again, and he gestured angrily at the maps. "If you would cooperate and tell us where the reptiles' piece is, maybe I would be willing to stop hunting Simon."

"But I thought you were doing it for his own good—to protect him?" said his mother.

"I am. However, you don't seem to be terribly convinced, so I thought you would appreciate this . . . compromise. If you help me, I will do as you request and leave Simon alone."

His mother sniffed and looked at the maps. "I've already told you, the reptiles didn't trust me with their piece's location. I had it long enough to make a convincing copy, and that's all."

She was lying. Relief spread through Simon. Orion might have captured her, but he hadn't broken her. She still had some fight left.

But if she was human and out of her cage, then why was she still here? Why hadn't she run away? Simon cautiously flew from one perch to another, this one several feet closer to his mother, and he spotted a collar around her neck. It looked like it was made of some sort of metal, and judging by the way she moved, it was heavy enough to hold her down in eagle form—or even break her delicate bird bones.

"You must have overheard something," said Orion. "I know you listen, I know you watch. I know you would never allow the reptiles to hide their piece without knowing exactly where they were going to put it."

"You give me way too much credit," she said, and she pointed to a spot on one of the maps. "If I were a reptile, I would have buried it in the mountain, just here—"

"We've *searched* the mountain." Orion slammed his fist on the table, and several birds took flight. "We've searched every location you've suggested."

"Then maybe it isn't here anymore," she said. "Have you considered that, Father? Have you considered the possibility that the reptiles moved the piece to stop this very thing from happening?"

Orion gritted his teeth. "You know what I have considered? How to make you see that I'm trying to help your sons."

"Help them?" His mother laughed, but there was no humor to it. "By what, assembling the Predator so you can murder Nolan and take his power for yourself?"

"Celeste is the one who wants to kill him. *I* have no desire to hurt anyone, let alone my own family."

"Keep telling yourself that," said his mother bitterly. "One day you might actually believe it."

Orion limped toward the tunnel that led back to the gathering room. "If you imbeciles can't find Simon, then I will," he called to Perrin and Rowan. "Perhaps then, Isabel, you'll be more willing to share what you know."

"You just said you have no desire to hurt him," said Simon's mother.

"I don't, but I will do what I must to defend my kingdom from Celeste. One of us *will* assemble the Predator, and if she gets there first, I promise you she will stop at nothing to destroy us. If you won't cooperate in order to protect the thousands of Animalgams whose lives rest in our hands, then perhaps you'll cooperate to protect your son."

Orion exited, leaving silence in his wake. Simon's mother touched the collar around her neck, adjusting it. Around the edges, Simon spotted skin rubbed raw, and anger boiled inside him.

"I have a drink to finish," muttered Perrin, and he trudged out of the room. Rowan offered Simon's mother a small smile, but he didn't say a word as he followed Perrin back into the tunnel.

Once alone, Simon's mother took a deep breath and exhaled, gazing at the maps. Picking up a book from the top of the stack she'd brought in, she headed back the way she'd come. Simon waited until she was gone before swooping after her.

His mother took a narrow spiral staircase downward, and Simon followed, careful not to make a sound. It wasn't until she stepped into a private office that she finally relaxed and sat down on a worn sofa.

"You're not supposed to be in here," she said, her eyes closed. It took Simon half a second to realize she meant him.

"I'm not the greatest at following rules," he said. She must have recognized his voice, because she twisted around, her eyes widening in surprise. He shifted back into a human.

"Nolan?" She stumbled to her feet, capturing him in a tight hug. Her metal collar rubbed against his skin, and he clung to her, burying his face in her hair. Even in the desert, she still smelled like fallen leaves and the forest.

"Simon," he corrected sheepishly. She pulled away enough to look at him, searching his face.

"But—you were a hawk. Not an eagle."

Simon nodded, and for a long moment, they stared at each other. Her mouth fell open. "It's you? You're the . . . ?"

"We both are."

His mother paled, and she sat him down on the couch, her hands never pulling away. "Who else knows?"

"No one," he said. "Not even Nolan. He hates me enough already. If he thought I was taking that from him, too—"

"Good." She leaned over to scan the empty hallway, and her voice dropped to a whisper. "You can't tell anyone, Simon. I mean it. You shouldn't even have told me. You must keep this secret at all costs, do you understand?"

Simon hesitated. Right now, staying quiet was easy, but if there was ever a day when Orion came after his brother—or his uncle, or his friends—Simon couldn't promise he wouldn't do everything in his power to save them. "I don't want anyone to hurt Nolan, Mom."

"I'm doing my best to make sure no one will. But even the people who claim the Beast King's heir poses no threat would revolt at learning there are two." She touched his face, her blue eyes watering. "I'm so sorry, sweetheart."

She had nothing to be sorry for, as far as Simon saw it. He set his hand over hers. "We have to get you out of here."

His mother nodded. "Is the pack waiting outside?"

"The pack?"

"Yes. Malcolm and Vanessa and the others . . ." She trailed off, and her eyes widened in horror. "Oh, Simon. Don't tell me it's just you."

"It's not," he said quickly. "My friends Ariana and Jam and Winter—they're here, too. Not *here*, exactly, because they can't fly, but they're at the Stilio. They're helping me."

His mother pressed her lips together, as if stopping herself from blurting out what she really wanted to say. At last she managed, "You weren't supposed to come alone. I can't believe—Simon, do you understand how dangerous this is?"

"It doesn't matter," he said, and he stood. "I'm going to get you out of here. Orion can't find the pieces without you, and we can look for them on our own. Together."

His mother's expression grew pinched, and she touched her collar. "If Orion thinks the reptiles or the mammals took me, it'll be all-out war."

"It's going to be war already," said Simon. "We have to destroy the Predator, Mom. That's the only way to keep Nolan and the whole Animalgam world safe."

"I know, sweetheart. Believe me, I know." She watched him for the space of several heartbeats. "I can't shift. The collar will crush me."

Simon examined the metal ring. He might be able to hold it while she turned into an eagle, but if he messed up, he could break her wing or worse. His frustration grew as he spotted the keyhole at the back of the collar. Maybe he could steal the key—

Wait. He didn't need to steal anything. Hastily Simon dug through his pocket, producing the lock picks Jam had given him on the train. His mother blinked.

"Where did you get those?"

"Jam. He got them from Ariana—she's a spider. Hold still."

Simon began to work the shallow lock gently, the way Jam had taught him. The collar was heavier than he'd expected, and the lock was far more complex than the one he'd practiced on with Jam. A bead of sweat trickled down his cheek. He didn't know how long Orion would be gone, but they didn't have all night. His hands began to shake, but at last he heard a soft *click*, and his mother gingerly opened the collar and pulled it off.

"Much better," she said, touching the raw patches on her skin. "We don't have much time—"

"Leaving so soon? But things were just about to get interesting."

Simon whirled around. Standing in the doorway was Orion.

16

SITTING DUCKS

"Really, Isabel, I'm perplexed as to why you're so eager to abandon our efforts," said Orion, limping toward the pair of them. "I'm doing this to protect Simon, after all, and to ensure that when the time comes, he has a kingdom to rule."

Grabbing Simon's wrist, she pulled him behind her, and Simon felt her nails digging into his skin. "I was just about to come find you," she said in a falsely cheerful voice. "It seems Simon found his way here after all."

"How delightful." Orion's gaze flickered to her bare neck. Perrin appeared behind him, a silent guard. "I only wish he had allowed the flock to escort him."

"I don't trust Perrin," said Simon tightly. "Or Rowan. Or any of the flock."

"That's a pity, since one day you will be the one to command them." Orion began to circle the pair slowly. "Why did you come back, Simon?"

"Because—" His mouth went dry. "Because I want to be a family again. Malcolm and Nolan, they try, but—but they're not you and Mom."

"I see. And how did you know where we were?"

"Malcolm—Malcolm heard rumors," lied Simon. "He believed them, so I thought I would come down here to try to find you."

"You came all the way to Paradise Valley on a maybe? How touching." Orion smiled, and though Simon's mother circled with Orion, trying to keep herself between the pair of them, Orion eventually outmaneuvered her and grabbed Simon's shoulder, yanking him away with surprising force.

"Don't you dare—" began his mother, but Perrin stepped beside her. Two more men lingered in the hallway behind him, and she fell silent.

"Now," said Orion, clutching Simon so tightly that a jolt of pain ran down his arm. "Why don't you tell me where the reptiles' piece is, Isabel, so we can put this bit of ugliness behind us and be the family Simon wants us to be?"

"I told you, I don't know," said his mother.

From his belt, Orion pulled a long knife with a jagged edge and rested it against Simon's throat. His mother turned sickly pale, and Simon couldn't breathe. "How about now?" said Orion. "Does this jog your memory?"

"You won't do it." His mother's voice shook.

"Won't I?" He pressed a little harder. "Are you sure you want to test that theory?"

Before that night in Sky Tower, Simon would have never imagined that anyone, even Orion, could hurt his own family. But he hadn't only murdered Darryl. He had dropped Simon from the roof, too, on the off chance that would be the moment he shifted. Orion hadn't been wrong, but Simon had still seen the darkest side of his grandfather—the side that would stop at nothing, not even killing his own blood, to assemble the Predator. And Simon knew without a doubt that Orion wasn't bluffing.

"He's your heir," said his mother. "You can't live forever, and if you kill him, your kingdom will be picked apart by vultures until there's nothing left."

"You'll be there, won't you, darling?" said Orion. "And as much as you insist you want nothing to do with us, I know you. I know you won't let your kingdom fall to the wayside, not when it would mean war and unfathomable loss."

"Try me," she said with a snarl. The two of them stared at each other for the longest moments of Simon's life. He could feel the sharp edge of the blade pressing against his skin, only a slip away from opening an artery, and the fiery knot in his chest constricted.

He could shift into a wolf, or a bear, or anything with fangs and claws, and he could tear Orion apart before his grandfather knew what was happening. Or he could change into a snake and squeeze the life out of him. Or he could become a spider and disappear into the rock. His mother didn't have to give Orion what he wanted. Simon didn't need her to protect him, not like this.

But even as his nails began to grow and sharpen, his mother glanced at him, and he could see the warning in her eyes.

Keep this secret at all costs.

Simon clenched his fists, the claws digging into his palms. Even if he *could* bring himself to kill his own grandfather, Perrin was still there, as well as the guards standing in the doorway. He didn't think he could kill them, too, no matter what Orion was threatening. But what else was he supposed to do?

His mother seemed to realize the same thing—that they were stuck. Seconds ticked by, and eventually she sighed, defeated. "The mountain is where the reptiles used to keep it, inside a hollowed-out boulder where no hikers could reach. But Simon overheard the council saying the piece was moved when I copied it in March, four years ago." She glanced at Simon. "The same way the underwater kingdom moved its piece after I copied it in September, two years ago."

Simon knew she was lying—the council had said they'd kept it in the exact same place—but there was something insistent about the way she looked at him, something he couldn't figure out.

Orion adjusted his grip on the knife. "Are you certain that's all you know?"

"I swear," she said.

At last Orion released Simon and returned the knife to its sheath. "Good. That wasn't so hard, was it? You'll show me the boulder. It's unlike the council to reveal such a secret in front of members of another kingdom, is it not? Perhaps Simon heard wrong." Orion studied her suspiciously with his good eye. "While we're gone, Perrin will see to Simon's comfort."

His mother grabbed him as soon as Orion let him go, pulling him close. "I'm not leaving my son," she said.

"It'll be fine, Mom," said Simon. "Just do what he says."

"There's a good lad," said Orion, and he ruffled Simon's hair. "Come along, Isabel. Do I need to tell you what will happen to Simon if you try to fly away?"

She shook her head, and Orion limped toward the doorway.

"Good. We'll be back shortly, and you two can catch up all you'd like then. Perrin, can I trust you not to let him slip away this time?"

"Yes, sir," said Perrin stiffly. "I won't take my eyes off him."

Reluctantly Simon's mother let go of him. "Get out of here however you can," she whispered in his ear, so only he could hear. "I love you."

"I love you, too," mumbled Simon, and he watched her join Orion as they headed back toward the spiral staircase. But he couldn't leave, not without her.

Perrin grabbed him by the elbow and led him to a small cavern, and though it was light on furniture, several cages lined the rock walls. Bird cages, Simon realized. This might as well have been the bird kingdom's dungeon.

"Shift," ordered Perrin, and Simon stared at him blankly. "Into your Animalgam form. *Shift*."

"And what if I say no?" said Simon.

"Then we have more than one collar, and it would be my pleasure to chain you to the wall."

Simon considered his options. A collar would be more difficult to escape from than a cage, and maybe if he seemed cooperative, Perrin wouldn't keep such a close eye on him. Slowly he shifted into a golden eagle, and when Perrin opened the door to a large cage, he hopped inside.

"I don't trust you," said Perrin as he shut the door and secured the lock.

"You probably shouldn't," agreed Simon. "If you're still around when I become the Bird Lord, the first thing I'm going to do is fire you."

"We'll see about that." Perrin scowled and settled into a chair at the entrance to the prison, pulling out a rolled-up paper from his boot to read. Simon pretended to familiarize himself with the food and water dishes— both half-empty—but instead he watched Perrin, checking to see how often he looked up from the paper. There didn't seem to be any discernable pattern, though Simon did notice that every time he ruffled his feathers, Perrin immediately focused on him.

So disappearing would be more difficult than he'd

anticipated, and even if he were able to shift without Perrin noticing, getting out of Beak Peak undetected would be next to impossible. No doubt the flock would be suspicious of any new animal that appeared, from a snake to a fly to a rat, and Simon couldn't be too careful. But he also had no choice.

He would wait for his mother to return first, he decided as Perrin turned the page. He couldn't leave without her, and the only way they would be able to escape was if they sneaked out. Otherwise Orion and the flock would be on them like buzzards, and no matter how fast they could fly, Simon didn't doubt that there were members of the flock who could fly faster.

Minutes ticked by. He tried to remain alert, but the more he watched Perrin, the more Perrin watched him in return, so eventually Simon closed his eyes and buried his beak in his feathers the way birds did when they slept. It felt oddly comfortable, and twice he nodded off for real, only to be jolted awake by the rustle of newspaper. Simon figured he had to take a break sometime. Right now, Simon simply had to wait him out.

"Here, thought you might be thirsty."

Simon cracked open an eye and peered between his feathers. Rowan stood in the doorway, holding out a bottle to his father. Perrin took a deep drink and sighed. "Are they not back yet?"

"Not yet. Sun's coming up soon."

"Have you sent anyone after them?" said Perrin, and his son nodded.

"I've checked on them twice, and other members of the flock are watching them. He's examining every rock himself. Doesn't trust us to do it for him."

Simon stayed perfectly still. He must have slept more than he'd thought if it was almost dawn. "He'll give up eventually," said Perrin.

"He won't," said Rowan. "Members of the flock have spotted Celeste outside Phoenix. We think the council tipped her off. If she's still on friendly terms with Rivera, she'll have no problem getting the piece's new location from him before we're able to find it. The rest of the council may not go along with it, but Rivera worships her. He'll believe her if she insists she's only protecting the piece from our kingdom."

A flash of Rivera's face appeared in Simon's mind, and his voice whispered, *I'll alert the Alpha.*

He hadn't meant Malcolm.

Rivera was leading Celeste straight to Simon—and directly to the reptiles' piece.

With his heart in his throat, Simon willed himself to stay still and keep his breathing even. Perrin, on the other hand, didn't bother hiding his panic. "We must alert Orion at once," he said, standing and dropping his newspaper on the chair.

"He already knows," said Rowan. "That's why he's still

out there digging around. He's convinced there's a clue, or that Isabel is lying about the council moving the piece."

"If Celeste and her loyalists attack, we're sitting ducks," said Perrin, and he peered at the rows of cages. "Stay here. Make sure the boy doesn't cause any trouble."

"But—"

"I said *stay*, Rowan."

Perrin rushed out of the dungeon, leaving Rowan lingering in the doorway. The younger man paced back and forth for a moment, and at last he muttered, "You're in a cage. Where are you going to go?"

Though he was talking to Simon, he didn't seem to expect an answer. With a muttered curse, he hurried after his father, leaving the prison unguarded.

Simon didn't hesitate. As soon as Rowan was gone, he shifted into a fly and, once he'd slipped the bars, back into a golden eagle. It was a risk, but there were other eagles in the mountain. With any luck, he would blend in.

He made it to the large open cavern with the long tables, only to discover it was empty. Maybe it was the late—or early—hour and everyone was asleep, but as Simon flew to the tunnel that led out of Beak Peak, he had a horrible feeling he knew exactly where the flock was.

He wasn't wrong. As he soared out of the mountain and into the crisp morning air, he flew straight into a mob of countless birds flying around the peak. Every single member of the flock must have been there, prepared to fight.

Simon merged with them silently, joining another golden eagle as it glided through the air. To his relief, no one batted an eye at him. Even if the flock knew he was at Beak Peak, they must have thought he was still locked up.

Though every bone in his body screamed at him to fly toward the safety of the hotel, he couldn't leave without his mother. Circling the mountain, he searched for her, only to spot another pair of golden eagles on a cliff, inspecting a large rock.

"Sir, we must get to safety," said a hawk as he danced around anxiously. Perrin. "If Celeste is in the area—"

"Let her come. If she wants a fight, I'll give her a fight," said Orion, examining a crack in the rock with his good eye. "Does this look natural to you, or man-made?"

Members of the flock tightened their perimeter around the three of them, and Simon sucked up his courage. He would only have one chance to take them by surprise, and this was it.

He dived toward the rock, landing clumsily on top of it as his talons scraped the stone. Orion, engrossed in studying the boulder, didn't look up. "Mom!" he cried. "Let's go!"

"Simon?" She tilted her head in surprise, but instead of arguing, she spread her wings, and they took off together. "What are you *doing*?"

Behind them, Orion screeched, and the flock exploded into the air, chasing after them. Simon didn't dare look back.

"I'm not leaving without you," he said. "Come on, it'll be safe at the hotel."

His mother's beak clenched with determination, and she dived down the slope of the mountain. Simon flapped his wings, matching his mother's pace. He could see the lights of the resort. If they flew fast enough, they could make it. He wasn't sure what they would do when they reached the balcony and the flock caught up, but they had to try.

Together he and his mother soared through the air at breakneck speed, hurtling toward the hotel. Simon was practically dizzy with excitement. He had done it. He had really rescued his mother. Only another quarter mile and—

"Stop!" Orion's cry filled the quiet morning sky, and Simon felt something tug at his tail feathers. At the speed he was going, it was enough to throw him off balance, and he tumbled through the air, struggling to catch himself on the currents. But his human mind had taken over now, shoving his instincts aside, and all at once, he had forgotten how to fly.

"Don't you *dare* touch my son."

His mother slammed into Orion, and together they tangled as they half flew, half fell. Simon watched out of the corner of his eye, utterly useless—he had enough trouble simply staying upright as the ground grew perilously closer. There was nothing he could do to help his mother.

The resort appeared faster than he anticipated, and Simon angled his feathers, trying to land. His talons caught tufts of grass as he somersaulted toward a pond, skidding to a stop inches from the water's edge.

"Mom!" he shouted, and as soon as he was on his feet, he spread his wings to take off once more. But to his surprise, his mother rocketed straight toward him, Orion nowhere in sight. The flock dived toward a point beyond the borders of the hotel, and Simon spotted a figure he thought might be a golden eagle crumpled on the ground.

His mother landed beside him and shifted back into a human. Simon did the same, and she caught him in a hug. "Are you all right? Are you hurt?"

"I'm fine," said Simon. "We have to go, Mom—once we're inside—"

"I'm not going with you, Simon."

"I—what?" Her words hit him like a fist to the gut. "Mom, I'm not leaving—"

"No. I'm the one leaving, Simon."

He gaped at her, struggling to catch his breath. "I don't—I don't understand—"

"And I don't expect you to." She looked over toward the border of the resort. The flock had gathered around the silhouette of an old man, and a bitter, twisted part of Simon hoped he was dead. "I need to stay with Orion. He's right, you know—someone is going to find the pieces, and it can't be Celeste."

"So you're going to help him?" said Simon in a strangled voice.

"No. I'm going to help *you*." She brushed a blade of grass from his cheek. "I was hoping you would be older. I never wanted to burden you now, not when you're still so young, but we don't have a choice anymore. You have to assemble the Predator, Simon. You're the only one who will destroy it once it's whole."

"But you know where the pieces are," he said, the words thick in his throat. "We can find them together—"

"As long as I'm with you, Orion will stop at nothing to hunt us both down. Do you understand?" She jutted a finger toward the flock. "Every bird in the country will be our enemy. No place will be safe, not even the Den with Malcolm. It will be *war*, and we will lose. But if I'm with him—if I distract him and keep him focused on finding the pieces before Celeste—he'll never know you're looking, Simon. Neither of them will."

His eyes watered, and he stared at her, not believing what he was hearing. "You told me to come here and find you, Mom."

"No, Simon. I told you where to find the reptiles' piece." She cupped his face. "I know it's difficult to accept, but destroying the Predator is my life's work."

"And you care more about some stupid weapon than being a family with me and Nolan?" Simon jerked back, and his mother dropped her hands. A dark, pained expression passed over her face.

"Yes. I care more about keeping you both alive and safe

than being there to make you breakfast each morning." She pressed her lips together, but her voice never wavered. "You know I've never been much of a mother, Simon. That life was stolen from us before you were even born. I was lucky, having as much time with you two as I did, but—" She blinked hard. "Darryl was your family, not me. And now Malcolm and Nolan are. I hope one day I'll fit into that equation, but right now, while the pieces of the Predator are still out there, while Orion and Celeste are still after them—I have more important things to do than to be your mother."

Simon watched her numbly, his entire body shaking. If his leg hadn't been throbbing from his landing, and if he hadn't been able to feel the dewy grass against his ankles, he would have guessed this was all a dream. A nightmare. But it was real. It was actually happening.

His mother wasn't coming with him.

"I love you more than life itself. Never forget that," she said as she slowly backed away. Her blue eyes glittered with tears, but Simon didn't know what to believe anymore. "Find the pieces, Simon."

She began to shift, and Simon lurched toward her, tripping over the dirt. "I can't, Mom."

"Yes, you can." She rose into the air. "You have everything you need already."

"But—"

"If you don't, Orion or Celeste will. Now go, while the flock is distracted."

"Mom—"

"*Go.*"

She flew beyond the borders of the resort, straight toward the flock. Over the edge of the fence, Simon could see Orion sitting up now, and hot betrayal snaked through him, burning him from the inside out.

His mother was choosing Orion over him. Simon didn't care why—she was leaving him again, like she had done countless times before. No matter what he did, no matter how hard he tried, she always left him behind.

His vision blurred as he stumbled across the grass, and when he reached the nearest door, he grasped the handle like it was the only thing keeping him upright. Several members of the flock cried out, and wiping his eyes angrily, Simon squinted into the sky, which was only now beginning to lighten along the horizon. Orion shifted back into an eagle, and the flock formed a protective circle around him as they flew back toward the mountain, taking his mother with them.

No, they weren't taking her anywhere. She was choosing to go. And with that fact weighing heavily on him, Simon shifted back into a golden eagle and flew up toward the balcony that opened to his and Jam's suite. His mother wanted him to assemble and destroy the Predator— fine. He would do it, but not for her. He would do it for Nolan. He would do it to protect his brother, since he was practically all the family Simon had left.

Shaking off his grief and misery as much as he could,

he forced himself to focus. His mother had insisted he had everything he needed to find the pieces, but what did he have? A notebook he'd already memorized, a pocket watch that didn't work, the hundred and twenty-four postcards she'd sent—

Something sparked in Simon's mind, and he landed on the balcony. It was crazy, but maybe, just maybe—

He knew how to find the reptiles' piece.

THE ALPHA RETURNS

Simon dug through the pockets of his backpack, searching for the stack of postcards. They were right where he'd left them, wrapped in a rubber band and sorted by date, and he quickly flipped through the familiar pictures.

His mother had said the reptiles' piece of the weapon had been moved in March, four years ago. He knew that was a lie, but it must have meant something. Four years ago, he had been in third grade. His mother had visited him twice that year: once on Christmas Eve and once on his birthday. But she had sent postcards every month, the same way she had since he was two.

As soon as he spotted the picture, he knew he had found the right one. A snake with red, black, and white bands hissed on the postcard, and on the back, below the date, his mother had written in her familiar handwriting:

The Kingsnake is, as its name suggests, the king of all snakes. Immune to its venomous cousins, it is feared among its kind for eating other snakes, lizards, and birds.

That was all she had written that month—not even a "Love, Mom." But it was all the information Simon needed.

The piece was in the room with the Kingsnake statue.

"Jam." He dashed into the bedroom. "Jam, wake up."

He turned on the lights and froze. The bed looked slept in, with the sheets wrinkled and an indent on the pillow, but Jam wasn't there.

"Jam?" Simon darted through the rest of the suite and checked the bathroom. It was empty. "Jam!"

A soft knock sounded on the door, startling Simon. He rushed to unlock it. "Jam, where have you—"

He stopped. Winter stood on the other side, dressed in designer clothes with her hair freshly washed. A new purse hung from her shoulder, but despite her expensive accessories, there were dark blotches under her eyes, and she looked like she'd slept even less than Simon.

"I thought I heard you," she said, pushing past him and closing the door. "Where have you been?"

"I—" Simon tried to find the words to explain, but he could barely admit to himself that his mother had abandoned him again, let alone Winter. "Where's Jam?"

"Rivera came to check on you after the council meeting finished late last night," she said. "When he found out you were missing, he was furious. He took Jam and Ariana somewhere—I think he wanted to interrogate them."

The room began to spin. Simon didn't want to think about what Rivera might do to get the truth out of his friends. "Where are they?"

"I don't know," she said. "He didn't tell me."

"Can you ask him?"

"I would, but he's been gone all night."

Simon reached for the door. "I need to find them."

Winter stepped in front of him, blocking his way. "The guards are out there, remember?"

"Then I'll use the back door," he said, heading toward the balcony instead. Winter hurried after him.

"Simon—"

"What?" He whirled around. "What do you want me to do, Winter? I'm not leaving them." Not like his mother had left him. "Celeste is on her way. We don't have time to wait around for Malcolm to get here, and I'm not letting the council hurt my friends."

Winter rolled her eyes. "I was just going to say good luck."

The bubble of anger inside him deflated. "Oh. Thanks. Don't tell anyone I was here, okay?"

"Like I was going to."

Winter held the balcony door open as Simon shifted into a golden eagle and took flight. It was growing lighter out now, and he soared around the edge of the hotel until he spotted the secret Animalgam entrance. Landing in the bushes, he shifted back and crawled out from the foliage, nudging the button toward the ground with the toe of his shoe.

The door opened, and he hurried inside. The Animalgam lobby was all but empty, save for a woman behind the front desk. "Excuse me," she called. "Excuse me, you shouldn't be in here."

"You're right—I need to be in there," said Simon, and he raced past the elevators toward the heated room that housed the pit of serpents. The woman shouted after him, apparently unwilling to leave her post, but he kept going, only skidding to a stop after he'd crossed the glass bridge and reached the statue of the Kingsnake. The thought of being so close to the piece and passing right by made him curse with frustration, but he would figure out a way to get it as soon as his friends were safe.

The door to the council room was closed, and Simon sneaked up to it, pressing his ear against the crack. The low murmur of voices filtered through, and he gripped the handle, trying to make out what they were saying.

". . . at this for hours," rumbled a familiar voice. Crocker, the council member with the cane. "Have the guards check again. If he isn't back by now, Orion must have him."

"I will not accept that," said Rivera sharply, and Simon pictured his pinched face. "The Alpha is nearly here, and she is expecting us to protect the boy."

"What would you like for us to do? Go to the mountain and fetch him?"

"If we must."

"Your Honors!" Ronnie the bearded dragon's voice sounded from nearby. "The flock is here—several of our lookouts spotted Orion himself flying nearby."

A murmur ran through the room. "Return the children to the snake pit immediately," said Rivera.

"That's hardly necessary," said Crocker. "They'll be secure in their rooms."

"I am not taking any more chances," said Rivera. "The snake pit. *Now.*"

Footsteps sounded on the other side of the door, and fast as he could, Simon darted behind the massive Kingsnake. It was just in time, too—the guards Simon recognized from the night before, Rosencrantz and Guildenstern, marched an exhausted-looking Ariana and Jam into the statue room. They stopped beside the moat of vipers and cobras, however, and while one guard held on to Ariana and Jam, the other pulled the glass bridge up.

"In you go," said the shorter of the two. "Make way—and stop your snapping. They're not food. Move your tails, too. Don't want to get stepped on, do you?"

Ariana paled, but she bravely led Jam underneath the platform. The guards set the bridge back in place, and

Simon waited until they returned to the council's chambers before he moved to the edge of the moat. "Ariana? Jam? Can you hear me?"

A cobra rose up threateningly, spreading its hood as a tangle of other serpents slid beneath it. "Not an inch closer, or I'll have you for breakfast, boy," it said in a thick accent.

Simon backed away. How was he supposed to sneak past hundreds of snakes? Even if he shifted and they thought he was one of them, he had no idea how to get Ariana and Jam to safety.

He shoved his hands in his pockets, his fingers brushing up against the pocket watch. The closer to the statue he moved, the warmer it became, and he paced around the base. There had to be something he was missing.

"Simon." A female voice sent a chill down his spine, and a claw-like hand settled on the back of his neck. "What a delight."

Celeste. The former Alpha of the mammal kingdom, and the woman who had held his brother captive for ten years while forcing his mother to collect the pieces of the Predator. Simon twisted around. Her icy blue eyes met his, and she smirked.

"I've been looking for you, my dear," she murmured, her nails digging into his shirt. "Why don't you come with me to speak with the council?"

"I know why you're here," he said through a clenched jaw. "I'll tell them if you don't let me go."

"You'll tell them what, exactly? That I'm here to protect

my grandson from a tyrant bent on using him for his own evil ends?"

"That you want the reptiles' piece," he said. "That you're trying to assemble the Predator and take over the Animalgam world."

Her expression softened, and with her free hand, she patted his cheek. "Oh, darling. I've already taken great care to explain to them my only intention is to block our mutual enemy, Orion, from finding the pieces. If they called me here to protect you, surely they must be sympathetic to my side of the story."

Simon's mouth went dry. "You can't do this."

"Can't do what? I'm not here for the piece, Simon. I'm here for you. Without you and your brother, the Predator will do your grandfather next to no good. But if he has to come to me to get you . . . well, that changes things, doesn't it?" She smiled and smoothed her dark hair. "Come. Let's greet the council."

Celeste pushed Simon forward, and he stumbled, fighting her every step of the way. Despite her slight frame, however, she was much stronger than him, and across the glass bridge they went. When they reached the door to the council's chambers, Celeste didn't bother knocking. Instead she pushed it open as if she had every right to be there, and the murmur of voices inside stopped.

"Celeste?" Rivera stood from his place at the round table. "We weren't expecting you so soon. And—" His brow furrowed. "You have the boy?"

"Was he missing?" said Celeste, feigning confusion, and she forced Simon into an empty seat at the table. "He does have a tendency to disappear from time to time, I'm afraid. Nothing a leash won't solve."

"You can't trust her," said Simon, wrenching his shoulder from her grip. "She wants the piece as much as Orion does—"

"So claims the heir to the bird kingdom's throne." Celeste lingered behind Simon, making no move to sit. The council members bent their heads together, whispering as she continued. "I have no interest in your piece, ladies and gentlemen of the council. I only ask for safe passage back to mammal territory. If Orion discovers I have his heir in protective custody, he will stop at nothing to kidnap him from me."

As much as Simon hated Orion, he was pretty sure he would've been much safer stuck in Beak Peak than wherever Celeste intended on taking him. "I'm not going anywhere with her."

"Hush, darling," she murmured. "I am your Alpha, and like it or not, you will obey me."

"I'm not a member of your kingdom," said Simon fiercely. "I don't have to listen to you. And anyway, in case you forgot, you're not the Alpha anymore. Malcolm is."

"Is that true?" Crocker leaned forward. "We heard there was a disturbance in the hierarchy of the L.A.I.R., but it seems reports of a new Alpha have failed to reach us." He lowered his stare onto Rivera, who raised his chin defiantly.

"There was an—unfortunate incident between Celeste and her remaining son," he admitted. "But I saw no need to bother the rest of the council with the details, not when it will certainly resolve itself once the unrest dies down."

"So you *are* no longer the Alpha of the mammal kingdom," said Crocker, and several of the other council members fidgeted uneasily. "That certainly changes things."

"Does it?" Celeste sniffed. "Nearly the entire mammal kingdom continues to follow me. My son's leadership is only recognized by the pack—"

"And what is an Alpha without a pack?" said Crocker. Celeste stiffened.

"I believe we are getting off track, gentlemen. Regardless of my *temporary* status, Simon is still my grandson, and I am here to take him home, where it is safe. Once we have arrived, I will send my best fighters to help you eradicate the pestilence of feathers from your territory. All I ask in return is for assistance getting my grandson across the desert."

The council began to whisper to one another again, and dread coiled in the pit of Simon's stomach. "I *said* I'm not going with her," he repeated, louder this time.

"She is your family. We must respect that," said Rivera, and others nodded in agreement. He looked around the room. "Does anyone oppose the Alpha's most generous offer?"

"She is not the Alpha anymore," said Crocker, staring directly at Simon. "The boy does not want to go with her. Whatever his reasons may be, I will not force him into the custody of someone he does not trust."

"If we were to play that game, no child in the country would want to stay with their guardian at some point in their lives," said Celeste. "Particularly at Simon's age."

The murmur from the council grew louder, and Rivera said sharply, "All in favor of granting the Alpha and her grandson safe passage in return for her assistance ridding our territory of the flock?"

"Aye," the council chorused. Simon felt his face grow hot with frustration.

"All opposed?"

Crocker raised a single finger, never taking his eyes off Simon.

"Then it's settled. We will escort them to mammal territory and assist them with any defense against the flock." Rivera nodded to Celeste. "I will see you to the lobby myself."

Feeling like he was walking to his execution, Simon stood at Celeste's urging and let her nudge him toward the door. Rivera followed them, along with half the council, though Crocker remained seated, clutching his cane.

"I'll send my best soldiers to aid you as soon as we reach safety," said Celeste to Rivera. As they walked across the moat of snakes, Simon eyed the glass bridge. He wanted to yell for Jam and Ariana, to let them know he was all right and they weren't alone, but he couldn't help them now. Not with Celeste and nearly the entire council surrounding him.

He would escape the first chance he got. If Orion had let him slip through his fingers with the entire flock standing guard, surely he could shake Celeste. He only had to wait for the right opportunity. But how long would that take? Hours? Days? Weeks?

As they marched through the corridor and into the lobby, Simon racked his brain, trying to think how he could alert his uncle to their location. But when they exited the hotel and stepped beneath the early-morning sunlight, Simon stopped suddenly.

Malcolm stood in the middle of the path, his face twisted with fury. Zia leaned against the wall, inspecting her nails, while half a dozen other mammals from Colorado lurked nearby, several lounging at the edge of the fountain. Allies, Simon assumed. Or hoped.

Celeste's grip on Simon's arm tightened painfully, and she took several steps backward until they were once again inside the empty lobby. "Hello, son. I'm afraid you're too late for the meeting," she murmured in her icy voice.

"The only one who's too late is you, Mother," said Malcolm as he and the other mammals moved forward, cutting off Celeste's intended route. "Are you all right, Simon?"

"I'm fine. How did you find us?" said Simon, torn between relief and fear. Rivera had called Celeste, after all, not his uncle.

"I followed you here. We've been watching the hotel all night, trying to figure out what you four are up to," said Malcolm.

"Thought you might need backup if things got out of hand," added Zia, who didn't look the least bit bothered by any of this. "We saw you go into the lobby earlier, but storming the hotel without good reason didn't seem practical. You've got your provocation now, though, don't you?" she added, glancing at Malcolm. Clearly this was something they'd been arguing about.

"This is absurd," said Rivera, his voice booming but a note higher than normal. "You can't attack the council—"

"I would be very, very careful about telling me what I can and cannot do right now, Rivera." Malcolm advanced on his mother. "Hand over Simon. If you don't, I have no problem taking him from you. What will it be?"

The rest of the mammals filtered into the lobby, forming a barrier between Celeste and the door. They may have been misfits and a ragtag collection of fighters at best, but Simon had seen them in action. Individually they weren't all that threatening, but together, he didn't doubt they could take on a fully grown wolf. With Malcolm's help, Celeste didn't stand a chance.

She must have known it, too, because she remained silent for several moments, seemingly assessing the situation.

"It isn't up to me, son. The council has already made its decision, and as you are standing on reptile territory, you must respect their authority."

"They have none over Simon," said Malcolm, and the muscles in his arms twitched.

"They have Ariana and Jam locked up with the snakes," said Simon suddenly. "The council's been interrogating them—"

"Enough," barked Celeste. "If you try to take Simon from me, the force of the entire reptile kingdom will rise against you. Is that what you want, Malcolm?"

"If that's what it takes," he said, and with a growl, he shifted into a hulking wolf. "This is your last warning, Mother."

"I'm afraid I can't let you do that," said Rivera. His body elongated and thinned, with his arms disappearing into his trunk while his legs fused together. Scales grew from his skin, and his face flattened and pupils sharpened until the largest cottonmouth snake Simon had ever seen lay on the lobby floor, his forked tongue tasting the air.

One by one, the other members of the council shifted. Lizards, crocodiles, alligators, vipers, iguanas—suddenly the lobby was full of reptiles.

"Have you ever been bitten by a venomous creature?" said Rivera, slithering toward the wolf that was Malcolm.

"I've put up with my mother for over thirty years. If I can survive her venom, I'm sure I can survive yours." Malcolm bared his teeth. "This is how it's going to be?"

"We have every right to defend our territory," said Rivera.

"And I have every right to defend my family," said Malcolm. *"Now!"*

In a flurry of howls and growls, the mammals shifted and launched themselves at the reptiles. Adrenaline flooded Simon's body as his uncle tore through the council, fur and claws flying. "Watch out!" he shouted as Rivera shot toward Malcolm, and the massive wolf turned in time to grab the cottonmouth in his jaws and fling him against the wall.

"That's enough of that," said Celeste, yanking Simon backward toward the elevators. He stumbled and tried to grab hold of a nearby couch to resist, but Celeste dragged him to the doors and jabbed a button.

"Going down?" said a familiar voice, and a cloud of orange fur tackled Celeste. Zia the fox.

Celeste shrieked, and as she tried to claw Zia off her, she released Simon. He sprang away, hesitating as Celeste shifted into a wolf. Zia clung to the back of her neck, holding on for dear life, but Simon could have sworn he saw a grin form on her muzzle.

"I've got this flea bag," said Zia. "You do what you came here to do."

There was something about the way she said it that made him think she wasn't talking about rescuing his friends. Either way, Simon couldn't bring himself to leave her alone with Celeste, and he shouted into the brawl. "Someone—over here!"

An armadillo and a badger raced toward them, and they too jumped onto the wolf's back. Celeste screamed, and Simon darted past her and down the corridor, running as fast as he could. Glancing over his shoulder, he spotted Zia on the ground, snarling and snapping at Celeste's hind legs, and he forced himself to keep going. The mammals could take care of themselves. His friends needed him, and he would only have one chance to help them. Even if it meant he wouldn't have time to find the reptiles' piece, he wasn't going to waste it. His mother might have been willing to give up everything to find the Predator, but he wasn't. Some things were too important.

THE VIPER PIT

Simon burst into the antechamber and rushed past the statue, stopping only when he reached the glass bridge. Dozens of snakes curled underneath, and Simon couldn't see any sign of Ariana and Jam.

"Hey—my friends are down there," he said, trying to lift the bridge, but it didn't budge.

"And?" said a rattlesnake with a shake of its tail. "You are not permitted to enter."

Simon searched for a button or lever he could push that would make the bridge open up, but he saw nothing. Frustrated, he stood and looked around. Even if he shifted into a viper and slipped past the snakes, he still had no way of getting his friends out of there. Ariana might be able to cling to his back as a spider, but Jam was a dolphin. He would still be stuck.

His gaze landed on the monstrous statue of the Kingsnake, and he sucked in a breath. It was crazy, but Rivera himself had said the reptiles worshipped the Kingsnake. It was the only shot he had.

Closing his eyes, Simon pictured the red, black, and white bands of the snake, and he felt his body slowly shift. It felt strange, losing his arms and legs, and his sense of smell grew sharper, but once the transformation was complete, he raised his head experimentally, and he could feel the strength in his new form. Even more so than the wolf, the Kingsnake was all muscle, and Simon felt as if he could take on a bear and win.

A gasp ran through the serpents close enough to see him, and several shrank back. "It can't be!" said the rattlesnake who had warned him off. Others rose from the pit, craning to get a better look as shock permeated the room.

"I need to see my friends. Open the bridge," said Simon in the most authoritative voice he could muster. Without hesitation, the rattlesnake pressed its nose against a well-camouflaged rock, and the glass bridge rose. The snakes melted back, revealing an opening at the base of the moat.

"I'm going inside for my friends," he said. "You're going to let them out without getting in their way or attacking, got it? And you will tell no one that the Kingsnake was here. Not even Rivera."

The rattlesnake bobbed its head, while dozens of other cobras and vipers clambered on top of one another in an attempt to get as far from Simon as possible. A sense of power and control surged through him, and he briefly wondered how far he could take this charade. When would they start to refuse him?

No. That wasn't why he was here. Taking a deep breath, he slid on his belly over the smooth rocks that led into the moat. The ground sloped downward, and in the low light, Simon saw countless other snakes slither out of his way. No wonder the council thought this was the safest place in their kingdom. Simon couldn't imagine anyone else getting this far alive.

The tunnel opened up into a small chamber beneath what must have been the very center of the room, and Simon spotted two figures huddled together near the edge of a square pit. He hissed, and the snakes surrounding them scattered, murmuring their apologies.

"Hello?" said Jam, his voice trembling. A thin sheen of sweat covered his face, and he wiped his forehead with his sleeve.

Ariana spotted Simon first, and she sucked in a breath. "Is that a Kingsnake?" she said. Jam squinted.

"I can't see. Are those bands red or orange?"

Now that he was down here, Simon knew he had no

choice but to reveal his secret to his friends. He could have slithered away and left them wondering, and part of him was tempted to do that, but Jam and Ariana had risked everything to help him. He trusted them with his life.

"Red," he said, and Jam's mouth dropped open.

"You sound *exactly* like our friend," he said, while Ariana froze, her gaze transfixed.

"It can't be," she said, and she leaned closer, her purple hair falling in her eyes. "*Simon?*"

Simon shifted back, winding up on his hands and knees near the edge of the dark pit. His human body felt oddly weak after the Kingsnake's, and he shook out his arms. "Right. So. I can do that, too."

"You—" Jam gaped at him and blinked several times. "How—"

"You're the heir," said Ariana, stunned. "Not Nolan."

"We both are," said Simon sheepishly, keeping his voice low. "I don't know how or why, but we can both shift into anything we want."

"That's—that's *incredible*," said Jam, adjusting his glasses. "How long—"

Something creaked above them, and Simon shook his head. "I'll explain everything later. Right now, you have to leave. The snakes will let you out."

"You're coming with us, right?" said Jam.

"There's one thing I have to do first."

"What could possibly be more important?" said Ariana,

and Simon slid his hand into his pocket. The closer he inched toward the square pit, the hotter his father's pocket watch burned, and though he had no idea how, Simon was sure it was trying to tell him the piece was nearby.

"Just trust me, okay?" said Simon. "Go. I'll be right behind you."

Ariana hesitated, but Jam grabbed her arm and pulled her toward the exit. Simon watched them go, and as soon as they disappeared into the light, he shifted back into the Kingsnake and slithered to the edge of the pit.

It was deep—ten feet at least, and filled with more vipers and cobras than Simon could count. He shuddered inwardly, but in the same strong voice he'd used before, he said, "Show me the piece of the Predator."

Despite the fact that they vastly outnumbered him, the snakes in the pit anxiously squirmed as far from him as they could get, with several abandoning their posts and hurrying to the safety of the moat above instead. Those that remained looked back and forth between Simon and each other.

"But—Your Majesty, we have sworn to protect it," said a coral snake with red, yellow, and black bands.

"By giving it to me, you are protecting it," said Simon. The vipers and cobras still hesitated, and he added, "Rivera ordered it. He's waiting now."

Reluctantly the snake shifted aside, and the ones beneath it did the same. Layer after layer of serpent moved until at last, at the very bottom of the pit, Simon spotted a triangular crystal glinting against the stone. It glowed from within as if calling to him, and he took a deep breath. The reptiles' part of the Predator.

"For you, Your Majesty," said the coral snake in a trembling voice, though it made no move to touch the piece. Knowing he had no choice, Simon slowly descended into the pit and over the waiting serpents, trying not to wince at the dry sound of scales against scales.

With no hands to carry the crystal, he grabbed it in his jaws and slithered back up. By the time he reached the top of the pit, he felt sick and dizzy with fear, but the flat faces staring back at him looked even more terrified.

"Simon!" shrieked Ariana from above, and his entire body went cold. Fast as he could, Simon slithered toward the exit, his heart racing.

Right before he reached the moat, he shifted back into a human and shoved the reptiles' piece into his sock. It burned against his skin like his father's watch, but he didn't care. He didn't have time to hide it, and he couldn't risk carrying it in his pockets, not when that would be the first place someone would look for it. His sock would have to do for now.

"Ariana, what—" he began as he stepped into the harsh light, shielding his eyes.

"Hand it over, or your friends will die," said a cold voice. Rivera. He stood at the foot of the glass bridge, and he grasped Ariana's and Jam's elbows. Both struggled against him, but their movements were sluggish.

"What did you do to them?" demanded Simon. He had seen Ariana and Jam take on fully grown adults and win; there was no way Rivera, with his skinny frame and the cut on his forehead spilling blood into his eyes, could have possibly held them both off without help.

"I bit them. As did several of my friends," said Rivera, as if discussing nothing more than what he was going to have for breakfast. "If I don't give them the antidote soon, well—we can only hope they don't suffer. Now hand it over before I lose my patience."

Simon's vision swam, blurring around the edges. "I don't know what you're talking about."

"Yes, you do," he said. "I don't know how you got it, and I don't know how many of my brave guards are dead down there—"

"I didn't kill anyone," said Simon, and Rivera sniffed.

"Hand it over."

"I don't—"

"*Hand it over.*"

"Are you deaf or just extremely stupid? He said he doesn't have it," said a new voice, and Rivera began to turn.

"Who—"

Thwack.

Rivera's expression went blank and, seemingly in slow motion, he crumpled to the floor. Winter stood behind him, clutching the handles of her new designer purse like a weapon, her face pale but her eyes fiery.

"I really hate bullies," she muttered, and she looked at Simon. "You have it, right?"

He nodded numbly, rushing forward to help Jam and Ariana sit. "We need to find the antidote."

"It's in his pocket," said Winter, and she dug through Rivera's jacket until she found several syringes. "Last night he told me he keeps multiple doses on him at all times, in case someone tries to assassinate him."

"Wonder who would ever want to do that," grumbled Simon. Uncapping a needle, he winced as he stuck it in Jam's arm and pushed the plunger. "What do you have in that thing, anyway? A bowling ball?"

"Books," said Winter as she tried to administer another dose to Ariana, but she batted Winter's hand away and took the syringe shakily.

"I can do it."

Ariana's words were slurred, and Simon could have sworn she'd gone cross-eyed, but after fumbling a moment, she managed to inject the antidote into her arm. "Are you okay?" he said.

"I'll live," she said woozily. "We need to get out of here."

Even if Simon believed her, one look at Jam's vacant gaze told him neither of them was going anywhere right now. "You two stay here. I need to go help my uncle."

"And what am I supposed to do? Babysit?" said Winter.

"Unless you'd rather go out and fight a bunch of alligators and cobras," he said.

She blanched. "Don't be ridiculous. There aren't any real cobras in the United States," she said, making no move to join him.

"Tell that to the dozens I just saw in the moat. Help Jam and Ariana onto the couches in the council's chambers. I'll be back soon," he promised, but before he left the room, he approached the serpents huddled together at the far end of the moat. "You know who I am?"

"The Kingsnake," they murmured, inching away.

"Exactly," said Simon. "I need your help."

A minute later, he ran past the elevators and into the lobby with at least a hundred snakes slithering after him. The fighting had mostly stopped now, and several mammals and reptiles nursed their injuries off to the sides of the room. In the center, amid broken furniture and torn artwork, two gray wolves circled each other.

Simon's breath caught in his throat. Malcolm's fur was matted with blood, and he limped heavily, favoring his front leg. Celeste, despite being ambushed, looked strong and whole as she bared her long teeth, saliva dripping from her muzzle.

"Don't make me kill you, son," she growled, her claws clicking against the marble floor.

"I'd like to see you try," said Malcolm.

It was the rooftop with Darryl all over again, and Simon

· 260 ·

bit the inside of his lip so hard he tasted blood. Though the council members were giving the pair of wolves a wide berth for now, he had no doubt that if Malcolm managed to overcome his injuries and strike down Celeste, the reptiles would join the fight once more, and Malcolm would be too spent to make it out alive.

Fire filled Simon's veins, and his skin felt as if it was bubbling while he fought the burning knot in his chest with everything he had. He was half an inch from losing control, but part of him wanted to. He wouldn't stand by and watch another uncle die, and if that meant the entire Animalgam world knew his secret, fine.

"Now!" he cried, and the snakes that had followed him shot forward toward the pair of wolves. Malcolm danced out of the way, but Celeste stood there, bemused as the serpents surrounded her.

"What's going on?" she demanded. "Rivera!"

"He's a little busy right now," said Simon, flexing his hands as his fingers threatened to once again curl into claws. "If you don't leave immediately, these snakes are going to bite you. And they're going to keep biting you until I tell them to stop."

Celeste stared at him. "How—"

"They're my friends," he said. "And none of them will let you hurt Malcolm."

"What is the meaning of this?" said an alligator near the edge of the room. "The snakes are under our command—"

"We follow the boy. The small wolf must leave," said a diamondback with a shake of its rattle, and the other snakes hissed in agreement.

Slowly Celeste backed away. "This isn't over," she growled, and a handful of mammals stepped aside, leaving her a clear path to the door.

"Sure about that?" said Zia, still in her fox form. Celeste snarled, but made no move to attack as she saw herself out.

The remaining members of the council all watched silently, seemingly dumbfounded as the vipers and cobras drove Celeste through the exit and closed the door firmly behind her. Even Simon was stunned it had actually worked, and it was only when his uncle shifted back into a human that he managed to speak.

"Celeste isn't the Alpha anymore. Malcolm is," he said. "And you're going to respect that, all right?"

Several council members shifted back, including the alligator who had spoken out. They whispered to one another for a moment, their heads bent, and finally the alligator Animalgam spoke. "If the mammal kingdom recognizes Malcolm Thorn as their Alpha, then so shall we," he said grudgingly. "However, we had a deal with Celeste that we request the Alpha upholds."

"Orion's on the mountain," said Simon to his uncle. "He's been threatening the council. Celeste promised to take care of it for them."

"I'll send members of my kingdom to help. The flock

will be out of your hair in a few days," said Malcolm. His shirt was torn, there were deep scratches on his neck, and he cradled his right arm to his chest, but he still radiated strength and power.

"Thank you," said the councilman. "The sooner they are gone—"

"The piece!" A shrill voice rang from the corridor. Rivera stumbled toward them, running his hand over the wall to keep himself upright. A purple lump had formed on the side of his head. "The brat has the piece!"

Immediately all eyes turned to Simon, and the heat in his sock seemed to grow. "I don't have anything," he lied. "I have no idea what he's talking about."

"You took it." Rivera lurched past the elevators and reached for the edge of the front desk, barely managing a grip. "I know you took it."

"I was rescuing my friends," said Simon as the members of the council inched toward him. Several of the mammals began to growl. "I don't know where your piece is, but I do know you poisoned Ariana and Jam. They're okay now," he added over his shoulder to Malcolm, who limped to Simon's side. "Winter and I gave them the antidote."

"Is that true?" said Malcolm to Rivera. "You tried to kill the general's son and the Black Widow Queen's daughter? I suppose angering my kingdom wasn't enough for you, then?"

"I—" Rivera's face went white. "They were getting away—"

"I'm sure their parents will understand," said Malcolm, setting a hand protectively on Simon's back. "Now may we go, or do we have to fight our way out?"

"But he has the piece!" wailed Rivera, and he pushed off against the desk, staggering toward Simon. "You cannot allow him to leave—"

"As a matter of fact, I have just seen our piece with my own eyes," said Crocker in his low, rumbling voice. Leaning heavily on his cane, he walked toward them, his tortoiseshell glasses perched on top of his head. "It is exactly where it belongs, Rivera."

Simon tried not to let his shock show. If Crocker had really looked, he would have known the piece was no longer at the bottom of the snake pit. Whatever Crocker's reasons for helping Simon were, though, he wasn't going to argue.

"But . . ." Rivera looked wildly from the council to Crocker to Simon. "He has it—he must—I saw him—"

"The piece is safe," hissed the diamondback, shaking its rattle from its spot on the marble floor. Though the snakes continued to keep their distance from Simon, he felt an enormous swell of gratitude for their loyalty.

"It seems to me, Rivera, that you have sustained a significant head injury in this unfortunate misunderstanding, which has muddled your memory and clouded your judgment," said Crocker. "We will have a doctor examine you, and once you are well, we will discuss your place within the council. I doubt the general and the Black Widow Queen will take kindly to hearing about your treatment of their children, and the last thing we need is to risk endangering our peace treaties with the underwater and insect kingdoms."

The members of the council murmured among themselves, several nodding in agreement. Rivera's eyes widened, and it may have been the concussion or the shock of losing everything in one fell swoop, but either way, he sank to the floor and buried his face in his hands. Crocker limped around him as if he were nothing more than furniture.

"I will make sure the doctor sees to the injured mammals as well, and you are welcome to stay for as long as your recovery demands," he said to Malcolm, bowing his head. "My deepest apologies. Now that we are aware of the shift in power in your kingdom, I assure you such mistakes will not happen again."

"Thank you," said Malcolm, bowing his head in return. "You have our continued friendship. Now, Simon—bring me to Mr. Fluke and Miss Webster. I must insist a doctor see them first."

"Of course, of course," said Crocker, and he gestured down the hallway. "Ronnie, have the receptionist call the doctor immediately."

The bearded dragon appeared from behind a framed painting that had fallen off the wall. "Aye, mate," he said in his thick accent, and he ran off at an impressive speed, clearly eager to get as far from the mammals as possible. Or maybe it was the vipers. Simon couldn't tell.

Simon led his uncle to the council's chambers, where Ariana and Jam already looked far better than they had before. Simon filled them in on everything that had happened in the lobby, and while Ariana looked decidedly smug at Rivera's fate, the color drained from Jam's face all over again.

"There are *how many* snakes loose in the hotel?"

"Don't worry," said Simon. "They're back in the moat now, and I don't think they're ever going to bother you again."

"I should hope not," grumbled Malcolm. "Come on—let's get you back to your room. As soon as the doctor clears you two, we're taking the first flight back to New York."

This time, Simon didn't argue. After everything that had happened, he wanted nothing more than to put as much distance between him and Paradise Valley as possible. Part of him—a much bigger part than he wanted to admit— ached at the thought of leaving his mother behind, but she had left him, he reminded himself. She had chosen to stay with Orion.

As they shuffled out of the council chambers, Simon spotted Crocker and Zia speaking quietly in a corner, their heads bent together and Zia's hand on his arm. Did she have something to do with why Crocker had lied for him? It was crazy, but after the past three days, Simon wasn't willing to rule anything out.

The doctor insisted Jam and Ariana would be well enough to travel the following day, but in the meantime, he ordered them both to rest. Though Ariana argued, swearing she felt fine, Jam disappeared to take a long bath, claiming the desert air had dried him out.

"So," said Malcolm over lunch in the living room of their suite. "Are you coming with us, Winter, or have you decided to stay with your grandfather?"

"He's not my grandfather," she said, wrinkling her nose as she took a sip of tea. "I mean, maybe biologically, but blood isn't everything."

"No, it isn't," agreed Malcolm quietly. "Sometimes the family you choose is far better than the one you're born into."

"Yeah, sometimes it is," she agreed, catching Simon's eye. He quickly looked away, tearing off a piece of roll for Felix to eat. The little mouse had spent nearly an hour berating him for leaving in the first place, and Simon couldn't blame him. If Felix had disappeared like that, he would have worried, too.

"Does that mean I should buy another ticket to New York, then?" said Malcolm, and Winter nodded.

"Actually—" Simon paused, his gaze drifting to the purse sitting at Winter's feet. "I need to talk to Zia first, but do you think we could stop in Chicago?"

"Chicago?" said Malcolm. Winter groaned.

"Simon, no—"

"You know it's the right thing to do," he said, and to Malcolm he added, "I wouldn't ask if it wasn't really important."

His uncle sighed and took a bite of his burger. "If it means that much to you, I can make sure our flight connects in Chicago."

Winter muttered a few choice words under her breath and stabbed her salad. "This is a terrible idea."

"Probably," said Simon, but he had to try. Even though he couldn't have his mother, he could make sure another family had each other. Safe and sound.

19

CITY MOUSE

The next morning, they all gathered in the lobby at dawn. Several members of the council joined them to say their good-byes, and Crocker patted Simon on the head, insisting he keep up the good work. Simon's curiosity nearly got the better of him, and twice he had to stop himself from asking Crocker why he had lied to the council. Maybe Crocker hadn't realized he was lying, Simon rationalized; maybe he thought he really had seen the piece of the Predator in the snake pit.

Zia waited near the door, her arms crossed and her foot propped up against the wall as she watched Simon approach. Four stitched-up claw marks ran down her exposed shoulder, and every time Simon looked at her, he was reminded once again of what she had risked to give him the chance to save his friends.

"So, back to the big city," she said. "Knew you weren't much of a country mouse."

"The desert's a little sandy for me," said Simon, and she grinned. Pulling a card from her pocket, she offered it to him.

"If there's ever anything you need, call, all right?"

Simon took it dubiously. "Thanks," he said, tucking it into his pocket.

"I mean it." She straightened and unfolded her arms, leaning in closer to him. "You're not always going to get this lucky. If there's ever anything I can do—anything at all— you *will* let me know. You're not alone, Simon. Remember that."

A shiver ran down his spine, and he nodded, now certain she knew far more than he realized. However, with Malcolm hovering only a few feet away, trying to extract himself from an especially long good-bye courtesy of one of the female councilmembers, now wasn't the time to ask Zia for details.

"Actually, there is something you could do for me," he said, and she raised an eyebrow.

"That was fast."

"You said anything," he pointed out, and she grinned again.

"All right, then. What'll it be?"

Simon explained the situation to her, and by the time Malcolm finally joined them, they had hashed out a plan. It was a stupid plan full of plenty of holes, but Simon had to trust that it would all work out.

The drive through Phoenix was quiet, but once they arrived at the airport and reached their gate, Malcolm said to Simon, "Want to help me grab snacks for everyone?"

Simon glanced at his friends, who were all seated together with their suitcases. While Jam and Ariana had their eyes closed, still exhausted from the day before, Winter gave him an encouraging nod. Simon reluctantly stood. It wasn't that he didn't want to spend time with his uncle; he just had a sinking feeling Malcolm would ask questions, and Simon wasn't sure he would have answers.

"Nervous?" said Malcolm as he led him to a kiosk across from the gate.

"About what?" said Simon. The reptiles' piece of the Predator rested inside one of his socks in his backpack, and every time he thought about it, he felt a little nauseated.

"This is your first flight, isn't it?" said Malcolm, and Simon exhaled.

"Oh—yeah. It's okay, though. I mean, I'm a bird, right? I shouldn't be scared of flying."

Malcolm ruffled his hair with his good arm. "That's the spirit." Though he grabbed several snack packages seemingly at random, he took his time choosing the drinks. "Are you ever going to tell me what you were really doing in the desert?"

The question came so casually that at first Simon thought he hadn't heard his uncle right. He picked out a bag of trail mix and said calmly, "I told you, Winter wanted to see her family."

"And yet she's getting on a plane back to New York with us," said Malcolm, inspecting the label on a bottle of juice. "You're not in trouble, Simon. Well, you are—you're grounded for the rest of your life—but it's not going to get any worse if you tell me the truth, I promise. I only want to help you."

Simon opened and shut his mouth, and at last he mumbled, "I was trying to rescue my mom."

"Isabel?" Malcolm looked at Simon sharply. "She's in Paradise Valley?"

"Orion still has her," he said miserably. "I tried to get her out of there, but she didn't want to come. She said—she said stopping Orion from putting the pieces of the Predator together is more important than being my mom."

Malcolm was quiet for a long moment, and at last he picked out a few drinks. "Nothing is more important to her than being your mom, Simon."

"But she said—"

"I don't care what she said. If you needed her, she would be there in a heartbeat if she could."

"I do need her," he said, his throat tightening and his voice dangerously close to breaking. "She's my family."

"She's not your only family. You know that, right?" Malcolm stooped down so they were as close to eye to eye as they could get. "Things haven't been easy, and it's been an adjustment for all of us, but you are and always will be my family, too, Simon. And I know Nolan can be—difficult at times, but he loves you, too. Things will get better. It might take a while, but you'll start to feel more at home a little every day until one morning, you'll wake up, and all of this will be normal."

Simon wasn't sure he ever wanted a life without Darryl and his mother to be normal, but he didn't have much of a choice. He'd done everything he could. Now, somehow, he had to learn to accept it.

"And Simon," said his uncle, pausing before heading toward the checkout line. "Isabel may not be here, but she has never stopped being your mom. It's just that right now, for her, being your mother means staying with Orion so she can *protect* you and your brother. Everything she's doing, everything she's risking—that's exactly what a parent does. If she could do all that and still be here with you, she would be. I guarantee it."

A lump formed in Simon's throat, and he didn't trust himself to reply. Once Malcolm had paid, they gathered up the snacks and drinks and headed back to the gate. Winter gave him a searching look, but he purposely sat several seats down from her as they waited to board. Malcolm was right, and the aching, bitter weight he'd been carrying around for the past twenty-four hours started to diminish.

The plane was smaller than Simon had expected, and he squeezed in beside Malcolm, who was about two sizes too big for his seat. His uncle mercifully didn't ask any difficult questions on their flight, and Simon managed to nap. By the time they landed in Chicago, it was early afternoon, and both Jam and Ariana seemed to have recovered.

"I can't believe you're doing this," said Winter as they all climbed into a taxi, and Jam leaned forward to give the driver directions. "They don't deserve it."

"They don't deserve living on the streets, either," said Simon.

As the cab maneuvered through the heavy traffic, the four of them filled Malcolm in on everything that had happened in Chicago, or at least as much as they could with the driver listening. Malcolm's frown deepened the more they went on, and once they'd finished, he said, "Do me a favor and don't tell your parents."

"Are you kidding? My mom is going to practically burst with pride," said Ariana.

"The general will probably kill me, but he'll also be glad I took some initiative," said Jam sheepishly.

Malcolm didn't look convinced, and as they pulled up to the dingy theater, he said, "Maybe I should go in."

"You'll scare them off," said Simon, hopping onto the broken sidewalk. "Stay here. I'll be right back."

"I'm coming with you," said Winter, jumping out after him. Together they found the covered opening in the brick wall, and Simon led the way through the darkness.

He half expected the raccoons not to be there. It was midday, after all, and there were probably all kinds of pockets to pick and Dumpsters to raid on the streets. But when he pushed open the squeaky door, he spotted Bonnie perched on the edge of the stage, her body tensed like she was ready to flee.

"Relax—we're not here for anything," said Simon.

Bonnie exhaled sharply. "I thought you were the cops." Climbing to her feet, she strode over. "What do you want?"

"I brought you something," he said, pulling an envelope from his pocket. Bonnie took it curiously, while Winter wandered across the stage.

"Don't touch anything," said Bonnie over her shoulder as she pulled out the contents of the envelope. Her forehead knitted. "Train tickets? What am I supposed to do with these?"

"They're to a town in Colorado, near New Mexico," said Simon. "It's a safe haven for mammals who don't belong anywhere else."

Bonnie stuffed the tickets back inside and thrust the envelope toward Simon. "We're not leaving."

Simon refused to take them. "There's a woman there—Zia

Stone. She knows people who would be willing to take you all in. Together. No one's going to separate you. You'll have all the food you want, beds to sleep in, people to help you—it can't be easy watching and worrying about your brothers all the time, right?"

Bonnie scowled, though she slowly pulled the tickets out of the envelope again. "They say they won't separate us now, and maybe they won't at first, but once it becomes too much for them—"

"So run away and come back here if that happens," said Simon. "But it won't. Zia gets it, and she swore you three would stay together. My uncle, Malcolm—he's the Alpha of the mammal kingdom, and he asked for regular updates. If anything goes wrong or isn't okay, he can take care of it for you. I promise."

Bonnie stared at the tickets, and a piece of short bleached hair fell into her eyes. "Why are you doing this?"

"Doing what?" said Simon.

"Helping us. We stole from you. We took your friend's *shoes*."

"Yeah, but you also saved me from the flock. You helped us when we needed it, and you stole because you needed the money. Or the shoes. I don't know. You're out here on your own, and you don't have to be. I just want to help."

Bonnie bit her lower lip, and at last she tucked the envelope into her back pocket. "I'll think about it."

Simon knew that was as close to a yes as he was going to get. "Great. Zia will meet every train for the next week, so you have time."

Suddenly a pot clattered to the floor, and Winter straightened beside a pile of things stacked in the corner of the stage. "I'm taking this back," she declared, holding up her purse—the one Orion had given her. "You can keep the credit card. Use it as much as you want. In fact, max it out."

"Already did." Bonnie smirked, and to Simon, she added, "Thanks."

"You're welcome. Say hi to Billy and Butch for me."

"Will do," she said, and Simon and Winter trudged back through the dark corridor and into the alleyway, where the taxi waited for them.

Before Simon opened the door, he turned to Winter. "When we get to the airport, I need to talk to you."

"About what?" she said, but he shook his head and climbed in beside Jam. She had the good sense not to bring it up in front of the others, but Simon could tell she was dying to ask.

As soon as they reached the gate for their flight to New York, Simon announced, "I need to go to the bathroom."

"Me, too," said Winter.

Simon gave Jam a look, and several seconds passed before his eyes widened with realization. "Oh! I have to go, too."

"I could always pee," said Ariana, and together the four of them hurried away before Malcolm asked any questions.

Simon found the nearest family bathroom and, ushering his friends inside, he closed and locked the door. "I have to tell you all something."

"Is this about—" began Jam, and Simon nodded.

"Winter doesn't know yet."

"I don't know what?" she said, frowning.

Simon set his backpack on the tiled floor and unzipped the pocket, and Felix poked his head out curiously. "What's going on?"

"Both of you, watch," he said. Taking a deep breath, Simon began to shift. At first he took his usual form of a golden eagle, and Winter rolled her eyes.

"In case you didn't know, I can do that, too," she said. But then his body began to change again, this time into a snake. And then a mouse. And then a turtle, and a squirrel, and a fly, and finally he shifted back into a human.

"Can you do that?" he said with a nervous grin. Winter stared at him, her eyes the size of saucers.

"You—you're—"

"Yeah." He hesitated. "Jam and Ariana found out yesterday, but I wanted you to know, too. You're my friends, and I trust you."

Felix let out a long-suffering sigh. "Terrific. Another reason for someone to try to kill you," he muttered before disappearing into the backpack once more. Simon zipped the pocket back up, glad he hadn't made more of a fuss. He wasn't sure he could take another lecture from Felix right now.

"I guess this isn't something you want announced in the middle of the dining hall?" said Ariana, and Simon shook his head.

"No one else knows. Not even Malcolm and Nolan. If anyone else finds out—"

"No one will," said Jam fiercely, pushing his glasses up his nose.

Ariana nodded in agreement, but Winter continued to stare, stunned. "I can't *believe* you didn't tell me! How many times do I have to prove I'm on your side?"

"I know you are," he said. "I just—didn't know how. I'm sorry. You know now, though. You all do. And—" He faltered. "I have the reptiles' piece, too."

"Good. One down, four to go," said Ariana. "If we're going to look for the rest, we have to come up with a better plan."

"First, we need to figure out where to go next," said Jam, and Simon remembered what his mother had said in Beak Peak.

The underwater kingdom moved theirs after I copied it in September, two years ago.

She hadn't only told him how to find the reptiles' piece. She'd told him how to find the underwater kingdom's piece, too.

As they left the bathroom, Jam and Ariana argued about which kingdom to focus on now, while Simon fell into step beside Winter. "I'll try my best to make sure Garrett doesn't bully you anymore."

"As long as your best doesn't include turning into a bear and eating him." After a pause, she added, "Actually, I wouldn't mind that."

Simon smiled. "Thanks for coming back. I mean it."

"Thanks for telling me about the—thing," she said, gesturing toward him. "Does that mean you're technically a snake, too?"

"I can be," he said. "I think I belong to all the kingdoms and none of them at the same time. It's a little weird."

"It's a little cool, too. And dangerous." She stopped before they reached Malcolm, who had his nose in a newspaper. "You're the best friend I've ever had, Simon. Before I met you, I didn't feel like I belonged anywhere, but now—" She turned red. "If you tell anyone I said that, I'll eat your rat."

"Mouse!" squeaked Felix from his backpack. Simon grinned.

"Your secret's safe with me," he said, and a voice over the loudspeaker announced their flight was about to begin boarding. "Time to go home."

"Time for you to face the music," said Winter. "I bet Nolan's furious you left him behind."

Simon made a face. "Probably." Despite everything he'd

been through, somehow enduring whatever Nolan had in store for him seemed like the scariest part of all. But no matter how upset his brother was, he owed Nolan an apology and an explanation. Simon could only hope he understood.

GREAT WHITE LIE

Nolan didn't understand. Not at all.

The moment their plane touched down in New York City, a knot of dread formed in Simon's chest, and it only grew tighter the closer they got to the Central Park Zoo. The pack was waiting for them inside the Arsenal to escort them to the secret level below, and as Simon crossed the bridge that led to the underground academy, he spotted several sharks circling the water, all on high alert.

"With Celeste on the run, we're not taking any chances," said Malcolm, and Simon's hopes sank. There was no way his uncle would let him go flying now. But, he supposed, he'd had no chance of Malcolm ever letting him do anything fun again since the moment he had run away to Arizona. Simon would have to find another way to stretch his wings.

Malcolm saw him to his room, and before Simon could even pull off his backpack, Nolan stormed in from the bathroom they shared.

"Where have you been?" he demanded. "Malcolm said you made it to Penn Station, but then I don't hear anything from you for *days*."

"I'm sorry," said Simon, setting his bag down on his bed and opening the zipper so Felix could climb free. "I really am. But I found out Mom was in Arizona—"

"Mom? You know where Mom is, and you didn't tell me?"

Nolan's face fell, and Simon felt a stab of guilt so deep in his gut that he blurted out the whole story. Minus the part about the pieces. And being the Beast King's heir, too. Simon described everything that had happened in Chicago and Colorado and Paradise Valley, but when the time came to recount what had happened as he escaped from Beak Peak, he paused.

"Then what?" said Nolan. He'd taken to pacing angrily across the carpet. "Did Mom get away? Is she here? Or did you let Orion take her again?"

"It wasn't—it wasn't like that," said Simon. He sat down on the edge of his bed, unable to admit to Nolan that their mother had chosen to stay with Orion rather than come home to them. It hurt Simon badly enough as it was, and he was used to her leaving. She'd left his whole life, again and again, until he'd come to expect it.

But this was the first time she hadn't been there for Nolan. No matter how miserable Simon was, he couldn't take that hope from his brother, too.

"I tried," he said at last. "But—they caught her, and she wouldn't let me help."

His brother's face twisted into a sneer. "I would have never let them take her again. If I had been there, she'd be free right now."

Simon clutched his hands together so tightly he could feel his fingers throb. "Yeah, probably," he mumbled. "I'm sorry I lost her."

"You should be," said Nolan. "You should have told me you were going. I would have come with you."

"But—"

"You're not the only one in this family who can go out and fight, Simon. I'm not helpless, but you and Malcolm act like the second I step foot outside the Den, someone's going to kidnap me, and you're never going to see me again."

"What if that does happen?" said Simon. "What if Celeste finds you, or Orion?"

There was a dangerous glint in Nolan's eyes. "Then I'll tear them to pieces before they get the chance to hurt me. Or you, or Malcolm, or Mom."

"You can't, though," argued Simon. "You can't ever kill anyone. If the truth about what you are ever comes out, the only hope you'll have is to prove you're nothing like the Beast King. Otherwise the entire Animalgam world is going to try to take you down, and I can't lose you, all right?"

That brought Nolan up short, and he studied Simon, his expression softening. "Then what makes you think I can lose you?"

The pair of them stared at each other. For the past two months, Simon had thought Nolan wanted nothing to do with him. But maybe Simon was wrong.

"She's my mom, too," mumbled Nolan at last. "I want to help. I know you'd rather have her than me and Malcolm, but—"

"That's not true," said Simon, his voice cracking. "You're part of my family, too. It wouldn't be complete without you and Malcolm."

"Then stop pretending I don't exist. You and your friends act like you're too good for me—"

"What?" Simon shook his head. "*You're* the one acting like you're too good for us. Have you seen what Garrett's been doing to Winter?"

"She sticks up for Orion. He's the one who took Mom, and she thinks it's no big deal."

"She knows it's a big deal. She helped me try to get Mom back," said Simon. "He abandoned Winter, and she doesn't have anyone except us, all right? You don't have to make it worse."

Nolan gritted his teeth so hard a muscle in his jaw twitched. "Fine. I'll tell Garrett to lay off."

"Thanks," said Simon, and he averted his eyes, focusing on a loose thread hanging from his backpack. "You can sit with us whenever you want, you know. There's always room for you. And Garrett, too, if he's nice."

"Garrett's never nice," muttered Nolan. "Just—promise me that next time, you'll let me come with you."

Simon opened his mouth to say there wasn't going to be a next time, but that was a lie. As badly as he wanted to protect his brother, if he kept pushing him away like this, that was only going to make Nolan do something stupid. He still couldn't tell his brother about also being the Beast King's heir—that would only give Nolan another reason to hate him—but next time they had to leave to find a piece, Simon could include him. Zia was right, after all. They wouldn't always be as lucky as they had been on this trip. Maybe having Nolan would tilt the scale in their favor.

"I promise," said Simon. "I'm sorry."

"I know," said Nolan, and he sighed. "We'll get her back. He can't run forever."

Simon hoped more than anything that his brother was right. "I miss her. Is that weird? I only got to see her once or twice a year, but—I miss her."

"It's not weird. I miss her, too. I don't know how you did it, never getting to see her like I did."

"I don't know, either," he admitted. "You adapt, I guess. It never goes away, and some days are worse than others, but you get used to it."

The way he was getting used to Darryl's death. The way he was getting used to Nolan and Malcolm and the L.A.I.R. and a new life he'd never asked for. Sometimes, when he thought about it, it all became too much. Today, however, with Nolan standing across from him, he managed to push the overwhelming fear aside. Not everything that had happened was terrible. He had, after all, gotten a brother out of it.

"Come on," said Nolan, and he turned away, rubbing his eyes. "Dinner's going to be ready soon, and if I'm sitting with you, we'll need to grab a bigger table."

Simon hesitated. He still had to unpack and hide the piece, but it could wait. Felix would watch it for him. Right now, he was going to have dinner with his brother. "Yeah, all right. We'll have to warn Winter, though."

"I'll make Garrett apologize. He's been a jerk lately anyway," said Nolan, and they headed out into the atrium together. It would take a long time for them to work out everything between them, but for the first time in weeks, Simon was hopeful.

• • •

At dinner, everyone was surprised to see Simon and his friends, and student after student came up to them, asking where they'd been. On the plane ride home, they'd discussed cover stories, finally settling on something as close to the truth as they could get: Winter had wanted to go to Arizona, and they'd helped her. She seemed fine with it, especially since it placed her in the spotlight, and for once, even Nolan seemed all right with not being the center of attention.

By the time Simon returned to his room, he was exhausted. It had been a long day, and he was eager to catch up on the sleep he'd missed during their trip, but first he had something he needed to do.

Pulling the collection of postcards from his backpack, he flipped through them until he found the card from September, two years ago. On the back was a picture of a great white shark, and Simon made a face, flipping it over to read his mother's handwriting.

Great white sharks are formidable predators, growing over twenty feet in length. Though they are responsible for the most attacks on humans per year, they do not typically see humans as prey. Great whites are, for the most part, a deeply misunderstood and feared species, but I wouldn't recommend swimming up to one and trying to befriend it no matter how chummy he might seem.

Terrific. Not only did he have no idea exactly where the piece was, but apparently he would have to fight a shark to get it. He groaned and slid the card back among the others.

"You wouldn't happen to know any great white sharks, would you?" he said to Felix, who meandered in through the bathroom.

"No, but I do know something that might interest you," said Felix. "Someone's rearranged your brother's room again. And that someone left a note on my pillow."

"They're my pillows, not yours," said Simon, but sure enough, a white envelope rested on his bed. Simon pulled out the note, which was written in scratchy handwriting he recognized as Malcolm's.

A member of the pack will always be watching you. Don't go far, and most of all, be safe.

Simon's heart skipped a beat, and it took everything he had not to immediately run into Nolan's room. Instead he pulled on his coat and boots, knowing if his mother or uncle were here, they would insist that he wear both in the November cold.

"I'll be back soon," he said to Felix. "If Nolan comes in, tell him I'm going to fly tomorrow morning, and he can come if he wants."

Felix tugged on his whiskers. "Don't get eaten."

"I'll try not," he said, and with a grin, he darted through the bathroom and into his brother's empty room. Felix was right—the bookcase that had covered the secret tunnel had been replaced by Nolan's desk once more, and whatever measures Malcolm had taken to close it had been reversed.

He didn't know why his uncle was giving him this privilege after everything he'd done to not deserve it, but Simon wasn't about to protest. Shifting into a mouse, he ran through the tunnel at top speed, relishing the sensation of his muscles and lungs burning. After his trip across the country, the Den had never seemed more claustrophobic. At least now, when he sneaked out, he could do it mostly guilt-free.

He paused long enough to shift into a golden eagle once more before stepping out into the Central Park Zoo, his talons scraping the stone courtyard. It was eerily quiet, and a snowflake landed on his beak. Closing his eyes, he tilted his head up toward the dark sky, letting the cold swirl around him. There really was no place like New York.

Eventually he flapped his wings and rose into the air. Rather than flying around Central Park, however, he only went a couple hundred feet, landing at the base of Darryl's statue. The stone wolf bayed at the moon, and Simon shifted back, patting its muzzle.

"Sorry I've been gone," he said quietly. "I went to Arizona

to find Mom. And I did, but—it's the same as it's always been, I guess. She's there, and I'm back here now."

He couldn't say anything else about his trip, not when a member of the pack could be listening. Even with the snow muffling his words, he couldn't take the risk, and instead he cleared his throat. "I think Nolan and I might get along more now. We just need to figure out how to stop getting in each other's way and—"

Simon frowned. Underneath the loose stone at the base of the statue, he spotted a rectangle of glossy paper, its edges damp from the snow.

Another postcard.

With trembling hands, Simon picked it up and angled it toward the light. On the front was a picture of a beach with the bluest waves Simon had ever seen, and the words *Greetings from Los Angeles* were printed at the bottom.

A lump formed in his throat, and he turned it over. His mother had only written two words.

I'm sorry.

Simon sank to the cold stone ground, reading those words over and over until he'd memorized every last curve of the letters. "I'm sorry, too, Mom," he whispered, and as the snow swirled around him, he tucked the postcard into the safety of his coat pocket and gazed up at the statue of the wolf. One day they would be a family again. They would never be whole, not without Darryl, but they would be together, and that was the important part. No matter what it took, Simon would make sure of it.